A SNACK IN THE SUN?

The sun's rays were blinding even with the protection of my new sunglasses, and I shaded my eyes with my hand, peering out at Foreverglades, visible beyond the expanse of tall grasses and tangled vines. A movement in the undergrowth next to the boardwalk caught my eye. I looked down. Two yellow eyes with black vertical pupils stared back at me. The head of the creature was huge, its broad, flat snout rounded at the end, its eyes twin bulges in the bumpy black hide. For a few seconds, we stared at each other, both frozen at the unsuspected intrusion into a private moment. Then it opened its jaws and hissed.

I glanced around quickly to see if a baby alligator was nearby, but from the size of the creature in front of me, I was guessing that this was no mother, but a bull alligator, and one that was close to twelve feet long. I shivered, my breath coming in short spurts. So I wasn't between a mother and a calf, but I was between the alligator and the water.

It must want the water; it's hot. Unless, of course, it's not hot? What if it's hungry? You'd make a tasty meal. . . .

Other *Murder, She Wrote* mysteries

DYING TO RETIRE

A *Murder, She Wrote*
Mystery

A Novel by Jessica Fletcher
and Donald Bain

based on the
Universal television series
created by Peter S. Fischer,
Richard Levinson & William Link

A SIGNET BOOK

SIGNET
Published by New American Library, a division of
Penguin Group (USA) Inc., 375 Hudson Street,
New York, New York 10014, U.S.A.
Penguin Books Ltd, 80 Strand,
London WC2R 0RL, England
Penguin Books Australia Ltd, 250 Camberwell Road,
Camberwell, Victoria 3124, Australia
Penguin Books Canada Ltd, 10 Alcorn Avenue,
Toronto, Ontario, Canada M4V 3B2
Penguin Books (N.Z.) Ltd, Cnr Rosedale and Airborne Roads,
Albany, Auckland 1310, New Zealand

Penguin Books Ltd, Registered Offices:
80 Strand, London WC2R 0RL, England

First published by Signet, an imprint of New American Library,
a division of Penguin Group (USA) Inc.

First Printing, April 2004
10 9 8 7 6 5 4 3 2 1

*To Ellen Edwards, editrice extraordinaire,
with many thanks from a grateful pair.*

Chapter One

Warm, humid air washed over me as I stepped from the airplane onto the steel steps leading to the tarmac. I squinted against the glare of the sun and shifted my coat to my left arm. I knew I should have bought new sunglasses. My old pair had broken when Seth Hazlitt had sat on them. It wasn't his fault. I'd come in the door and carelessly flung my coat on the chair to answer a ringing telephone. Later, when I went to hang the coat in the closet, I didn't see that the glasses had slipped out of my pocket. The armchair is Seth's favorite, and when he sat down after dinner—I'd baked a lobster casserole—we heard the snap of the plastic. He was up like a shot, but it was too late. One earpiece had broken off and both lenses were cracked. I'd told him it was no matter at all, and it wasn't. But I'd been remiss in not replacing them, and now here I was, my hand shading my eyes from the intense Florida sun.

"Would you like me to hold that coat for you, Mrs. F?"

"No, thanks, Mort," I said. "I can manage." The stairs had been sitting in the sun and the handrail was hot. I used the sleeve of my coat as a pot holder, stepped quickly down the portable staircase, and waited for the others at the bottom.

There were four of us who had come to Florida to attend the funeral of a former neighbor. Traveling with me were my dear friends Dr. Seth Hazlitt and Mort and Maureen Metzger. Mort is our sheriff back in Cabot Cove, Maine, and the funeral coincided with the week he and his wife had planned for vacation. "We'll pay our respects to Portia, and then me and the missus will go on down to Key West."

We'd been lucky to get a flight—this was Presidents' Day weekend—and the airport in Miami was so busy, there hadn't been a jetway available for our plane. Instead, the pilot had pulled the 767 to a stop away from the traffic of the terminal and we were instructed to deplane and climb aboard one of the fleet of buses waiting to take passengers to a doorway near the baggage area.

I unbuttoned the tweed jacket of my suit. It had been fourteen degrees and snowing when we'd left Boston's Logan International Airport. Most of the people boarding the flight carried winter coats, scarves, and gloves, there being little room in their suitcases to accommodate the heavy winter clothing. I would be happy to put away mine as soon as we arrived at Portia's condominium complex, where several unoccupied units would serve as accommodations for our stay, a suggestion from Portia's neighbor Helen Davison that had proved a good one. She'd given me the telephone number of Mark Rosner, the manager, who'd assured me that the apartments were nicer and more convenient than the local hotels, and besides, the hotels were all full. We'd agreed on a rate, and Mr. Rosner had arranged for a car from the airport and three furnished apartments in the same building, across the courtyard from the one Portia had shared with her husband of two years, Clarence Shelby.

"I'm surprised they had any units available," Maureen had commented when I'd called with the news. "Mort and I had to make our reservations for Key West a year in advance."

"Perhaps this part of Florida isn't as popular as the Keys," I'd said.

"Portia said it was beautiful, although she did complain about the bugs. Poor thing. She finally finds a nice guy and settles down, and then her heart gives out. There's just no justice."

"I wish she'd had a longer time to enjoy her life there, too," I said. "The warm weather was much better for her arthritis. In her last e-mail, she told me that instead of being locked in her house for weeks during the winter in Cabot Cove, she was out strolling along the boardwalk every day. Sounds wonderful, doesn't it?"

We filed into the air-conditioned baggage area and followed our fellow passengers to the carousel that had been designated for our flight.

"Any chance you can join us for a few days in Key West, Mrs. F?" Mort asked.

"We'll have to see," I said. "If Portia's husband needs a hand packing up her things, I'd like to offer to help."

"What about you, Doc?"

"I might, I might. Got a colleague of mine from medical school lives there. Been invitin' me for years. Could practice up on my golfin'."

"How's that going, Doc?"

Seth shook his head. "Wasn't too good, last summah. But I still have hopes to improve, that is if Dr. Jenny's still willin' ta see my patients in my absence."

After years of resisting anything close to retirement, Seth had taken a young physician into his practice.

Dr. Jennifer Countryman—Dr. Jenny, as she soon was dubbed—was perfectly suited to Cabot Cove. Her parents lived nearby. She'd already had her fill of big-city hospital work. And she loved the mix of medical cases a small-town practice provided, everything from a child with a splinter to an old man with senility, and all life's myriad woes and wonders between.

"I'm sure Dr. Jenny will manage just fine," I said. "She's always encouraging you to get out more."

"She's always harping on me to exercise, you mean." He frowned. "Don't think I don't know she's pulled you into this campaign."

"Oh, look," Maureen said, pointing to sign that read JESSICA FLETCHER PARTY. "That must be our ride."

"Probably a child," Seth growled. "Can't even see his head over all these people. I'm not riding with any crazy teenager, I'll tell you that right now."

I stood on tiptoe to see who our benefactor was, and when there was a break in the crowd, I waved to the sign holder. He was a wizened gentleman, barely five feet tall, with tufts of white hair fringing his bald pate and framing his jug ears. He wore a green T-shirt, khaki shorts, and purple-and-gray sneakers. When he spotted me, he scuttled over to where we stood, his lips parted in a big grin over the whitest teeth I'd seen since Tina Treyz's youngest child wore a Bugs Bunny mask for Halloween.

"Mrs. Fletcher, it's a pleasure. I'm Sam, Sam Lewis," he said, pumping my hand. He had a surprisingly strong grip.

I introduced him to Maureen, Mort, and Seth, and watched the surprise reflected on each of their faces as Sam briefly crushed their fingers.

"When you get your bags, meet me outside. Car's

in a no-parking zone and I've gotta move it before they tow me. Look for the pink Caddy."

He snapped a baseball hat onto his head and disappeared back into the crowd. I had no idea how long he'd been waiting, and hoped for all our sakes that his car was still there. It was another half hour before we'd assembled all the bags and showed the matching luggage receipts to the guards. Outside again, we had little time to adjust to the warmth and humidity before Sam pulled to the curb, hopped out of his car, and opened the trunk.

Sam's Cadillac was a vintage model with huge fins trimmed in chrome. Seth walked around it, admiring the highly polished surface. "Nice vehicle you got here," he told Sam. "Haven't seen one of these in years."

"She's a beauty, isn't she?" Sam said, running a gnarled hand over the sleek pink fender. "Got it from old friend in South Beach about five years ago. They took his license away from him, poor guy. First they said he couldn't drive at night. Then they said he couldn't drive in the day." Sam shook his head.

"Get in a lot of accidents, did he?" Seth asked.

"Never got into an accident at all," Sam replied, "but I hear he left a lot of them in his wake. Police got tired of pulling him over for driving too slowly. They grounded him permanently. And he was only eighty-seven, a youngster." He winked. "Tough luck for him, but good luck for me."

Mort hauled his heavy suitcase to the back of the car, his face red from the effort. He and Maureen had vowed to take only one piece of luggage on this trip, but it was a big one, and didn't have wheels. Sam rushed to pull the suitcase from Mort's hand.

"That's okay, Sam. I've got it," Mort said. "This one's a backbreaker." He wrestled the suitcase into the trunk, stepped back, and dusted off his hands.

Maureen's eyebrows disappeared under her bangs as she looked up. "I told him we should use two bags," she muttered just loud enough for her husband to hear.

Sam took my rolling bag, nestled it next to Mort's, and swung Seth's suitcase on top. The trunk of the car could have taken double our load. We pressed Seth to take the front passenger seat, and after he cranked a bit about wanting to be a gentleman and letting me sit there, he complied. We were on our way.

Sam's method of driving was a bit unnerving. He could barely see over the steering wheel and drove very slowly until the traffic light up ahead turned red. Then he pressed his foot down on the accelerator to catch up with the cars stopped at the light, jamming on the brakes at the last minute.

"You must be tired after comin' all this way to pick us up," Seth said to him. "Would you like me to spell you awhile? I can drive and you can give me directions."

"Are you kidding? Driving this boat is the most fun I have all day," Sam said, pounding on the dashboard affectionately. "You just sit back and relax and I'll show you the sights."

Fortunately for us, once out of the airport, heavy city traffic kept Sam from racing between lights, and we did as he said, sitting back to take in our new surroundings.

Miami in February is a joy to New Englanders whose winter experience revolves around snow, ice, and cold, and more snow, ice, and cold. As we neared the coast, the balmy air wafted in through the partially opened windows—we'd convinced Sam to lower the air-conditioning—and we breathed in the sweet, briny aroma of salt water and sun-softened earth, admiring the passing landscape of tall palm trees, flowering bougainvillea, and pastel buildings. At first we had only glimpses of blue, but when we reached Biscayne Bay, the sun-sparkled water stretched out before us. Familiar sounds accosted us—the lines of sailing boats docked in the harbor jangling musically against the masts. Familiar sights drew our eyes—the white triangles of sails and other boat shapes moving on the water. Yet it was all new and different. It was the same Atlantic waters that washed the rocky coast of Maine we'd left that morning, but here the blue was turquoise, not slate; the air was warm, not frigid. I felt a combination of pure excitement and deep relaxation flow into me.

"Thought I'd give you a bit of the scenic route," Sam chirped from the driver's seat. "Now I'll take you home."

We drove south on Route 1 and then west, moving inland, then southeast again, passing a succession of strip malls and housing developments, emerging onto a flat plain of scrub vegetation that was not nearly as beautiful as the carefully tended tropical gardens in and around Miami. Sam's driving seemed to smooth out as the distance between traffic signals lengthened, or perhaps I was just too tired to let it affect me. I was weary from the early-morning start to make our flights, and that, coupled with the mild weather and vibrations from the big car, lulled me to sleep. I awoke when the Cadillac bounced over thick ridges set in the road to slow vehicles. Ahead was a huge archway set into a white coral wall. A sign that spanned the arch read, WELCOME TO FOREVERGLADES. The development was a series of two-story pink buildings, set at angles to each other, each grouping of three forming a courtyard within which a grassy sweep was broken by a pattern of walkways, park benches, and numbered signs. The road through the development was curved, perhaps to break up the hard edges and straight lines of the buildings, or maybe to take advantage of the slight hill from the top of which we could see the blue waters of the intercoastal waterway. We passed a large white building, a fenced swimming pool, and a set of three tennis courts.

"That's the rec hall," Sam explained. "It's got a good-sized gym, classrooms, meeting rooms, a computer center, and a big kitchen. They offer lots of classes, and we even have formal dances. That's where our Residents' Committee meets."

He pulled into a parking spot alongside one of the courtyards. "If we'd kept going," he said, pointing farther down the road, "we'd come to the village. Everything you need, market, post office, hardware store, beauty shop, pharmacy—even a pizza parlor. We got all the comforts." He opened the car door, got out, and went around to unlock the trunk.

The rest of us climbed out slowly, our muscles cramped from having sat for so long.

Sam had the luggage on the sidewalk before we could assist him.

"Thanks for picking us up, Sam," I said. "What do we owe you for the ride?"

"Was no trouble at all. You're friends of Portia's. Here for the funeral, right? I can't charge you for that."

"Were you a friend of hers?" Seth asked.

"I knew her pretty well, but she was closer with my wife, Minnie." He looked down at his sneakers.

"Do you know where the funeral service will take place?" I asked.

"I know where. I just don't know when," he answered. "There's a chapel in the village. You can walk there from here."

"Well, would your wife know when the funeral is?" Maureen asked.

Sam took off his baseball cap and rubbed a hand over his face. He seemed to be weighing his words. "They haven't set a date for the funeral yet."

"Why not?" Mort asked.

"Something's wrong, isn't it?" I said.

"I guess you could say so."

"Well, out with it, man," Seth said. "What is it?"

"There's a little problem."

"What problem is that, Sam?" I asked.

"The police haven't released the body yet."

Chapter Two

"I'm sorry, Jessica. I know I should have mentioned something, but Clarence was so sure we'd have Portia back for the funeral that I thought it could wait till you got here."

Helen Davison was a beautifully dressed African-American woman. She wore a slim black skirt and a purple, raglan-sleeved blouse, the color of which complemented her café-au-lait skin. Her gray hair was pulled back into a chignon at the base of her neck, a tidy but severe look for someone whose profession was styling hair.

We were standing in what had been Portia's—now Clarence's—apartment, where an informal gathering was taking place.

"This is like a wake without the body," Seth had proclaimed when we'd walked in early on the evening after our arrival in Florida.

There were two dozen people there, sitting on Portia's pink-and-green flowered sofa and coordinating Bergere chairs, or standing in small groups in the L-shaped living room, which had a lovely view of the bay. A woman with long curly black hair, dressed in a gauzy skirt and peasant blouse, ferried casseroles, coffee, and plates of homemade baked goods from the kitchen to a table in the alcove that served as a dining area.

Among the people perched on brown metal folding chairs, brought in for the occasion and lined up along one wall, were identical twin brothers. I gauged them to be in their late thirties. Dressed alike in royal blue T-shirts over khaki trousers, they also wore Day-Glo-orange baseball caps, which matched their wide suspenders, and thick leather belts. Each balanced on his lap a plate with three cookies, two chocolate and one peanut butter. They were talking with a man who looked like a bodybuilder in an ill-fitting white button-down shirt and red bow tie.

"What exactly happened, Helen?" I asked. "I understand an autopsy was performed. Do you know the results?"

"I don't."

"What is it the police are looking for?"

"I only know they found Portia near the boardwalk that runs along the edge of the bay."

"She wrote to me that she used to walk there every evening," Maureen said.

"That's right. It's only a quarter mile from here. That's why she was so opposed to a development going in, because it would block access to the water for our residents. But that's another story. Apparently she never made it home that night."

"Didn't her husband notice when she failed to return?" I asked.

Helen shook her head. "Clarence had just gotten home after a week up north. He said he'd gone to bed early and didn't miss her till the morning. By that time she was gone."

"Oh, how awful," Maureen said.

Helen blinked back tears. "I only pray she went quickly and didn't lie there in the sand, cold and frightened, waiting for someone to come."

"But when I spoke to you on the phone, you said she died from a heart attack."

"That's what we all assumed, Jessica. Everyone knew Portia had a weak heart. We were all concerned about her. She was, too. Lord knows how many supplements that woman swallowed, handfuls at a time. 'Boosting my cardiac health,' she used to say."

Seth, who had come away from the table with a sampling of goodies on a plate, overheard Helen's comment. "She would have been better off just taking the medicine I prescribed for her," he said, joining our conversation, "and leaving all that other junk out of her system." He bit down on a brownie.

I introduced him to Helen.

"It's nice to meet you," she said. "Were you Portia's doctor back in Maine?"

"Ayuh," he said, wiping his mouth with a napkin. "For thirty-five years. But she's never been known to listen, so all my advice went out the window. Always ordering shark bones and snake oil from those fly-by-night pill catalogues like they'd know more than a physician who's spent years studying what was healthy and what wasn't."

"I happen to think you're right," Helen said, "but most of the people here would disagree. The local pharmacy makes a fortune on its supplements. They have a whole section of the shop devoted to them."

"Just quackery, if you ask me," Seth said, and wandered back to the table.

"Helen, you don't think Portia might have accidentally poisoned herself, do you?" I asked.

"I truly doubt it. She was very well-informed about

supplements. She used to attend all the talks on complementary medicine offered by our Resident Wisdom lecture series."

"What's that?"

"We're not close to many cultural opportunities down here—Miami's just far enough away to be inconvenient—so we have to make our own entertainment. Our residents are pretty knowledgeable on a lot of topics—we come from all over—so we take advantage of our natural resource, and that's us. Resident Wisdom. We're the residents."

"We do that in Cabot Cove, too," Maureen said. "We have our own theater and local orchestra. Not as fancy as Boston, of course, but I think it's pretty good."

Helen laughed. "We don't have a theater or an orchestra, at least not yet. It's mostly lectures and the occasional field trip. But it gets us out of the house, and gives those of us who don't golf something productive to do."

"Still, you're very wise to come up with such a wonderful idea," I said.

"Portia was one of the ones who started the program. And she roped Clarence into helping out."

We looked over to where Clarence was talking to two women. He was a handsome man with sharp features, tall, thin, slightly stoop-shouldered, gray hair cut very short to camouflage its sparseness.

"He looks like a nice fellow," Maureen said. "How did she meet him?"

Helen shrugged and said in a low voice, "I don't know him very well, only what I've picked up at my beauty shop. I heard he had a gaggle of women after him when he moved down here—he's nice-looking, and he still drives. No money to speak of, but at least he had the good taste to marry Portia. He could have chosen any number of others, I understand."

Mort tapped me on the shoulder. "Excuse me, Mrs. F?"

"Yes, Mort. Have you met Helen Davison, a friend of Portia's?"

"How do, ma'am," Mort said, extending his hand. "Would you mind if I pulled Mrs. F away from you for a moment? There's something I think she needs to hear."

"Now, Mort, sweetie, that's not polite," Maureen said.

"I'm sorry honey bun, but it's important."

"That's fine," Helen said. "You go right ahead. Carrie probably can use some company in the kitchen. She shouldn't have to be serving all by herself."

"Why don't I come help you," Maureen said.

"Thank you. We can always use an extra hand."

"I'd like to talk with you again, Helen, if I may," I said.

"Of course, Jessica, anytime. I live just downstairs, on the first floor."

Mort, who had been impatiently hopping from one foot to the other, drew me across the room and down the hall to where Sam, our driver, was standing outside the master bedroom.

"Sam, please tell Mrs. F what you told me."

Sam looked over my shoulder to be sure no one else was coming. His eyes darted between Mort's and mine. "She trustworthy?"

"Who? Mrs. F? She knows more about crimes and criminals than half the police in . . . well, probably in the country."

"Mort, that's quite an exaggeration," I said.

"Maybe, but not by much," he conceded. "Of

course you can trust her," he told Sam. "You trusted me, didn't you?"

Sam coughed. "Yes, but you're an officer of the law."

"Well, Mrs. F has been my deputy many a time, I can tell you that. She knows all about murder." Mort looked at me. "Sam thinks Mrs. Shelby was murdered, and he thinks he knows who did it."

"Darn it! Let me tell my own story," Sam said. "I know it better than you. You're giving away the punch line."

"An accusation of murder is no joke," I said gently.

"Aw, I didn't mean punch line. I meant the meat of the story."

"Let's go in here," Mort said, herding us into the bedroom and closing the door.

The master bedroom was small, but pretty. Flowered wallpaper—pink roses and peonies—covered three of the walls and complemented a patterned rug. The fourth wall was all closets, with mirrored doors. A queen-size bed took up most of the space, and someone—probably Clarence—had made an effort to tidy up, making the bed with an aqua-and-pink-striped spread, which was slightly askew. A pair of maple dressers, covered with medicine bottles, was arranged side by side across from the bed. A green tufted chair was nestled in a corner. Mort pulled over the chair and indicated that I should sit. Sam perched on the edge of the bed.

"Go ahead, Sam," Mort said.

Sam nodded sharply at Mort and looked at me. "First, I gotta tell you that I'm working for the police."

"You are?" I said.

"Yup. It's very common down here. The cops're

always short-staffed and short-funded, if that's the right word. They use us seniors to man the phones and do the filing and such. They want us because we're reliable, you understand. No coming in late and giving excuses. I'm no teenager. You can see that for yourself. I'll be eighty-four next summer, although everyone tells me I don't look a day over seventy-five. And it's not volunteer, you know. They pay us, too. Not a lot, of course, but it helps with Social Security so measly. Don't get me started on that. It's barely enough to live on, even here in Florida, where the cost of living is a lot lower than in New York. That's where I used to live before I retired."

Mort, who'd been pacing behind my chair, stopped. "C'mon, Sam. Get to the story," he said.

"I'm getting there. Hold your horses." He looked at me. "No patience, these youngsters," he said, cocking his head in Mort's direction. "Everyone's in a hurry. It's always rush, rush, rush. In my day, people took their time about things, and—"

"Sam!" Mort was about to explode.

"And had more respect for their elders," Sam finished. He held up one hand. "Okay. Okay. Where was I?" He leaned down to tighten the Velcro strips on his gym shoes and straightened again. "Oh, yeah. So I work at the station house, answer the phones—there's also a dispatcher, but that's a young guy—and I hear these cops talking about Portia."

"What did they say?" I asked.

"That the medical examiner had ordered an autopsy."

"Isn't that common with an accidental death, or one where the circumstances are not clear?"

Sam frowned. "I don't know. I guess so."

"Do the police suspect that she was murdered?"

"I think so, and I think I know the guy."

"Who do you think murdered Portia?"

"Tony Colombo."

"Who's Tony Colombo?" I asked.

"He owns the pizza parlor down in the village, but it's his cousin does the cooking. There's something suspicious about that."

"Perhaps he has other business talents," I said. "Why do you think he murdered Portia?"

Sam squinted at me. "I've been keeping an eye on this guy. Let me give you a little history, first. I used to live in New York—I told you that already—and on the news they were always talking about the families. You ever heard of the Colombo family?"

"Are you talking about the Colombo crime family?"

Sam smiled at Mort. "She's a lot smarter than I thought."

"I told you," Mort said.

"Yup, that's who I'm talking about. The five families." He counted on his fingers as he named the families. "Bonanno, Lucchese, Gambino, Genovese, and"—he paused for effect—"Colombo. That's the New York mob. I think this guy is a hit man, sent down from New York to ice Portia."

I sighed. "Sam, why would the mob want to kill Portia?"

"She must have found out something incriminating about him. Colombo, that is. You may not know this, but Portia was on the Foreverglades Residents' Committee. She knew a lot about a lot of people."

"If he's a hit man, why would Tony Colombo bother to open a pizza parlor?" I asked.

"A cover. Not a bad one either. They make pretty good pizza."

"But, Sam," I said, "what evidence do you have

that the Tony Colombo who owns this pizza parlor is a member of a crime family? Colombo is a common Italian name. In fact, I know of a famous policeman with that name."

"Sure, sure. It's a common name, but this guy is a mobster."

"How do you know that?" I asked.

"I've been keeping him under surveillance ever since he got here, and he's acting very suspicious."

I glanced up at Mort.

"Sheesh, Sam. You told me the police were watching this guy, not that *you* were watching this guy."

Sam straightened up. "I work for the police. That's as good as."

"It's not the same thing, Sam," Mort said, barely controlling his exasperation. "You're not a cop. You're a volunteer."

"A paid volunteer."

"Yeah. Okay. A paid volunteer," Mort said, slapping his hands on his hips. "But you told me the cops were watching this guy because he was out to get Mrs. Shelby. That's not what you're saying now. I'm sorry, Mrs. F. I thought he had a real inside scoop."

"I do. I do," Sam said.

Our conversation was interrupted by a knock on the bedroom door. Seth poked his head in. "There you are, Jess. I was looking for you."

I stood up. "Well, you found me."

"Excuse me, Doc," Mort said, sliding sideways past Seth and escaping into the hall. "I think I hear my wife calling me."

"Sam," I said, "I appreciate your telling us the story. I'm not sure we have anything to worry about with Mr. Colombo, but let's wait to see what the police have to say when the autopsy report comes back. Okay?"

Sam saluted me. "Right you are, chief," he said, grinning.

"And Sam," I called after him as he walked into the hall. He turned. "In the meantime, let's keep this just among the three of us. I think the police would prefer that, don't you?"

"You don't have to worry about me. It'll be top secret." He ran his fingers across his lips as if zipping them up. "My lips are sealed. It'll just be the three of us."

"Thank you."

"What the devil was that about?" Seth asked, walking over to the bureau and surveying the items arrayed across the top.

"I'm afraid Sam has an active imagination," I replied, "and if he's not careful, he could get himself sued for slander."

"That bad, huh?"

"That bad."

Seth picked up a brown bottle and squinted at the label. "You know the big guy we saw talking to the twins?"

"Yes?"

"That was Mark Rosner."

"Oh. The manager. I'll have to go and say hello."

"It'll have to be tomorrow. He's already left." He put the bottle down and picked up another one. "Told me about the twins—Nuts and Bolts, he calls them. Real names are Earl and Burl Simmons. They're maintenance people here. One of them is a bit slow, he said. They've never been separated. Live together next door to the post office, and both work for the development."

"You certainly found out a lot about them in a short time."

"Ayuh. Always wear matching clothing."

"Their mother must have dressed them alike as children and they've kept up the habit," I said.

"He said they're very reliable, really run the place." His voice trailed off.

"What are you looking at so intently?"

"Portia's pills."

I joined Seth in front of one of the dressers. I'd noticed the bottles, but hadn't examined them. Two rows of prescription medicines and nutritional supplements in various-size bottles were lined up across the top. On a mirrored tray in front of them, along with her watch, earrings, eyeglass case, and wedding band, was Portia's white plastic pill organizer with sections designated for each day of the week, two of which were open and empty. Seth flipped up the lid for Wednesday, and peered at the array of pills and capsules.

"See anything of interest?" I asked.

"I'm just wonderin' about these ones here," he said, poking his finger into the compartment. "Can't imagine why Portia would be taking this with a bad heart."

I heard a metallic jingling sound before a deep voice from behind us said, "Excuse me. Is there something you need?"

Clarence stood in the doorway, a scowl on his face, one hand rattling the change in his pocket.

"Hello, Clarence. We met earlier," I said, going to the green chair and pushing it back into the corner Mort had taken it from. "I'm Jessica Fletcher, one of Portia's friends from Cabot Cove, and this is Seth Hazlitt."

"I know who you are. What I don't know is what you're doing in my bedroom."

Seth put a hand under my elbow and pushed me toward the door. "Mrs. Fletcher was feeling a mite peaked," he said, his Maine accent thickening, "what with the flight and the long ride from the airport. So we ducked in heah so she could set a spell. She'll be right as rain in a bit. No need for you to worry."

"Why did you tell him I was sick?" I asked when we were back in the living room.

"Got us out of the room without having to explain, now, didn't it?"

"It did," I said, "but I think we may want to look around again sometime."

"Not necessary," Seth said, giving me a secret smile. "I've got what we need."

"You do?"

"Ayuh." He pulled his hand halfway out of his jacket pocket, his fingers wrapped around Portia's white pillbox.

"What are we doing with that?"

"Thought I might stroll down to the local drugstore and ask the pharmacist about a couple of Portia's pills."

"Is that really necessary?"

"Well, I just can't understand why a woman like Portia would be taking something athletes used to use. If I'm right, that is, about what kind of pills I saw."

"Portia? Taking pills that athletes use?"

"Used to. Not anymore."

"Why not anymore?"

"Probably because it killed them."

Chapter Three

"Harry, Mrs. Rodriguez is coming in for the insulin. Where'd you put it?"

"It's under W in the prescription box."

"And where's the Saint-John's-wort?"

"Aisle three, second shelf. Who wants it, Ronnie?"

"Mrs. Lazzara."

"If she's taking any diet meds or antidepressants, tell her she can't have it. There could be a danger of interaction."

"Okay."

"And if she buys it, tell her no red wine, aged cheese, or chicken livers."

"What was that again, Harry?"

"Hang on a minute. Let me come talk to her."

Seth and I had gone to Weinstein's Pharmacy in Foreverglades Village, ostensibly to find sunglasses for me and extra razor blades for him, but as Sam probably would have put it, we were "casing the joint." The pharmacist, Harry, was filling prescriptions behind the counter in the back, while a cherubic man named Ronnie and his daughter, Sandy, handled the customers out front. Fully half the store was a gift shop, overflowing with a wide variety of attractive items. I could have done all my Christmas shopping there without walking out the door. The other half was a drugstore, a small portion of which was stocked with traditional products like shampoo and foot powder, electric toothbrushes and headache remedies. But by far the largest section was devoted to vitamins, minerals, herbs, and other nutritional supplements, some with exotic names like hawthorn, ginseng, goldenseal, and feverfew.

"I might like those on you," Seth said, "if the label didn't cover your nose."

I looked at myself in the mirror and grimaced. The sunglasses I'd chosen to try on, like all the ones on the display rack, had a green label tied to the nosepiece.

"Isn't it silly?" Sandy said. "That's the way they come in, and there's nothing we can do about it." The young woman handed me another pair and I tried them on. In addition to the label dangling between the lenses, there was a round sticker on one lens with the letters UV in red.

"I think you might like these better," Sandy said, taking the glasses and handing me a pair with tortoiseshell-patterned frames. "The lenses change from dark to light when you come indoors," she said, "so they help your eyes adjust. They're very popular here. I'm sure they've prevented a lot of falls with the older folks. Besides, they're a nice shape for your face, and a good color for your complexion."

"All that?" I said, laughing. "Sold! I'll take them."

"Is there anything else I can help you with?"

"I don't think so. We'd like to talk to the pharmacist when he has a moment."

"Harry? Sure. He's with a customer right now, but he shouldn't be more than a minute. I'll tell him you're waiting to see him."

While Seth dug money out of his pocket for the razor blades, I thanked Sandy, paid for my new sunglasses, and eavesdropped on Harry's conversation with Mrs. Lazzara, a diminutive lady in tennis whites.

"Libby swears by the Saint-John's-wort tea," Mrs. Lazzara said. "Gives her a real lift."

"Yes, but she isn't on blood pressure medicine and you are," Harry said, taking the box from her hand and replacing it on the shelf.

She frowned. "I want to try it."

"I know you do," Harry said, gently escorting her farther down the aisle. "Unfortunately, the Saint-John's-wort contains hypericin, and that's thought to act just like the MAO inhibitors. You really have to watch your diet if you're taking that. Something as common as bologna, or that pickled fish you like, could cause a rapid rise in blood pressure, the last thing you need. You're a good customer. I want to keep you around a little longer."

Mrs. Lazzara's frown turned into a smile. "Are you flirting with me, Harry? I like that in a young man."

Harry, who was probably in his fifties, smiled. "How about the Marrakesh Mint tea I recommended last week?" he asked. "Did you like that one?"

"That was good advice about the Saint-John's-wort," Seth said to the pharmacist, after Mrs. Lazzara had left and Harry came to assist us.

"I could sell it to her, but knowing what I do, it would have been unethical," the trim, good-looking pharmacist said. "I carry the supplements and I believe in their efficacy, but as in all things people ingest, they have to know what they're taking and why, and most important, they have to be aware of the potential for interactions."

"Glad to hear you say it. I'm Dr. Hazlitt, by the way. This is Mrs. Fletcher."

"We were friends of Portia Shelby's," I said, "and came down for her funeral."

"I was sorry to hear about Mrs. Shelby," Harry said. "She was a real firebrand in the community, and a very kind lady as well. I'm sure you'll miss her. My condolences."

"Thank you," I said.

"How can I help you folks?"

"I wanted to show you a particular tablet I found," Seth said. "I think I know what it is, but I wanted you to confirm it. You're the expert."

Harry smiled. "Expert, huh? That's very flattering, Doctor, and you only just got into town. I must have quite a reputation. I'm not sure if I can identify it on sight, but I'll try." He held out his hand.

Seth dropped a pill on Harry's palm.

"Oh, this," Harry said, poking at the little blue pill. "I don't sell it."

"What is it?" I asked.

"It's a popular diet pill," he replied. "I used to carry these kinds of diet pills, and they'd fly off the shelf, but I stopped stocking them when a couple of football guys died and it turned out they were taking something like this."

"What's in it?"

"It's a combination of ephedra and caffeine. Some consider it fairly safe and effective for healthy people who want to lose weight."

"Would you recommend ephedra for someone who had a heart condition?" Seth asked.

"I wouldn't recommend ephedra to anyone; that's why I stopped selling it. This pill also has caffeine in it, and the combination is a powerful stimulant. Definitely not safe in my opinion, especially for someone

with a bad heart. Could die from that." He gave the
pill back to Seth, saying, "I wouldn't take it if I were
you. There are safer ways to lose weight. If you follow
me, I can show you some of the things we do recommend for our overweight customers. And I have a
wonderful booklet with easy exercise routines. The retirees have a pretty good gym over at Foreverglades.
Have you seen it?" He was halfway down the aisle
before he realized his error.

Seth sputtered. "Me? I wasn't talking about me. I'm
not retired, I don't have a heart condition, and I'm
not looking to go on a diet. And if I want exercise, it
won't be in a gym."

"Oh, sorry," Harry said, flushing. "I thought that's
why you were asking. . . ." He trailed off, obviously
embarrassed.

"Can you believe it, Jessica? I ask a simple question
and he has me on a diet. Next thing you know, he'll
be telling me to dye my hair."

"Now, Seth, it was a natural mistake," I said, trying
not to look down at his ample stomach. "The man
certainly didn't mean to offend you."

"And besides, I do exercise," Seth barked to Harry.
"I play golf." He straightened his posture, pulling his
shoulders back and stomach in. I wasn't sure how long
he could hold that pose. "Anyway, I found out what
I needed to," he said, starting for the door. He nodded
at Harry. "Thank you, sir. Appreciate the information.
Coming along, Jess?"

"Why don't you see if they have a table at the coffee shop next door," I said, not quite ready to leave.
"I could use an iced tea, and you'd probably like one,
too. I saw the nicest candle in the other aisle, and I
want to buy it for Charlene Sassi. She loves candles.
Go on ahead. I'll meet you in few minutes."

"Don't be dillydallying. Time's a-wasting," he said, looking back at me while he pushed through the door, nearly knocking over a red-haired woman in a suit.

"I never dillydally," I called after him.

"Sorry, Mrs. Fletcher," Harry said. "I just assumed he was talking about himself."

"Don't worry about it, Harry," I said. "He'll get over it. And I think he may need a reminder every now and again to follow the same advice he gives to his patients about diet and exercise."

"But he was upset, and I feel bad that I insulted him."

"He's not the type to hold a grudge. He'll forget about it."

"I hope so. Is there anything else, Mrs. Fletcher? I've got to get back to filling prescriptions. Sandy can help you with the candles."

"Just one or two more things, Harry. It's a lovely store. Tell me, have you had it a long time?"

"Moved here right when Foreverglades opened, about ten years ago. This place was a wasteland after Hurricane Andrew blew through, but the government put up a lot of money to rebuild, and Foreverglades was the first community to take advantage of the funds available. We've grown quite a bit since then. Have a whole village now, shops, library, police department—even a chamber of commerce."

"You must have a good-sized clientele with the development right next door. It's restricted to those over fifty-five, isn't it?"

"I see what you're thinking, and I thought the same thing myself when I first came here. Older people tend to need more medicines, it's true. But the people who live here are pretty healthy, and they want to stay that way. That's why I stock so many supplements. They're a bright bunch, read a lot, do research, and over the years I've brought in what they said they wanted. Law of supply and demand. That's how business runs."

"But I can see you're careful with them. You stopped selling the ephedra."

"Got to know your customers. That's the key. But you also have to protect yourself from lawsuits. You'd be amazed how many people are ready to go to court at the drop of a hat."

"So when did you stop carrying the diet pill, Harry? Was it recently?"

"It was right after I heard about those football players. Probably about a couple of months ago."

"And up until then, did you keep records of who bought it?"

"Well, if they charged it to their account, I did. But if they paid cash, I wouldn't have kept a record of that."

"But if someone asked you who might have bought the diet drug, could you tell them? For instance, do you recall if Mrs. Shelby purchased the pills?"

"I don't remember her buying them."

"But if she had an account here, you could look it up, couldn't you?"

"Oh, I couldn't do that. Breach of ethics to reveal private information about clients. No, I'm sorry, Mrs. Fletcher. I couldn't do that."

"Of course. I would never ask you to go against your principles."

"We sold a fair amount, I can tell you that. Just because people get older doesn't mean they don't want to look their best. You can ask Donna when she comes in. She runs our cosmetics counter. Lipsticks, eye shadow, face powder. Perfumes, too. Big business, cosmetics, second only to the supplements. Yes, ma'am."

Harry laughed. "They're a lively lot over at Forever-glades."

Seth was halfway through his iced tea when I joined him, and from the crumbs on the plate in front of him, I'd say Harry's faux pas hadn't had an impact on my friend's dietary habits.

The coffee shop was busy, and I recognized several people I'd seen at Portia's apartment the night before. It was only ten-thirty in the morning, late for breakfast and early for lunch, at least by Maine standards. But every table was taken. Customers could help themselves to sections from the local newspaper, which hung from wooden dowels on a rack next to the cash register. Those who wanted the paper all to themselves could buy one from a stack on the counter. Reading the news and drinking coffee seemed to be a major activity.

"Did you buy the candle for Charlene?" Seth asked, eyeing my empty hands.

"No. I completely forgot. But I can go back another time."

"Find out what you wanted to know?"

"Well, he stopped selling the diet pills a few months ago, but he wouldn't tell me who had bought them."

"I would have said Portia was too smart a woman to take a such a chance with her health. Obviously I would have been wrong."

"I don't think you're wrong. And, anyway, Portia didn't need to lose weight. I think we should have a talk with her husband."

A shadow fell over the table. "You're Jessica Fletcher, aren't you?"

I looked up into the face of a lady in her midsixties who was evidently one of Sandy's customers at the cosmetics counter in Weinstein's. Vivid blue eye shadow and black mascara framed large brown eyes. Bright red lipstick matched her fingernails. On her left wrist was a stack of gold bangle bracelets. Tucked in her right arm was a little dog with white curly fur and black button eyes, its red leash wrapped around her hand. "I'm Monica Kotansky. My sister Carrie and I live in Foreverglades around the corner from the Shelbys. I recognized you right away from the picture on your books. I'm a great fan. Is this your husband?"

Seth struggled to his feet. "Dr. Seth Hazlitt at your service. Mrs. Fletcher—Jessica—is an old friend. Would you care to join us?" He was holding in his stomach again.

"A doctor! How nice." Monica pulled out a chair and sat sideways in it, the dog on her lap. She crossed her legs and let a silver high-heeled pump dangle from her foot.

"What a cute little fellow," Seth said, leaning over to pat the dog on the head.

The dog growled. Seth jerked back his hand.

Monica pouted. "Ooh, I don't know what got into him," she said. "Snowy is a bichon frise. They're very friendly dogs." She lifted the little dog and kissed his muzzle, leaving a trace of lipstick on his fur. She smiled up at Seth. "Well, *I'm* delighted to meet you," she said. "But I can only stay a minute. I have an appointment with my massage therapist."

"Can't imagine why you would need a therapist. You look like a very healthy girl to me," he said, returning the smile and sinking into his seat.

"Woman," I corrected, thinking that if I disappeared, neither of them would notice.

"Of course. A healthy woman."

"A massage makes you feel so good," Monica said, rolling first one shoulder and then the other, thrusting her bosom forward. "And it keeps the muscles in shape. Don't you think so, Doctor?"

"Oh, absolutely," Seth said. "It's important to keep your muscles in shape."

"I work out, too," she said, pushing a strand of blond hair behind her ear. "A woman can't be too careful about her figure."

A light came into Seth's eyes. "Do you use the gym at Foreverglades?"

"Every morning from six to seven."

"Someone was just suggesting I stop by the gym to see the facilities."

"Ooh, I'd be tickled to death to show you around. I know all about the equipment."

"And were you a friend of Portia's?" I asked, deciding it was time to join the conversation.

She tore her eyes away from Seth's for an instant. "Oh, poor, poor Clarence," she said. "He lost his first wife in a boating accident, and then Portia drops dead on the beach. That man must just hate the water."

"I wouldn't be surprised," I said. "Tell me, Ms. Kotansky—"

"Oh, you must call me Monica. And I'll call you Seth. Is that all right, Doctor?" I'd lost her again.

"Absolutely. My pleasure."

She placed the dog on the floor, unwinding the leash from her hand, and rose. Seth rose as well. "I hate to run, but I don't want to be late for my appointment. So nice to meet you, Jessica," she said, still looking at Seth. "And if I don't see *you* at the gym early tomorrow morning, I'll catch you later at the funeral."

"What funeral?" I asked.

"Why, Portia's, of course," she said, finally turning in my direction. "Hadn't you heard? The police have released her body."

Chapter Four

Every seat in the small chapel was taken, and the air inside was stifling. Seth, Mort, Maureen, and I sat halfway back, having arrived early. But those who'd come ten minutes later had to content themselves with standing along the sides in front of the tall stained-glass windows, or leaning against the back wall on either side of the entrance. It was gratifying to see that Portia had made so many friends since moving to Florida from Cabot Cove, following her mother's death.

"All-powerful and merciful God, we commend to you Portia Shelby, your servant. In your mercy and love, blot out all the sins she has committed through human weakness. In this world she has died; let her live with you forever."

The minister closed his prayer book and invited Portia's friends to offer remembrances of her. Several people stood and moved to the front of the room, waiting for a turn at the lectern to eulogize our old friend and neighbor.

The first to speak were the Simmons twins, Earl and Burl. They'd donned identical black T-shirts for the occasion and had removed their fluorescent orange baseball caps, revealing light brown hair parted on the side and plastered down. Their slacks and sneakers were also black, but the caps clutched in their hands and matching orange suspenders rendered their coordinated outfits more appropriate for Halloween than for a funeral.

"We liked her," said Earl, or maybe it was Burl. His brother stood by his side, nodding. "She was a nice lady. Whenever we did work for her, she tipped us real good."

"Real good," his brother agreed.

There was a ripple of laughter from the audience.

The speaker pushed his brother aside and leaned into the microphone. "And she never made fun of us," he said.

The twins sat down and others took their place.

I had thought of Portia Carpenter—that was her maiden name—as a quiet woman, self-confident, yes, but never particularly outspoken on issues. Unmarried, she had been Judge Ralph Mackin's secretary for many years. The judge was a man who appreciated efficiency and frowned on ostentation. Portia had suited him perfectly. Conservative in dress, appearance, and demeanor, she had run his office like a well-oiled machine, retiring only when her failing eyesight made it too difficult to read the fine type in the law books for the citations required by the judge. At her funeral, I discovered another Portia, one I was sorry I hadn't known before. Her new friends praised her leadership, her energy, her fortitude in the face of tremendous odds against her.

"Portia was never one to leave the fight to others." The speaker was Minnie Lewis, Sam's wife. She was taller than her husband, her short steel-gray hair carefully coiffed and her pale blue eyes enlarged by thick glasses.

"When the management threatened to evict Gertie

Joule if she didn't get rid of her cats, Portia challenged the no-pets rule and won. When Portia discovered that some of our seniors weren't eating properly, she organized the Lunch Club, recruiting those of us who still cook to demonstrate how to make delicious, healthy meals. That's where I met Portia, and that was the beginning of our Resident Wisdom program."

As I listened to Minnie's eulogy, another sound caught my ear. Monica Kotansky, in a sleeveless black dress, Snowy perched on her lap, lifted a handkerchief to her eyes, her gold bangle bracelets jangling as they slid into each other. She had seated herself in the first row, across the aisle from the new widower, Clarence, who sat alone. The soft clatter of her bracelets caused Clarence to glance over at Monica, who gave him a wan smile and wiggled her fingers at him. Clarence lowered his eyes. Carrie, who had been helping out in the kitchen at Clarence's apartment and now sat next to Monica, tugged on her arm and whispered something in her ear, causing Monica to straighten in her seat and lift her chin, assuming an attitude of interest in the speaker. The dog struck the same pose.

I wondered if Monica Kotansky had been one of the women Helen Davison had said pursued Clarence before he married Portia. If so, how long would it be before she again tried to gain his interest? I looked around at the roomful of mourners. Were there others here already thinking of Clarence as a potential husband now that his wife was dead? Had Portia worried about holding on to Clarence? Had she tried to lose weight, thinking she would make herself more appealing to him? If so, she may have paid a terrible price for vanity. I hoped that wasn't the case, but the presence of a dangerous diet drug among her daily pills was disturbing. Of course, the autopsy would tell us more, if we were able to get a copy of the results. I made a mental note to suggest to Mort that he check with the police to see when the report was expected back.

"Portia was an inspiration, and I was proud to call her friend," Minnie continued. "I can think of no better tribute to Portia than for us to follow in her footsteps and take up the torch she has had to lay down. If we accomplish that, we will have honored her memory in the most significant way."

The eulogies were succeeded by a final prayer, and the minister announced that Portia had requested a private cremation. Friends were invited to the Shelby apartment for a luncheon in her memory. In addition, the Residents' Committee would meet in the boardroom the next afternoon to discuss a fitting tribute. All those interested were welcome to attend.

"What a lovely service," Maureen said, fanning herself with a program as we slowly followed the crowd up the center aisle of the chapel. "People said such nice things about Portia. I never knew she was such an activist, did you?"

"She was on the chamber of commerce committee that raised money to buy our new squad car," Mort said. "I remember that."

"She may have wanted to get involved with other community projects," I said, "but just didn't have the time. She took care of her mother for so many years. And Ralph kept her pretty busy managing his office and doing research for his cases."

"Just as well," Seth said, shrugging off his jacket. "She had a weak heart. Too much stress might have done her in. Maybe that's the trouble down here. Too much stress and heat."

"I thought retiring meant less stress," Maureen offered.

"Might be the opposite," Seth said, wiping sweat from his face. "All this heat can make you crazy."

Just then Earl and Burl pushed passed us, barreling up the aisle, so close to each other that the stomach of one pushed into the back of the other.

Seth raised his eyebrows at me as if to indicate that here was a case in point.

We'd almost reached the back row when a man standing off to the side caught my attention. Arms folded, he held a baseball cap by its peak, and leaned against the wall, studying each of us as we made our way up the aisle. Younger than the others attending the funeral—except for the twins—he had the shadow of a heavy beard on his face, and was dressed in a rumpled jacket, tie askew. There was something world-weary in his expression, some combination of watchfulness, endurance, and resignation.

"He looks like a policeman," I said, more to myself but loud enough for Mort to hear.

"Who does?" he asked.

"That man over there."

"What makes you say that, Mrs. F?"

"There's a look people in law enforcement get," I said.

"What kind of look?"

"I don't know. Maybe it comes from being exposed to the worst of human frailties. It's hard to explain, but I recognize it."

"Do I look that way?" Mort asked. "If you didn't know me, would you know I was a sheriff?"

I laughed. "I certainly wouldn't know your title."

"Mrs. Fletcher! Mort!" Sam Lewis had joined the

man with the baseball cap, and was waving to us. "Over here."

"Go ahead," Seth said. "It's too hot in here for me. I've got to get some fresh air."

"We'll catch up with you outside," Maureen said, taking his arm. "Please don't be too long, Mort. You know me and the sun."

"I'd like you guys to meet my friend Zach," Sam said when Mort and I had joined them.

"I understand you're friends of Mrs. Shelby's from Maine," Zach said. He extended his hand and I took it. He looked to be in his midforties, with dark hair and even darker eyes.

"That's right," I said. "I'm Jessica Fletcher. This is Mort Metzger. He's our sheriff back home in Cabot Cove."

The men shook hands. "Name's Zach Shippee."

"Zach's a detective with the Foreverglades Police Department," Sam said. "We work together on a lot of cases."

A policeman! I resisted giving Mort a smug glance, but he winked at me. "I'm surprised a place as small as Foreverglades has a police department of its own," he said to Zach.

"We're actually a division of the Miami-Dade Police Department. Foreverglades is in Dade County, so it falls under the MDPD's supervision."

"That makes sense."

"Zach's a big fan of your books, too, Mrs. Fletcher," Sam said. "In fact, he said he'd lend me one."

"Actually, it's the wife who's the big fan," Shippee said with a pleasant smile. "She's read all of your books. I've read a couple of them, though. Sam didn't know that you're a famous author."

"I don't know about being famous," I said, "but it's nice of you to say so."

"Just wanted to make sure you guys met," Sam said. "I've got to go now. I'm the designated driver for Clarence."

"Has he been drinking?" Mort asked, looking at his watch.

"No, no. What I mean is I'm supposed to drive him somewhere. He doesn't have his car here."

"I'll come out with you. Maureen's probably getting impatient. Says she wilts in the sun. Nice meeting you, Zach."

"Same here," Zach said. He turned to me. "Our friend Sam there would make a great character for one your books," he said. "He could be your lead character, the one who always manages to solve the crime before the cops do. I wish *we* could work that fast."

"You could," I said, "if you had to meet my publisher's deadlines."

He laughed.

"May I ask why you came to Portia's funeral?" I asked.

He shrugged. "It's a small town. The department likes to pay its respects."

"Does that mean you send a representative to everyone's funeral? Given the average age of the residents of Foreverglades, I imagine you could spend a lot of time at memorial services."

He gave me a wry smile, but didn't respond.

"Would your presence here have anything to do with the results of the autopsy on Portia?" I asked.

"There's a little matter of privacy here, Mrs. Fletcher. I can't very well discuss the deceased with you, especially not before I've spoken with her husband."

"I can be trusted not to reveal the results, but I agree. You need to notify Portia's husband first."

"Appreciate your discretion."

"When will you give him the autopsy results?"

He scratched his jaw where the beginnings of whiskers were evident, although it couldn't have been more than four or five hours since he'd shaved. "I didn't exactly say that's what I was going to talk about with him, did I?"

"No, but the police did release the body for the funeral, so you must have obtained whatever information you were looking for."

"Some of it, anyway," he said. "I'm not really sure when I'll talk to Mr. Shelby. I might not get 'round to it till tomorrow or the next day. We don't want to be accused of being insensitive."

"I'll have to check in with Clarence then, to ask when you've spoken with him."

"Good idea." The chapel was empty and he pushed off the wall and started toward the door, indicating I should precede him. "Let's go outside. You must be hot. This place is like an oven."

"Feels good, after the winter we've been having in Maine."

"A lot of the Northerners say that."

"I guess that's why so many move to Florida."

"It's really nice now, but you wouldn't like it quite so much in the summer," he said, opening the door for me. "Everybody stays indoors. Too hot and too humid."

"Ironic, isn't it? We stay indoors in the winter and you stay indoors in the summer."

A lovely breeze greeted us as we stepped out onto the portico. The chapel was located halfway up a gentle rise with a clear view of the sparkling water. I took a deep breath and let it out. "Portia said she loved it here. I can see why. Had you ever met her?"

"Um-hmm," he said, suppressing a smile. "Your friend was a really feisty lady."

"What do you mean?"

"I mean she wasn't afraid to make waves. Always calling us on some infraction by the management. She must have lived with the contract under her pillow. Drove the guys down at the station house crazy. But she got that developer to bow down every once in a while. Course, now she can't get in his way anymore."

"Are you hinting at something, Detective?"

"Not at all. Just making an observation. I've got to run. It was nice meeting you, Mrs. Fletcher. I'll have something good to tell my wife at dinner. She's always complaining that I never talk about my work."

"Glad to be of service," I said.

"Will you be staying long?"

"Why do you ask?"

"If you plan to stick around Foreverglades for a few days, I could bring you one of my wife's books and you could autograph it for her. Would you mind?"

"It would be my pleasure. My friends and I came down for the funeral together. We're all staying at Foreverglades, number twenty-three. I'm on the top floor, two B."

"I'll try to get over there, but if I miss you, you have a good trip back north." He smoothed down his dark hair, damp from the heat, put on his baseball cap, and trotted down the steps.

"Thanks," I called after him.

Portia's friends stood talking in small clusters in the courtyard of the chapel. Helen waved me over and introduced me to Sam's wife, Minnie Lewis, and to Amelia Rodriguez, who worked in Helen's beauty shop. Amelia was younger than her companions, and wore her ebony hair in an elaborate style, partly pinned up with wispy curls around her face. Apparently another customer of the cosmetics counter at Weinstein's Pharmacy, she was heavily made up, but with a far more deft hand than Monica Kotansky's more obvious efforts with eye shadow and mascara.

"Can you believe how hot it was in there?" Helen asked. "If I hadn't used half a can of hair spray on Olga Piper, her beehive would have been tilting to one side."

"My hair held up pretty well," Minnie said, patting the back of her head. "You did a nice job."

"Thanks," Helen said, turning her friend around so she could inspect her work. "It still looks good."

"Never mind hair. Did you see who was inside?" Amelia asked, a frown on her face. "What *cojones,* if you'll excuse me for saying so. I don't know how he has the nerve to show his face." She spoke in rapid-fire English with a distinct Spanish accent. "If Portia was alive, she'd drop dead all over again, seeing him here."

"Who are you talking about?" I asked.

"DeWitt Wainscott," Minnie said. "He's a real estate developer."

"He's trying to build on the property between Foreverglades and the bay," Helen said. "Portia was spearheading our opposition to the project when she died."

"That's him over there," Amelia said, pointing to a

man in a dark gray suit talking to a stout woman I'd
seen somewhere before. He was of medium height
with a paunch hanging over the waistline of his trousers. He wore a light green bow tie, and when he
pushed back the side of his jacket to pull a handkerchief from his pocket, I spotted a set of chartreuse
suspenders with little flowers embroidered on them.
"I don't know how my sister-in-law can stand working
for the man," she added.

"Is that your sister-in-law he's talking to?" I asked.

She nodded. "*Sí*, that's Marina, *mi cuñada*."

Amelia's sister-in-law was as tall as her boss, her
red hair neatly pinned in a bun. She wore a gray suit,
and held an open briefcase from which she handed
him a sheet of paper.

"How long has she worked for him?" I asked.

"Too long. Look at her. She even dresses like him.
He built Foreverglades. That's how we came here. We
lived in Miami before, but he promised my brother a
job on the construction site, and then he hired my
sister-in-law as his secretary. He tried to hire me, too,
but I wouldn't work for him."

"What did he want you to do, style his hair?" Minnie laughed.

"He's barely got any left to do a comb-over," Amelia said, giggling.

"It sounds to me like he's been good to your family," I said.

"Good? This is a man who makes all kinds of promises and never keeps them. The only one who ever
earns any money when he's around is DeWitt Wainscott. My brother has been laid off so many times, his
head is spinning. But now that Marina works for the
pig, she don't want to move anywhere else. My

brother went back to Miami, and they're getting a divorce."

"When Wainscott built Foreverglades, he gave his word he'd never put up anything between our development and the water," Minnie said. "Now he's talking about building three high-rise buildings, which will completely block our views. People are already leaving Foreverglades."

"So much for his word of honor," Helen said. "Look at that." She swept her arm toward the expanse of blue water. "It'll be gone. I didn't come down here to see big buildings all the time. I could have stayed in Chicago for that."

"Fullero!" Amelia spat. "Cheater! And then, if that's not insult enough, he's going to put a fence around it with a guard at the gate. We won't be able to get to the beach from the village. We'll have to go all the way down to a new road that's not even built yet."

"Plus, if you're not careful, you could run into an alligator going that way," Helen said. "Did you hear about the woman up in Perrine who lost her foot? Came out of her house in the afternoon to cut some key limes for a pie and there it was, crossing her lawn on the way to her pool. The thing was about five or six feet long, and—whomp!—bit her on the ankle, going clear through to the bone."

"How dreadful," Minnie said.

"We should sue him for breach of promise," Amelia said.

"Who?"

"Wainscott."

"I think you mean breach of contract," I said, trying to keep up with the ricocheting conversation. "Did he have a contract with you stating his intentions not to build?"

"We thought so," Amelia said. "*Naturalmente,* his lawyers say it doesn't really promise anything. They say it's all in the little print or something."

"You mean the fine print?" I asked.

"Try standing in a shop all day without a foot," Helen muttered.

"*Sí.* That's it." Amelia nodded at me. " 'Can't stop progress,' he says. The big crook."

"Croc? No, they're alligators. Girl, I tell you, I'm looking out for alligators every time I walk to the bay," Helen said. "They really scare me."

"Portia wasn't scared. She was the bravest person I ever knew," Amelia said, sniffling.

"He looks so sad, doesn't he?" Minnie said, handing Amelia a tissue.

"Quién?" Amelia asked, blowing her nose.

"Clarence."

Clarence, who stood by the door of Sam's pink Cadillac, shook hands with the minister, and accepted the sympathies of several of his neighbors before climbing in the backseat.

"Where is he going?" I asked.

"Probably to the place where they do the cremation," Minnie said. "The undertaker has a hearse for the coffin, but no limousines. So Sam fills in when a limo is needed. He's supposed to charge for the car service, but he never has. 'Not for funerals,' he says, 'and not for friends.' "

"That's very kind of him," I said.

"He's such a mensch," she said fondly. "That means 'good guy' in Yiddish. He started the service as a way to earn a few extra dollars—the nearest limousine company is over in Florida City—but he's such an easy target for a sob story that I don't think he's earned a penny yet. Anybody gives him a good excuse, or even a terrible one, and he drives them for free. I wouldn't care except that gas guzzler is going to break us if it doesn't earn its keep. Parts for that old heap are not cheap."

"Ooh, Minnie, you made a rhyme," Amelia sang out, smiling.

"I did?"

"Who's going over to the Shelbys'?" Helen asked.

"Everyone," Minnie said, rummaging around in her handbag.

"Amelia and I have to get back to the shop," Helen said. "We probably have ten people waiting by now."

"Well, come by when you're done," Minnie said, pulling out her sunglasses.

"What time do you figure Clarence will be back?"

"Doesn't matter. Carrie has the key, but she'll need help setting up. I'm going over there now."

"Okay, see you both later," Helen said, and she and Amelia crossed the street and started up the hill toward her beauty parlor.

"Would you like my help, too?" I offered.

"Oh, no, no," Minnie said. "You're a guest. Bring your friends by in about an hour or so and we'll feed you." She walked off toward Foreverglades.

The crowd in front of the chapel had dispersed. My friends were nowhere in sight. But the vista of Biscayne Bay from this vantage point was captivating. The day was clear and the sun shot little sparks of light off the choppy water. I dug my new sunglasses out of my bag and put them on. Portia had loved this view. She had been fighting hard to keep it so everyone in Foreverglades could see the water, walk along the shore, and enjoy the beauty of nature. How sad that what is called "progress" by some was going to spoil it for others. Detective Shippee had characterized Portia as a "feisty lady." Had her heart given out because of her determination to keep this beautiful view unblocked?

Chapter Five

I originally intended to follow Minnie back to Forev-erglades, but when I reached the intersection at the base of the hill, I gave in to the lure of the water, and set my steps toward the shore. Tall grasses lined one side of a concrete sidewalk that wound its way to the bay alongside an unpaved road, which ended in a small, pebble-strewn parking lot. An L-shaped dock jutting into the water was anchored to concrete slabs sunk into the mud. Two dozen boats were tied up to the dock. An aluminum dinghy, its lines looped around a piling, was available for owners of boats moored offshore to reach their vessels.

At the head of the dock, down a short flight of steps, a narrow boardwalk veered off to the left, back in the direction of Foreverglades. Sand had been dumped in a long crescent-shaped section to create a man-made beach, but the thick vegetation had not been kept in check, and tendrils of green crept under the low boardwalk as though trying to reclaim the land. Farther down, the sand ended, palm trees rose from the thick grass, and the boardwalk, with a waist-high railing, curved out over the water, ending in a circular gazebo. A large white sign had been braced in the damp earth about ten yards off the boardwalk. On it was the message: SITE OF THE FUTURE WAINSCOTT

TOWERS, A NEW GATED COMMUNITY. TWENTY-ONE-STORY BUILDINGS, FEATURING RESIDENCES OF DISTINCTION. Someone had circled Wainscott's name with red spray paint and scrawled *Liar* above it, the thick paint dripping down from the letters like blood.

Beyond the sign, I could see the pink buildings of Foreverglades, and sympathized with their tenants' plight. The construction would not only block their view and cut them off from the waterfront, but it was bound to destroy the peaceful existence they currently enjoyed. Residents of three high-rise buildings would probably double the local population. They would crowd the shops, create traffic congestion with their cars, and overwhelm the small beach and the boardwalk on which I stood. I thought of Portia, and how much she loved the place she had found for herself in Florida. Change is difficult for many of us, but for people who have spent years planning for their retirement and carefully selected the environment they wanted, it's harder still to have threats made against their long-anticipated lifestyle.

Deep in contemplation, I meandered down the rough planks of the boardwalk—the footwear I'd worn for the funeral was not conducive to walking in the sand—and made my way toward the gazebo. As I approached the weathered wooden structure, I realized I wasn't alone. A figure stepped away from the railing he'd been leaning over. At first I thought he was holding a fishing rod, but then I realized it was just a long stick he'd been playing with in the water.

"What are you looking at?" I asked.

"Someone threw some litter in the water. I hate to see that," Detective Shippee said, leaning his stick against an upright and sitting on a bench, his back to the bay. "It's so beautiful out here, isn't it?"

"Spectacular."

"The best part is how quiet it is. You can sit here sometimes and the only sounds you'll hear are those made by nature—the birds, the insects, the water lapping up against the pier."

"I know," I said. "There's something about being on the water that soothes the soul."

He smiled sadly. "It's a pity it won't last."

"You're talking about the development?"

He nodded.

"I can understand why my friend fought against it," I said. "It's going to change the whole character of the area."

He frowned and crossed his arms. "Yeah, well, money talks, and Wainscott walks all over anyone who gets in his way."

"What do you mean?"

"The local zoning commission caved in to everything he proposed."

"Weren't the Foreverglades residents there?"

"Oh, yeah. They held public hearings, and you better believe those were well attended. Your friend Mrs. Shelby was a very persuasive speaker."

"But not persuasive enough?"

"She could rally the troops, but she didn't have the wherewithal to finance the war. She came pretty close, though. Wainscott must've spent a fortune on lawyers after she got started, but he's probably used to it."

"Has he done this before?"

"Many times, I'm sure. He has more lawyers than the local municipalities can ever hope to mount a defense against."

"But he still has to comply with the law."

"The law can be very flexible, especially when it has an arsenal of lawyers aimed at it."

"I'm sorry to hear it."

"He did the same thing in Key West. The city was opposed to a development that he proposed. He'd already bought the land and was damned if they were going to stop him. So he made them all kinds of promises. He was going to protect the environment, open shorelines to the public, stuff like that. Of course, once he broke ground, he broke all his promises, too."

"Couldn't the government sue him?"

"They could, but he had a secret weapon."

"His lawyers."

"Yup. By the time Wainscott's lawyers got through, they would have been tied up in court for years. It would have cost the citizens of Key West a fortune in taxes to pay for it."

"So the government gave in?"

"I'm sure Wainscott made a few concessions just to mollify them, but this is not a man you want to buck. There was an accident down there I'm still not sure about." He stood up and leaned over the railing, looking down into the water. "But accidents happen. Anyway, it's in the past. We can't recapture that, can we?"

He seemed distraught, and I wondered if Portia's death had truly saddened him. "My friends must be wondering where I am," I said. "I should get back to Foreverglades. Portia's husband is hosting a luncheon for her friends. Sounds to me like you fit that description. Why don't you come with me?"

"Maybe another time," he said.

We walked back toward the dock together. I scanned the landscape around us, thinking about Portia's evening constitutionals.

"Looking to see where your friend died?" Detective Shippee asked.

"Actually, I was."

"One of the boaters saw her lying in the sand and called the shore patrol. They found her over here." He pointed to where the tall grass ended and the artificial beach began. "Luckily there were no alligators around at the time, or it would have been a mess."

"Are there alligators here?" I asked.

"Yes. See those tracks?" He pointed to some markings on the sand.

"You mean they come right out on the beach?"

"We're trespassing on their property, not the other way around," he said. "There are alligators all over Florida. They've been here for thousands of years."

"Yes, but I would have thought—"

"They usually come out at night. I keep telling that to the folks who like to stroll on the boardwalk in the evenings. We've got an old bull around here the animal control people have been trying to trap for a year, but he always gets away."

I pictured Portia lying on the beach, ailing, and shuddered at the thought of her so vulnerable to attack.

Detective Shippee did not ease my mind when he said, "They prefer to catch their prey in the water, but they *are* meat eaters and they're not averse to— Well, never mind."

"Then she wasn't alive when they found her."

"No."

"How long had she been dead?"

"Don't know for sure. She died sometime during the night."

"Heart attack?"

"You're pushing into classified territory, Mrs. Fletcher."

"I know. I'm sorry. But I get the feeling that something about Portia's death is bothering you."

He snorted. "Don't let my captain know. He'll have a fit."

"Detective Shippee, is it possible Portia's death was not from natural causes?"

"Meaning?"

"Meaning that someone killed her, perhaps because she fought the development."

Detective Shippee stared out at the water for a long time before he answered. Then he hunched his shoulders and looked back at me. "People have been killed for a lot less, Mrs. Fletcher."

Detective Shippee took his leave, but I remained on the boardwalk instead of returning to Foreverglades as I'd intended. I retraced my steps to the gazebo and sat inside, protected from the heat and glare of the sun, listening to the lapping of the water and thinking about Portia. What a sad end to a life filled with purpose and sacrifice. She had found her true calling here in Florida among the other retirees. She had captured the leadership role that life and circumstances had denied her when she'd lived in Cabot Cove. In Foreverglades she took charge; she was a heroine to those she championed, but her body could not keep up with her ambition. She would have wanted to go down swinging. Instead, she collapsed on the beach she was trying to save for her fellow residents.

But can we ever choose how we die? And if we could, what would we want? To die in our beds, surrounded by loved ones? My husband, Frank, had left this world that way. I wasn't sure his death was any easier given knowledge of its approach. We mourned his death together for months before it occurred. Perhaps Portia had departed quickly without pain or even consciousness of life ebbing away. I hoped so, for her sake.

I stood up slowly in the way we have when our thoughts sit heavily on our shoulders, and wandered back down the boardwalk to the place in the sand where Portia had died. The sun's rays were blinding even with the protection of my new sunglasses, and I shaded my eyes with my hand, peering out at Foreverglades, visible beyond the expanse of tall grasses and tangled vines. A movement in the undergrowth next to the boardwalk caught my eye. I looked down. Two yellow eyes with black vertical pupils stared back at me. The head of the creature was huge, its broad, flat snout rounded at the end, its eyes twin bulges in the bumpy black hide. For a few seconds we stared at each other, both frozen at the unexpected intrusion into a private moment. Then it opened its jaws and hissed.

I forgot the heat of the sun as a chill crept over my body. Goose bumps rose on my arms and I felt as though my hair stood straight out from its roots. As my heart pounded in my ears, I tried desperately to remember the rules for encountering a wild animal. In Maine, the newspapers annually print advice on what to do when confronted by a bear or moose. *Pretend this is a moose, Jessica,* I told myself. *What are the rules? You should do . . . what? Rule number one: You should stay at least fifty feet away. Well, it's too late for that now. Rule number two. What was rule number two? Oh, yes. Never get between a mother and her calf.*

I glanced around quickly to see if a baby alligator was nearby, but from the size of the creature in front of me, I was guessing this was no mother, but a bull alligator, and one that was close to twelve feet long. I shivered, my breath coming in short spurts. So I wasn't between a mother and a calf, but I was between

the alligator and the water. That was probably its goal.
The black hide I'd always seen pictured in photographs as shiny and wet was neither. It was dusty-
looking, with streaks and patches of dried mud.

*It must want the water; it's hot. Unless, of course, it's
not hot. What if it's hungry? You'd make a tasty meal,*
I thought, gulping, my throat as dry as the alligator's
back. Would Seth come looking for me? What would
he find if I couldn't get out of this? I'd gotten out of
many dangerous situations in the past. But how long
could my luck hold? *No, don't think that way,* I chided
myself. The rules. What were the rest of the rules?
Don't yell. That was rule number three. Loud noises
and wild gestures might startle the animal into at-
tacking. Not that I could yell at the moment. I was
too breathless. The real question was, Could I move
at all?

I started inching my way back down the boardwalk,
trying to hum softly, but the sound came out more as
a grunt than a hum. I maintained eye contact with the
alligator until the heel of one shoe caught on a plank,
and I stumbled.

The alligator hissed again. It had been crouched in
the grass. Now it rose up on its legs; even its long,
heavy tail was completely off the ground. The boardwalk was an easy step up for an animal this size.
Would it climb onto the wood and chase after me?

*Quick, what is the next rule? Run! That's it. Rule
number four is run. And get behind a tree. You can
run around a tree faster than a moose can.*

But I couldn't run in these shoes, and the only trees
around were behind the alligator. Carefully I raised
my foot and reached to remove one shoe, and then
did the same with the other. *At worst,* I reasoned, *I
can fling them at the alligator if it follows me.*

In my stocking feet I moved away slowly, putting feet and then yards between us, praying that I was near the railing, which began only when the boardwalk bowed out over the water. If the alligator followed me that far, I could vault over the side and escape. But where? Into the water, where his companions might wait?

The alligator placed one leg on the planks and then the other, hauling its heavy body onto the boardwalk, its belly sliding across the wood, one eye keeping me in view at all times. It lurched forward, flopped onto the beach, and lumbered toward the water, its massive tail making waves in the sand.

I felt the adrenaline drain away and began to shiver. My knees buckled and I sank gratefully onto the rough boards. Still, I stared transfixed, watching its progress, until the beast slithered silently into the water, and the knurls on its back and long pointed tail slipped below the surface.

Chapter Six

"Did he say he suspected foul play?"

"No, but I got the distinct impression he was thinking along those lines."

"And he wouldn't tell you what the autopsy report said?"

I shook my head. "He wants to talk with Clarence first, and I respect that, of course."

It was the day after the funeral and the weather was delicious. The skies were sunny overhead; a warm breeze off the water ruffled my hair as Seth and I had breakfast in an outdoor café in the village. Even though the Foreverglades apartments we'd settled in had full-sized kitchens, they were not stocked with food. We'd debated whether or not to stop at a market, but since we had no idea how long we'd be staying, we'd decided against it.

"The likelihood is that she died of congestive heart failure, Jess."

"I know."

"She was being treated with digoxin for many years, but if she was dosing herself with supplements, she could have been compromising its effectiveness."

"True."

"She wouldn't listen to me," he said, his voice rising. "I warned her about those things."

"Yes. You did."

"And on top of that, if she'd been taking those darned diet tablets, she could have unwittingly committed suicide." He pounded his fist on the table and the silverware jumped.

Several people turned around to see who was disturbing the peace. Seth seemed startled by their reaction. "Well," he said to me in a lower voice, "I'm just not a fan of all these pseudomedications."

It was our first opportunity to talk privately. We'd spent the previous afternoon at Portia's apartment, but there had been so many people crowded into the three rooms—not to mention the group of women who'd monopolized Seth's attention all afternoon—that conversation of this nature had been impossible. When I'd managed to squeeze past people in the hall and walk into Portia's bedroom, I'd found a lively political debate in progress among a half dozen of her friends. There was no way I could peruse the bottles on her bureau, which I'd hoped to do, with an audience watching me.

The brief conversation I'd had with Seth, Mort, and Maureen had, of course, been about my encounter with one of Florida's undomesticated residents. Maureen had turned very pale and shuddered—"Oh, my gosh, Jessica. How horrible"—and we feared she might faint. We assisted her to a chair, and Mort fanned her with a magazine while Seth took her pulse.

"How come I'm not doing this for you?" he said to me.

"You're welcome to," I said, holding out my arm.

He batted it away. "You get into more trouble than any ten people I know put together. Darned foolish woman." He sounded as if he were angry, but there was no use in pointing out that I had merely been walking in a public place in the middle of the day. I knew his gruffness was out of concern for my safety.

"I wish I'd thought to bring my gun," Mort said. "I could take care of that monster right now."

"You'd never have gotten it past the inspectors at the airport," I said. "Besides, the police are aware of the alligator's presence. They've been trying to trap it for some time."

"Until they do, they'd better put up a warning sign telling people to stay away," Mort said. "Did you report the incident?"

"I did," I said. "They were going to send out another team from animal control this afternoon. I hope they don't kill it."

"Why not?" Seth asked.

"As Detective Shippee said, we're trespassing on the alligator's territory, not the other way around. If they catch it and release it somewhere else, it can live in peace and not hurt anyone."

"Dead or alive, it's got to go," Mort said.

"I can't believe you have sympathy for the alligator," Maureen said, rallying. "You nearly got eaten. Don't you care?"

"On the contrary. I'm very grateful to be standing here," I said. "I'm not in the least insensitive to the danger I was in. Now that I'm out of harm's way, I'm able to think about the animal with compassion. Mort is right, however. It's got to go. Someone else might not be so lucky."

The four of us had agreed to forgo dinner—my revelation had spoiled everyone's appetite. Of course, the others had filled up earlier at the plentiful buffet Portia's generous neighbors had supplied. My stomach was empty. Nevertheless, I was grateful to retire to my apartment early. The rigors of travel, combined with the emotional impact of the funeral, not to mention my experience as a potential meal, had taken their toll. I'd gone to bed early, although dreams about yellow eyes with black slits down the center kept interrupting my sleep.

"What if Portia never intended to take the diet pills?" I asked Seth as I dug into a platter of bacon and eggs. "What if someone slipped them into her pillbox?"

"Wouldn't she have noticed?"

"I don't know. Her eyesight wasn't very good."

"It was good enough to put the pills in the container in the first place, wasn't it?"

"If she did."

"I think you're overreacting," he said, biting down on a flaky pastry and sending a sprinkle of crumbs and powdered sugar across his chest. "It's the normal sequence of events to order an autopsy if you find a body on the beach, but nine out of ten times it's going to be natural causes."

"You're right. I'm probably misinterpreting the detective's point of view. He never really said he suspected anything out of the ordinary in Portia's death. Still, it would put my mind at rest if I knew the results of the autopsy."

"Then you should get them. Maybe Mort can help."

"Maybe Mort can help with what?" Maureen asked, coming up to our table with her husband in tow. Completely recovered from her shock at my episode on the beach, she was carrying a colorful straw tote bag I hadn't seen before, and Mort's arms were full, holding a box and two shopping bags from Weinstein's Pharmacy. We pulled over two of the chairs from an empty table and they sat, Mort piling the purchases on the ground between his feet.

"What a marvelous find," Maureen said. "Have you been in there?" She gestured to the shop across the street. "Who knew a drugstore would have so many great things? They gift-wrap, and they ship, too, if you don't want to take your purchases with you. It's too bad we won't be down here before next Christmas; I could really go to town."

"I think you already went to town," Mort said, eyeing the pile. "Wasn't there anything here you could have shipped home? These'll never fit in the suitcase."

"We'll make room," she said. "We can roll up the table mats, and I can put the salt and pepper mills in your shoes. Anyway, I'll need the sunscreen and the face cream while we're here. And I didn't want to take a chance on the candles getting broken in the mail. Mmm. The coffee smells good. We haven't had breakfast yet."

"Do they have any doughnuts?" Mort asked, pushing his packages under the table so he could bring his chair closer.

Seth gestured to our waitress, and Mort and Maureen gave her their orders.

"Did I hear you wanted my help with something?" Mort asked.

"Remember the detective we met in the chapel yesterday?" I asked.

"Zach something, right?"

"Right," I said. "Zach Shippee."

"Couldn't believe it when Sam said he was a detective. You were on the mark there, Mrs. F, pegging him as a cop. Did he say something after I left?"

I related my conversation with the detective about Portia, and my encounter with him again at the beach before my infamous incident, pausing only when the waitress delivered Mort's and Maureen's breakfast.

Gossip is common currency in a small community. I didn't want my misgivings overheard, and certainly didn't want Clarence hurt by any unsubstantiated rumors.

"I don't know how much credence they give professional courtesy down here," Mort said, taking a sip of his coffee, "but it won't hurt to ask at the station house for a copy of the autopsy. I'll say it's for her doctor from back home." He nodded at Seth.

"Good point," Seth said. "She was my patient for thirty-five years. Guess that would give me a right to see the report." He wiped at the crumbs on his chest with his hand but only succeeded in smearing the powdered sugar.

"I appreciate that, Mort."

"No problem, Mrs. F. I'll find out where the station house is and stop by."

"You'd better go soon, Mort," his wife said, shooting him a look.

"No need to go rushing off right away," Seth said, dipping the corner of his napkin in a glass of water and dabbing at the sugar. "Finish your doughnut."

Mort pursed his lips. "Maureen's right. We thought we'd leave for the Keys today. I'll help her back to Foreverglades with the packages and find Shippee after that."

"I hope that's not a problem," Maureen said to me. "It's only a little over three hours from here to Key West if you drive straight through, but we don't want to do that. It's supposed to be a gorgeous route, and we thought we'd take our time and maybe see a bit of the other Keys. If we wait till tomorrow, we might get caught up in weekend traffic. The trip'll be a lot longer, and not as much fun."

"And I don't have my siren or bullhorn with me to

order the other cars out of my way," Mort said, laughing.

"You know, I could go to the police station myself," Seth said.

"No, no. Let me do it," Mort said. "It won't take that long."

Our conversation was interrupted by a voice calling, "*Buenos días,* Jessica."

I looked up to see Amelia waving at me from the door of the beauty shop, Helen's Curly Locks. She was wearing a pale blue smock over tight capri pants, and high-heeled slip-on shoes. Her hair was pulled smooth on one side of her face, with a cascade of curls hanging down the other. I waved back and she hurried across the street to join us, sliding her feet along the pavement so as not to lose her shoes. Seth and Mort stood when she approached.

"*Cómo está?* The shop hasn't opened yet, and I was going to get a Coke at the deli when I spotted you," she said.

"Why don't you join us for breakfast?" I said. "Have you met everyone?"

"You were all at the funeral," she said, "but we weren't formally introduced."

Seth did the honors. Amelia smiled at everyone. "I'll stay, if I won't be intruding. I don't want to interrupt anything."

"Not at all," Mort said, giving up his seat after Maureen nudged him with her elbow. "Watch out for the packages," he said. He pulled the last chair from the table next to us and, setting it slightly behind Maureen and me, reached between us to snag his doughnut.

"We were just talking about traffic," Seth said, sitting down again. "Nothing that can't be put aside."

"I saw you at Clarence's," Amelia said to him, "but

we didn't have a chance to meet." She sat up straight in her chair and beamed at him.

Seth cleared his throat. "Well, it's nice to meet you now," he said, coloring and absently brushing the front of his shirt with his hand. "Would you like some coffee?"

"*Sí, gracias.* That would be very nice."

He left his seat to find the waitress, and Maureen's eyes twinkled with amusement. "It was quite a crowd there, wasn't it?" she said to Amelia.

"*Dónde?*" Amelia looked confused.

"At the funeral, and later at the apartment," Maureen replied.

"Oh, that. Portia was very popular," Amelia said. "And now, with Clarence single again, there are a lot of ladies in Foreverglades who would like to comfort him, if you know what I mean. I heard three of them in the shop yesterday discussing what he likes to eat. *Caramba!* Can you give the woman a chance to get cold in her grave? Of course, she's not in a grave, since she was cremated. Irregardless, that Monica Kotansky has already been cooking meat loaf, lamb stew, and stuffed peppers—although she still owes Helen for her last haircut. If she didn't spend so much money on clothes, she could pay it. But anyway, we're getting a heat spell tomorrow, and it'll be too hot for stew, *sí*?"

If Maureen had thought to coax Amelia into talking on the chance the beautician might be reticent about joining our conversation, she was quickly disabused of that notion.

"Of course, they're not exactly strangers to each other, so I guess he won't mind," she continued.

"What do you mean?" I asked.

"Didn't she tell you? Monica was Clarence's girl-

friend before he married Portia, so it's not surprising
if he kept Monica on the side. Portia didn't like her,
but can you blame her? She kept a pretty tight leash
on Clarence, but I heard he managed to slip away
from time to time."

"How awful for Portia," Maureen said.

"There are a lot more women down here than men,
if you haven't noticed. My sister-in-law says that men
are always cheating on their wives anyway. Can you
believe her? I think it's just guilt speaking, because
she's divorcing my brother. Plus, she's got a crush on
her boss, although why anyone would be attracted to
that ugly *cochino*, I don't know. She even comes to
all the Residents' Committee meetings just to spy
for him."

Seth returned with coffee for Amelia, who kept up
a steady stream of gossip about her customers, her
neighbors, her family, the staff at the development,
and seemingly everyone she'd ever met since moving
to Foreverglades. The rest of us at the table began to
feel shell-shocked.

"Did you meet Mark Rosner yet?" she asked. "He's
the new manager at the development. Big muscles.
He's supposed to be a social director, but he looks
like a construction worker, and he can't dance to save
himself. He runs the socials at the rec hall, and he's
not happy unless he's got everyone on their feet moving. The ladies love to flirt with him. He's the only
one they can count on to entertain them while their
husbands are on the golf course. Frankly, I think he
may do more than just talk, especially with the single
ones, but I will not say any more about that."

Jumping into the pause in Amelia's torrent of chat-
ter, Maureen looked at her watch and gasped. "Oh,

gosh, will you look at the time? We've got to get on the road—and soon." She hoisted her new tote bag onto her shoulder. "Will you excuse us, please? I've got to pack and Mort has to run an errand. Amelia, it was so nice to meet you." She gave me and Seth a peck on the cheek. "We'll call when we get there to let you know the phone number where we're staying."

"I'll find you before we leave, Mrs. F." Mort winked at me. "Nice meeting you," he said to Amelia as he pulled the shopping bags out from under the table.

"I think I'll join Mort on his errand," Seth said, hastily throwing some money on the table and grabbing a bag out of Mort's hands. "Let me help you with those packages."

"I can handle them, Doc," Mort said, immediately recanting when he saw Seth's desperate look. "Oh, sure, take this one."

The men walked quickly after Maureen, who had all but sprinted down the block.

"There seems to be quite a social life down here," I said to Amelia after they'd left.

"It's a regular soap opera," she said, sipping her coffee, which must have grown cold. "He's very handsome."

"Who?"

"The doctor. Is he attached? I wouldn't want to step on your toes or anything."

I assured her she wouldn't be, but told her that Seth would have to speak for himself about his attachments.

"I hope you don't mind my telling you, but you could use a few highlights," she said, studying my hair. "Helen does a great job with blondes, and I do, too, if I say so myself. I could give you a couple of platinum streaks across the top. It would really brighten up your face. Why don't you come by the shop and make an appointment?"

"I may just do that," I said, patting my hair, "but I've got a busy schedule today. Anyway, this was nice, but we must have kept you too long. Won't Helen miss you?"

"Oh, she doesn't care," she said, just as the woman under discussion leaned out the door to the shop and called to Amelia.

"Please give her my best," I said, waving at Helen.

"What do I owe you for the coffee?"

"Nothing at all. It's our treat," I said.

Amelia clopped across the street to the beauty shop in her backless shoes, and I put on my new sunglasses. I left the waitress a generous tip—we had occupied her table for a long time—and after a quick glance at my reflection in the café window—I don't think platinum streaks are for me—I strolled down the hill, intending to stop by Clarence's apartment to talk with him. My visit was postponed, however, when I saw Sam getting into his pink Cadillac. He was wearing a black shirt, a cowboy hat, and silver reflective glasses, along with his usual khaki shorts and purple sneakers.

"Hi, Sam," I said when I came abreast of the car. "Where are you off to today?"

"Shhh," he replied, frowning. "How'd you know it was me?"

"Oh, wasn't I supposed to recognize you?"

"I'm working undercover today," he said, settling the hat low over his brow and checking himself in the rearview mirror. "Surveillance."

"Don't you think the pink car is a bit of a giveaway?"

"Nah. Lots of people in Miami have pink cars."

I didn't say that Foreverglades was a far cry, not to mention a far piece, from Miami, and that his giant Cadillac stood out like an elephant on a fishing boat.

"Wanna come along?" he asked.

"Where to?"

"Can't tell you here. Someone might be listening."

I looked up and down the block. "We're alone, Sam. I don't see anyone nearby."

"They've got spies everywhere. There could be a camera on us right now, plus one of them loud-speaker telephones."

"Do you mean microphones?"

"Yeah. Those. Well, get in if you're coming. I know you mystery writers like to hang out with the cops and see how it's done."

"I can't resist an offer as good as that, now, can I?" I said, walking around to the passenger door.

"You gotta be discreet, though," he said through the open window.

"Scout's honor," I said, raising my right hand.

Chapter Seven

Sam made a U-turn on the street and drove by the main shopping area of Foreverglades, screeching to a halt at every red light. We passed through the outskirts of the village till we reached another residential section where private homes, a mix of Spanish-style ranches and stucco bungalows, sat on small pieces of property. Anywhere else, it might have been an ordinary neighborhood. But the tall palms and lush tropical plantings gave the place an exotic quality to my eyes, accustomed to winter's leafless trees and the gabled architecture of New England.

"Is this still Foreverglades?" I asked.

"No. This is Bayview Heights," he said. "But it was built around the same time as Foreverglades."

Whoever named Bayview Heights was either overly optimistic, or had an ironic sense of humor. Most of the houses didn't have a view of the bay, and the land was as flat as the pancakes in Mara's Luncheonette back home.

Sam found the address he was looking for, a single-story, pink-roofed house with a double-car garage that took up most of the front of the property. He checked his watch and then slowly drove around the block, stopping two houses down from his surveillance target.

"It's almost ten-thirty. Watch this," he said. "You can set your clock by this guy."

"Who are we waiting for?" I asked.

"Shhh."

Sam adjusted the cowboy hat. It was too large, and kept slipping down to rest on the frame of his sunglasses.

I glanced at my watch. At precisely half after the hour, the double garage doors lifted up, and a black BMW backed out of the garage, down the driveway, and onto the street. I couldn't see the driver through the tinted windows of the sedan, but I was sure he'd seen us. Since we were the only car parked on the street, it was hard to keep from noticing a vintage pink Cadillac with chrome trim, driven by a short man in a cowboy hat whose head barely made it over the top of the steering wheel. Not to mention the crazy lady from Maine who'd agreed to accompany him.

The black sedan backed down the street until the car was parallel to ours. Then the passenger-side window rolled down, revealing the driver, a chubby man in his thirties with a prematurely receding hairline, wearing a short-sleeved tan shirt. He leaned across the seat and said, "Mornin', Sam. Got a girlfriend today, I see. Morning, ma'am."

"Good morning," I called back.

"I didn't write out my itinerary for you, Sam, but I have to stop at the post office; then I'm driving over to the farm stand to see what they got that's fresh, and then I'll be opening the restaurant. Got that?"

Sam, who'd been looking straight ahead, gave a sharp nod.

"Don't lose me now," the driver said. He rolled up his window and drove off.

"What just happened?" I asked as Sam pulled away from the curb and stayed a few car lengths behind the sedan.

"He knows I'm keeping an eye on him."

"So I gathered."

"So he helps me out sometimes."

"Who is he?"

"I told you already."

"You did?"

"Yeah. The other day at Clarence's."

"Is that . . . ?"

"Yup. Tony Colombo. The hit man."

"The man you *suspect* of being a hit man, you mean."

"That's the guy."

"Are the police aware of what you're doing? Do they know you follow this man?"

"Sure. He tried to stop me in the beginning— complained to the lieutenant—but I wouldn't give up. So now he sees how dedicated I am. He won't pull any more fast ones with me on his tail."

"And did he 'pull a fast one' before?" I asked.

"He got to Portia. I can't keep him in my sight twenty-four hours a day, and she insisted on walking down by the water after dark. I'm in bed by nine. I told her I couldn't protect her if she kept doing that, but she pooh-poohed me all the time. Now see what happened."

"Then you told Portia of your suspicions."

"Of course. She wouldn't listen to me. Portia was the stubbornest woman I ever met. She never listened to anybody once she got something in her brain to do."

"I've heard that before," I said. "Then again, her

persistence was sometimes helpful to the residents of Foreverglades, wasn't it?"

"I'll give you that. She did a lot of good. But in the end it killed her. I warned her not to walk alone at night. She insisted there were always other people around. But there wasn't anyone around to save her the night she died."

The BMW pulled into the parking lot of the Foreverglades post office, and Tony Colombo, holding a handful of envelopes, got out of the car and entered the building. Sam backed into another space in the lot and left the engine idling.

"Broke my Minnie's heart when Portia died. She was her closest friend. If it weren't for Helen, she would have gone completely to pieces."

"It's always sad to lose a friend."

"And they're not easy to make down here," Sam said, looking at me through his silver lenses and tapping the steering wheel. "Lots of people, but lots of cliques, too. This one doesn't like the way that one dresses, or her accent, or his golf game. That one accuses another of cheating at cards. The other day there was a fight over whose turn it was to dance with the building manager. It's like high school all over again."

"Uh, Sam," I said, trying to interrupt his tirade.

"I get so aggravated with them. That's why I decided to work at the police station. These guys are dealing with important things, not how warm the temperature should be in the pool or how many times you can use the tennis courts in one day."

"Sam? You're forgetting something."

"What? What am I forgetting?"

I pointed at Colombo's car, which was exiting the parking lot and making a right turn onto the road.

"Shoot! Why didn't you tell me?" He released the brake and we jerked forward.

"I just did."

Catching up with Tony Colombo was not a problem. He drove slowly, and Sam drove like a madman, swerving around cars and trucks until we were back on Colombo's tail well before he turned onto the road leading to the farm stand, which turned out to be a building unlike any other farm stand I was familiar with. Rather than an open shed by the side of the road, this farm stand was a warehouse with boxes of produce piled on tables, and a line of cars and trucks backed up to one side of the building.

"A lot of people come up from the Keys for this," Sam explained. "The restaurants and food stores all buy from here."

We followed Colombo inside.

While Sam got waylaid, bargaining with a man selling tangerines, I wandered the aisles, watching as Colombo continuously consulted his shopping list and examined the fruits and vegetables in the boxes, choosing what he would buy and cook that day. Testing green peppers with his thumb, he pulled out individual boxes and placed them near the door on one of the many red wagons—I had a similar one as a child—available to customers to bring purchases to their cars. He hoisted a net bag of onions over his shoulder and deposited it next to his stack of boxes. A carton labeled LIMES held small round fruit with mottled yellow-and-green skin.

In the middle of the market was a row of tables holding different kinds of lettuce and other salad greens, although many of them were not green at all. I was admiring all the different-shaped leaves and colors when I heard a voice next to me.

"Listen, if you're going to follow me around, the least you can do is be helpful," Colombo said, giving me his shopping list, along with two large bags of mixed greens. He lifted a tray of radicchio, which looked like a box of Christmas ornaments with the round red lettuces nestled in green paper, consulted the list I held—*tomatoes for sauce,* it said—picked up a bushel of beefsteak tomatoes, and headed toward the door.

I helped Colombo bring the vegetables to his wagon and waited while he argued with a vendor over prices. He pulled a wad of bills from his pocket and, after removing the rubber band around it, counted off what he owed, paid the man, and turned to me.

"You playing detective with Sam today?" he said, pocketing his cash.

"I'm just along for the ride," I said. "Has he been doing this a long time?"

"Who? Sam? Yeah. Ever since I opened Portofino—that's my restaurant, mine and my cousin's, anyway—he's been hanging around. Thinks I'm a member of the mob." He shook his head and laughed.

"So he's told me."

"Some people just hear an Italian name and assume the worst. You know what I mean? It's all because of the *Godfather* movies, and the books, too. I'll tell you something, that program on HBO, *The Sopranos?* Know it? That hasn't helped either. So here's little Sam, learns my last name, and thinks I'm going around whacking people like they do on television. But he likes our pizza, so I can't be all bad."

I laughed, too.

Colombo smiled back. "At least he isn't sitting home like my uncle Jimmy, who's retired now, and all he does is send corny jokes all over the Internet."

"Sam said you tried to stop him in the beginning."

"I didn't know who he was at first. I told the cops some wacko was following me. I wanted to know if he was dangerous. I'm gonna be moving my wife and kids down here eventually. Don't want no trouble, and don't want to have to worry about them. Know what I mean? But the cops say he's harmless—Sam, that is—just playing at being a detective. So I kid him along. No skin off my nose."

"That's very understanding of you."

"Yeah. Well, he's all right. I'm Tony Colombo, by the way, although I bet you already know that." He held out a beefy hand.

I shook it. "Jessica Fletcher. Nice to meet you."

"Same here. You new to Foreverglades?"

"I don't live here," I said. "I only came down for the funeral of an old friend."

"Mrs. Shelby?"

"That's right. Did you know her?"

"Everyone knew her. She was hard to miss."

"What do you mean?"

"She was a pain in the neck, if you don't mind my saying so. Don't get me wrong. She was a nice enough lady. Not like that husband of hers. What a cold son of a gun he is. She was okay. I even catered a couple of meetings up there in her apartment recently. But she got in my way."

"How could she do that?"

"How? Easy. There's supposed to be a new development going up by the water. She don't want it, and she stirs up all her neighbors. Tied up the project for more than a year now."

"I take it you're not opposed to high-rise buildings going in there."

"Opposed? I'm waiting forever for that. They promised us they would be up and occupied by now. That's why we came down here in the first place. You don't think we'd move thirteen hundred miles for the old turkeys in Foreverglades, if you'll pardon my expression. No! We got bigger plans. And we almost lost our deal with the landlord for the property next to the restaurant, thanks to your friend Mrs. Shelby. Soon as they break ground on those buildings, we're expanding. We got a no-compete deal with the village. They can't let another Italian restaurant in as long as we're there. Speaking of . . ."—he looked at his watch—"I gotta get back and start cracking the whip. We open at noon, and there's always people waiting. Tell Sam I'll see him later. Come by sometime. I'll give you a slice on the house. Best pizza in southern Florida. We make our own sauce. Everything fresh. See?" He pointed to the wagon piled high with produce as he pushed open the door.

I looked around for Sam. He was perched on a stool next to the table with the yellow limes, eating a tangerine and watching highlights from a basketball game on a portable TV. A man in a white apron stood next to him, cutting the limes and working a juicer.

"Mr. Colombo left, Sam," I said. "Do you want to go now?"

"Just a second," he replied. "I want to see them make this shot." He whooped when a player on the screen passed the ball to another player, who stuffed it in the basket, hanging for a split second from the rim. "That's the Miami Heat," he told me, hopping off the stool. "Their coach used to coach the Knicks in New York. I was real happy when he came down here."

"He ain't doin' so great this year," Sam's companion said.

"They've got a lot of injuries, but they'll get better. See you, Arthur." He waved to the man in the apron and we walked toward the door.

"Wait, Sam. You forgot your juice," Arthur said, running after him and handing him a bottle.

"Oh, boy. You saved my life. Minnie would have had my hide if I forgot this. Thanks."

"What is it?" I asked.

"Fresh key lime juice. Arthur juices the limes for me. They look like little lemons, but they're actually key limes. It's a different fruit from regular limes. Anyone ever gives you green key lime pie, you tell them it's a forgery. Key limes are yellow."

"I'll remember that."

"Minnie uses the juice for pie. There is nothing better in the world than Minnie's key lime pie. You could go from Key West to Key Biscayne and never find a better one."

We walked outside. The day was heating up, the contrast with the coolness inside the farm stand making the warm temperature more noticeable. The Cadillac was parked in the sun. Sam unlocked and opened the door for me, and a whoosh of hot air escaped the interior. "Give it a minute," he said. "Don't get in. I'll put on the AC and it'll cool down in two shakes."

He slid into the driver's seat, making yelping noises when his legs came in contact with the hot leather. Five minutes later, in cool comfort, we were on our way back to Foreverglades.

"So what did you guys talk about?" Sam asked when we were on the road.

"Beg pardon?"

"You and Colombo. What did he tell you?"

"Nothing much," I replied. "He's planning to bring his family down here soon."

Sam snorted. "I'll bet he only told you that to soften you up."

"He also said that Portia was organizing against the development, but that he's in favor of it."

"See? There's your motive."

"Just because he disagreed with Portia doesn't mean he wanted to kill her. Anyway, Portia died of a heart attack."

"There are ways to make it look like a heart attack," Sam said somberly.

"Well, I hope you're wrong," I said. "He seemed like a pretty nice fellow to me."

Sam dropped me off in front of number twenty-three. He was going home for lunch and then off to a Residents' Committee meeting in the afternoon. A fitting tribute to Portia was the main topic on the agenda.

I climbed to the second floor, put my key in the lock, turned it, and pushed the door open. I heard a scraping sound and looked down to see a white envelope with my name on it in Mort's recognizable scrawl. I picked it up, opened the flap, and pulled out five sheets of paper. At the top of the first page, it read, *Metropolitan Dade County, Office of the Medical Examiner, District 11. Name of deceased: Portia Shelby.* Seth had affixed a sticky note to the page. On it he'd written, *Damn those diet pills!*

Chapter Eight

"I think we need to talk with Clarence," I said.

Seth and I sat in the back room of Portofino having our dinner. We'd decided to eat early to avoid the crowds, but the place was filled to capacity, and we'd been fortunate to get the last table for two. A long line behind us waited to be seated. A box on the menu offered an explanation. We were just in time for the "early-bird dinner," which featured reduced prices on certain dishes for those who sat down before six o'clock.

Seth nodded as he twirled spaghetti around his fork. "You've been saying that since we got here, Jess. We can go over in the morning." He lifted his fork but the slippery strands of pasta slid back into his bowl. "I'm not sure it'll do any good," he added.

On the way to the restaurant I had briefed Seth on my visit to the Davisons earlier in the day.

I'd stopped by Helen and Miles Davison's apartment, which was on the first floor of Portia's building and across the courtyard from the unit where I was staying. Helen opened the door at my knock. She was clad in a white leotard with a towel slung around her neck. I could hear the plaintive wail of a jazz saxophone being played in the background.

"Have I caught you at a bad time?" I asked.

"Not at all," she said, drawing me inside.

"I wasn't sure I'd find you at home, but the lady who answered the telephone at your shop said to try."

"The Residents' Committee meets every Thursday afternoon, and that's a popular event," she said, wiping her brow with a corner of the towel. "I take advantage of the drop in clientele to take some time for myself."

"And I'm treading on it."

"Not at all." She beckoned me to follow her. "Your timing is perfect. I've just finished my yoga routine, and was about to make some green tea. I'm told it's full of antioxidants. I have no idea what they are, but they're supposed to be good for you. Would you like some?"

"I'd love some."

Over green tea and biscotti, long Italian cookies Helen told me were sold at Portofino, I guided the conversation around to what she knew about Portia's pill-taking habits.

"She used to take them by the handful, at least three times a day," Helen said, "gulping them down with a glass of water. I once asked her what they all were, but she only said they were a combination of her prescription drugs and supplements. Some were supposed to help her vision, I remember, but apparently they didn't work very well. She still needed Clarence to help fill the pillbox for her."

"Why was that?" I asked.

"Well, she couldn't read what was written on the bottles; her eyesight was that bad. Took her forever when she had to use a magnifying glass to check each pill, and then if she got them confused, she had to start all over again. She was grateful when Clarence offered to help her."

"Did she ever talk to you about taking diet pills?" I asked.

"Diet pills!" Helen laughed. "That woman didn't need diet pills. She was no Lana Turner, but her body suited her. Why would she ever want to take diet pills?"

"Sometimes when a woman has a new husband," I said carefully, "she may be more conscious of her looks."

"She never wore a drop of makeup or changed her hairstyle—and believe me, I tried to convince her to do that. 'I'm fine as I am,' she would tell me. You have to admire that kind of self-confidence. I seriously doubt she'd be interested in losing weight just to please Clarence, even if he'd had the nerve to say something, which I doubt he ever would. He's not my favorite person, Jessica, but he seemed genuinely fond of Portia."

"Why isn't he your favorite person?" I asked.

"Girl, you ask a lot of questions," she said, getting up to pour us more tea.

Before I could probe further, Helen's husband, Miles, leaning on two canes, joined us in the kitchen, and the conversation drifted away from Portia to Miles's passion, jazz.

Later that day, back in my apartment, I reread the autopsy report while waiting for Seth to pick me up for dinner. The medical examiner had ruled that Portia Shelby died from acute myocardial infarction, sometime around ten P.M., the heart attack most likely brought about by the presence in her system of ephedrine alkaloid and caffeine, two powerful stimulants known to cause ventricular arrhythmia and cardiac arrest. There was no ruling on the manner of death, since it could not be determined if the fatal combination was caused by an intentional overdose or an accidental one.

"I read the report, too," Seth said. "And I'm still not convinced she was murdered. However, I will withhold judgment until you come up with more evidence."

"I just think Portia was too smart a woman to have made that kind of mistake," I said, leaning over my portion of linguini with Bolognese sauce. "She would have known the danger of taking diet pills in her condition. Did she ever discuss her weight with you? Was it a concern?"

"Not that I recall." He made another attempt to wind the spaghetti around the fork, this time holding the tines against a spoon, but when he opened his mouth and lifted the fork, the pasta slipped away again. "I'd have to look up her medical records to be certain. I can call Dr. Jenny tomorrow and have her pull the file." He stabbed at a single strand of spaghetti, but missed. He looked up. "How the devil are you supposed to eat this stuff?"

I demonstrated my proficiency with fork and spoon on my own dish. Seth tried again, but without success. Disgusted, he picked up a knife, cut the pasta into small pieces, and used his spoon to scoop it up.

"Her medical record would be helpful," I said. "We need to gather as much information as we can before we approach Detective Shippee with our suspicions."

"Now hang on a minute, Jess. It's possible—I'll even say likely—that Portia did herself in with all those supplements."

"Do you really believe that?"

"Ayuh, I do. People do foolish things at times, even

those who are conscientious and intelligent. Mistakes get made, and there are consequences. You have to ask yourself why anyone would want to kill Portia."

"That's the question I can't answer," I said.

"You see? That's because she wasn't killed. She made a mistake and she died as a result."

We were silent for a while as we finished our meal. Seth sat back and eyed me.

"I'm for leaving for Key West tomorrow afternoon, next morning, the latest," he said. "Just for a long weekend. I'd appreciate if you'd come along."

"Have you heard from your friend?"

"Truman? I have, and he says he can't wait to see us. I told him we had friends visiting down there. Said to bring Mort and Maureen by; the more the merrier. He'll show us around."

"How thoughtful," I said. "When was the last time you saw him?"

"Must've been twenty years out from medical school, at a reunion, but he hadn't changed a bit. Regular fellow, maybe a bit stiff. He's a conservative type—never caught without a tie, as I remember. Hailed from Boston. That might explain it. Took over his father's practice—he was a doctor, too. Haven't seen him in as many years now, but we exchange cards and the occasional phone call."

"It's nice to keep up with old friends. Is he still seeing patients?"

"He keeps his hand in, consulting a bit, but for the most part, I think, he's retired. Big house in town. Said he's got more bedrooms than he knows what to do with, and he's wantin' us to stay there. I couldn't turn him down."

"He sounds very nice," I said.

"Well, will you come?"

"I promised myself I'd help Clarence pack up Portia's things, if he needs me," I said. "Let's see how it goes."

"From what I see, Portia has lots of friends who can help Clarence. But if you're bound to do it yourself, I can't stop you."

I hated to disappoint Seth. He'd spoken for years about this old friend of his who'd retired to the Keys. The opportunity to visit hadn't arisen—till now. But Portia's death was worrying me, and I knew I wouldn't rest until I'd learned more about Foreverglades and discovered who might have wanted to see her dead. Maybe I could do both, accompany Seth to Key West, and return to Foreverglades to look into Portia's death.

"Let me talk to Mr. Rosner tomorrow," I said.

"Which one's that?"

"The manager of Foreverglades. You met him at Portia's. He's the one who talked to you about the twins who work in maintenance."

"I remember now. Beefy guy. Looked like a boxer."

"I booked our accommodations through him. If I can arrange to stay here again when we come back from Key West, I'll come with you."

"Good enough," Seth said, smiling. "Can't see why they couldn't hold the rooms." He picked up the menu, which had been tucked behind the napkin dispenser. "Think they make good desserts in this place?"

"I wouldn't be surprised."

I looked around at Tony Colombo's business. Portofino was a combination pizza parlor, restaurant, and Italian deli. To reach the dining room we'd walked past a long counter. Behind it a young man dressed in white pressed a mound of dough into a round for the crust. He tossed it in the air to stretch it—to the admiring oohs of those waiting for a table—spooned on tomato sauce, sprinkled cheese over it, and slid the pizza onto a long paddle used to transfer it to the stacked ovens. Opposite the counter were stainless-steel racks filled with Italian foodstuffs: bottles of olive oil and wine vinegar, jars of red peppers, mushrooms, olives, and tomato sauce, packages of different shapes and colors of pasta, paper bags of biscotti and other kinds of cookies. Hanging from strings tied to the ends of the shelves were long salamis and balls of wax-covered cheeses. As I was taking in my surroundings, the proprietor walked through the swinging door from the kitchen in the back, stopping at each table to greet his customers.

"Nice to see you again, Mrs. Fletcher," Tony Colombo said when he reached us. "Did you try the salad?"

"Perhaps next time," I said. I introduced the men to each other.

"Enjoy your dinner?" Colombo asked.

"Very tasty," Seth replied.

"It's going to get even better. My cousin's got a chef coming down from New York who makes the best saltimbocca *alla romana* this side of the Atlantic." He kissed his fingers and hummed.

"Afraid I'll have to miss it," said Seth. "I'm driving down to Key West to see an old colleague. Been trying to convince my friend here to join me. We could both use a bit of relaxation."

"Key West is a great place," Colombo said to me. "Very popular with artistic types. Ernest Hemingway used to live there. 'Papa,' they called him. Sounds like he should have been Italian." He laughed. "He wrote a lot of books. You ever hear of him?"

I assured him I had.

"You really should go, especially since it's so close."

"I'll take that into consideration," I said.

He turned to Seth. "Don't let her tell you no. Gotta be forceful with these ladies."

I raised my eyebrows at my old friend.

"Any suggestions for dessert?" Seth asked, quickly changing the topic.

"Got the best spumoni in Florida," Colombo replied.

"I'm glad to hear it. I love spumoni," Seth said.

Colombo excused himself and moved on to the next table.

"Seems like a nice enough chap," Seth said when Colombo was out of earshot. "What was it he said I should try?"

"Spumoni."

"What is it?"

"It's a kind of ice cream."

"Sounds good to me." He looked around for the waiter.

The leading edge of the heat wave that Amelia had predicted was evident the following morning when Seth and I went to see Clarence. The air outside was very still and moist, with a noticeable odor of mold. Even though I'd just walked out of a cool apartment, the humidity enveloped me, immediately making the light linen dress I wore cling to my back. Seth, who's never bothered by the cold but has little patience for hot weather, was not pleased with the change in temperature.

"I trust Truman's house is air-conditioned," he said, escorting me across the lawn to Portia's building. "Never thought to ask him. Course, Key West is surrounded by water. Ought to be lots of ocean breezes, don't you figure?"

"I'm sure we'll be fine," I said. "It's not as if we don't have summer in Cabot Cove. You've managed well enough when it's hot in August."

"Not the same," he said. "It's a shock to the system coming into the heat down here from the cold back home. Takes some getting used to."

"Well, here's our opportunity," I said, laughing.

Seth opened the door to the vestibule, and waited for me to enter.

"Hold that door for us, please," a pair of voices called. It was the Simmons twins, Earl and Burl. Dressed in matching denim overalls, yellow shirts, and their Day-Glo-orange caps, they struggled to maneuver a maple dresser—one of Portia's, if I had to guess—around a bend in the staircase.

"Thanks," they chorused. They lugged the piece of furniture down the last steps, through the door, and out of view.

Upstairs I pressed on the doorbell and heard a series of sharp barks. Clarence opened the door. Monica's white dog stood between his feet barking and growling ferociously—or as ferociously as a ten-inch dog can muster—confident he could scare away the intruders. "Snowy! Get back," Clarence said, shooing the dog away. Snowy retreated to the hall where the bedroom was.

Clarence sighed. He looked tired. The skin on his face was drawn and pale, contrasting with the dark patches under his red-rimmed gray eyes. It was obvious he wasn't sleeping well. Fleetingly, I wondered if a guilty secret was keeping him awake. I then chided myself for such an unkind thought. He was suffering, a feeling I understood only too well. How many nights had I lain awake after Frank died going over our last conversations, regretting our disagreements, mourning the time I'd spent away from his bedside, jealous of anyone who'd shared his attention when I'd selfishly wanted his dying days all to myself? Sudden death, as Portia's was, is a terrrible shock. But even if you know death is imminent, even if you think you're prepared, the loss of a spouse is a terrible blow to bear. The world as you knew it is never the same again. Your compass is gone, and you wander lost and afraid. Years later, when life has gone on, and in many ways has been wonderful, there's always this little hole in your heart that never heals.

"I hope we're not disturbing you," I said.

"You wouldn't be the first," Clarence replied.

"We were hoping we might have a word with you."

He looked unsure whether to invite us inside, jingling change in his pocket while deciding. The sound of loud voices coming from the bedroom caused him to look back into the apartment. He sighed.

"What's going on?" Seth asked.

"Portia's friends," Clarence said, holding the door wide so we could enter. "That's what they call themselves anyway." He shuffled into the living room and collapsed on the couch, leaning his head back and closing his eyes. Seth and I took chairs facing him.

"They decided I couldn't dispose of her things by myself, and elected themselves to take over the task. I hope they're not planning to be here all day."

"If this isn't a convenient time for you, you should ask them to leave," I said, hoping he wouldn't apply my suggestion to us.

He raised his head. "It has to be done sometime, I

suppose. I guess now is as good as ever." He leaned forward, elbows on his knees, and pressed the heels of his palms to his eyes.

"No, it's not," Seth said, getting out of his chair. "I think you need rest more than you need help packing up. That's my prescription. Consider me your temporary physician." He walked out of the room. I heard frantic barking from the tiny sentry.

"What's he going to do?"

"I imagine he's going to ask them to leave," I said. "Is that all right with you?"

A trace of a smile crossed his lips. "It's more than all right."

A moment later Seth emerged from the hallway with three women in tow, Monica Kotansky—Snowy growling softly from the safety of his mistress's arms— her sister Carrie, and a third woman I hadn't met before but later learned was called Olga Piper. The trio had dressed carefully for their visit, looking more like guests at a party than a cleanup brigade, although two of them held green plastic sacks.

"Everything is sorted into bags now," Carrie called to Clarence. "They're all on your bed, and we're throwing away the garbage."

"It should be easy for you from here on out," Olga added. "The twins will bring up your old dresser from storage."

"Thank you, ladies."

"Oh, Clarence, I hadn't realized you weren't feeling well. I'm so sorry," Monica said, starting across the room.

Seth made a grab for her elbow but quickly pulled his hand away when Snowy thrust his snout forward and snapped at him.

"Snowy!" Monica chided, wrapping her fingers around her dog's muzzle. "You be nice to the nice doctor." She kissed the dog's nose and smiled coyly at Seth.

"You're being very kind to Clarence," he said, guiding her to the foyer but keeping his hands well away. "However, right now what he needs most is rest. I'm sure he'll be very grateful for all your assistance at a later date."

"But you and Jessica are staying," she complained as he held open the door.

"Not for long, I promise you," Seth said. "See you later." He gave her his best smile; she turned and blew him a kiss as she followed her friends down the hall.

Seth closed the door behind them, and we could hear their voices growing faint as they descended the stairs to the first floor.

"Bless you," Clarence whispered. "I didn't have the nerve to ask them to go, but I'm glad you did."

"If you'd like to lie down and rest, we'll go as well," I said, rising.

"No, it's fine," he said. "You're welcome to stay. I think there's coffee in the kitchen, if you'd like it. And help yourself to some cake, please. I've got enough to open a bakery." He went to the table in the dining alcove and began removing plastic wrap from the dishes.

"Don't fuss for us," I said. "Would you like a cup of coffee?" I asked, heading to the kitchen.

"I would. Black, no sugar," he said, thanking me again when I returned with three cups and handed him one. He took a sip, savored the taste, and swallowed. "Just before you came, Rosner, the building manager, was here, wanting to know my plans. 'Am I selling or staying?' he asks." He snorted softly. "As if I've already made plans. I'm barely awake, but I just can't sleep."

"You're going to lose strength if you don't get some rest," Seth said. "I can write you a prescription for a mild sleeping aid if you think you need it, but it would be better coming from your own doctor, who's familiar with your medical history. Want me to make the call?"

Clarence shook his head. "I'll be okay. I'm upset, that's all. It's been a nightmare since Portia died." He took another sip of his coffee and put the cup aside. "First the police hold on to her body and I have to postpone the funeral; then they finally release her, and now they're coming back and questioning me like I'm some criminal. She had a heart attack, for heaven's sake. She had a bad heart. Everybody knew that. Now the police tell me she was taking diet pills and they caused her heart to fail. That's news to me, but they don't believe me."

"Did you know she was taking diet pills?" I asked.

"She wasn't. Go look. The bottles are on her dresser. Oh, no, they're not. They're probably in some plastic garbage bag. And the Simmons twins took the dressers away."

"Did you want them to do that?" I asked. "We can ask them to bring them back if you didn't intend to give them away."

"No, don't do that." He waved one hand wearily. "They were all excited when Monica suggested I give them Portia's matching dressers. I have my own furniture in storage. Anyway, I don't need two dressers to hold my things."

I wondered why Monica was so eager to help dispose of Portia's furniture, but I didn't comment on it. Instead I asked, "What kinds of pills did Portia take?"

"Prescriptions?"

"No, the supplements. Do you remember?"

"Of course I remember," he said. "I helped her fill those damn pillboxes every day. We went over the catalogues together, looked up the drugs on the Internet on places like Healthy Stuff and Pills for Less, before we ordered them." He looked down at his hands and counted off on his fingers. "She took turmeric, bromelain, flaxseed oil—those are antioxidants—boswellia and nettle for arthritis, glucosamine, calcium, selenium, ginkgo biloba for memory, black cohosh. . . ."

"What was that for?" Seth asked.

"It's instead of estrogen replacement," Clarence replied. He'd run out of fingers.

"What's in it?"

Clarence shrugged. "We could look in the garbage bags for the bottles, if you really have to know," he said. "They're empty, however. Monica flushed all the pills down the toilet."

"Why would she do that?" I asked.

"She said she was afraid Snowy could get ahold of them. I didn't care. I don't take those things."

"But you let Portia take them," Seth said. I could hear he was making an effort to keep his voice neutral, and not to reveal his disapproval.

"It's not like you could forbid Portia to do anything she had in mind to do. But yes, I never objected because they really helped her. She used to say she was very healthy with one big exception. She told me she felt terrific, no pain, no shortness of breath. Her eyesight was bad, but she was still hoping for some improvement from the lutein. I don't know if I gave you all the pills. We can look inside, unless one of those harpies threw the bottles away, too." He hung his head. "That was nasty. I'm sorry. I know they're trying to be helpful. I just wish they'd leave me alone."

"You have to tell them that," I said. "You have to be a little forceful in protecting your privacy."

"You're right," he said. He was silent for a moment, then heaved a big sigh. "Now the police are on my back. This detective examined Portia's bottles like he was looking for poison, asking me all kinds of questions. Even took my computer with him." He stopped and looked up, his eyes going back and forth from Seth to me, his body suddenly rigid. "Are you working for the police?"

"No," I said. "We're not."

"We're old friends of Portia's; we told you that," Seth said. "And I was her doctor for thirty-five years, and—"

"And we're upset that she died," I interrupted, fearing Seth would launch into a lecture on the dangers of self-medication and the questionable value of herbal supplements. While I didn't disagree with him, it was not what Clarence needed to hear at the moment. "You said the police are on your back. Why is that?"

"This detective who came was irritated with me that I couldn't find all of Portia's pillboxes. She had three of them, and now one of them is missing. The police want to know where it is. I can't find it. He's called twice to ask me about it."

I glanced at Seth.

"I can answer that question for you," Seth said. He reached into his pocket and pulled out the white pillbox he'd taken from Portia's dresser.

Clarence looked stunned. "How did you get that?"

"I took it from your bedroom the other night," Seth said. His face was red, and I knew he was embarrassed. "I found a few pills in it I wasn't happy to see, and I brought one to the pharmacist to confirm what it was."

"You stole her pillbox?" Clarence was up on his feet, pacing. "The police have been all over me, suspecting me of God knows what, and all the time you had her pillbox?"

"I apologize," Seth said. "I'll call the police and tell them I was the one who took it."

"You're darn right you will," Clarence said, pointing his finger at Seth. "You can call them right now. Wait a minute. What pills? What pills made you unhappy?"

"They were diet pills."

"How do you know they were diet pills? What did they look like?"

"They were little blue pills," I said.

"She didn't have any blue pills," Clarence said.

"Seth took one from her pillbox and showed it to the pharmacist, who said it was a combination of ephedra and caffeine," I said. "He also said it would be very dangerous for someone who had a heart condition."

Clarence fell back on the sofa, his face even paler than when we'd entered. "So it's true," he whispered. "Why would she do that? Why would she keep it from me?"

"You didn't know she was taking diet pills?" I asked.

"No. I still don't believe it."

"Did she ever mention to you that she wanted to lose weight?"

"Never."

"Was she self-conscious about her body?"

"No. I don't think so. I don't know. I don't notice those things. She was no great beauty. She knew that.

But it never bothered me, and I never thought she was unhappy about it. It was refreshing for me to be with a woman who didn't make a fuss about her looks. I told her that. It was one of the things I liked so much about her." He labored to hold back tears.

I debated asking him about his reputation as a ladies' man. Two people had remarked on it, and Amelia had even suggested that Clarence had had an affair with Monica while he was married to Portia. Was it true? Or was it just the kind of vicious gossip that people with too little to occupy themselves will indulge in? Was Clarence the kind of man who needed attention from a lot of women? He was certainly good-looking, and it was easy to see he had already attracted a harem, ready to step into Portia's place.

Portia had been a plain woman, but a warm and kindhearted one, and someone who stood up for what she thought was right. Clarence must have appreciated that. He'd married her. Or had he been looking for something more, someone with enough money to support him, perhaps? No one had mentioned Portia's will, but she had no other family than Clarence. It stood to reason that he would inherit whatever was hers, the apartment, her pension, perhaps some investments or savings.

I looked into Clarence's handsome face and strained to divine his true nature. Was he sincere? Or was he putting on a performance for Seth and me? If so, he was an excellent actor. But even the finest actors occasionally forget their lines. I would wait and see.

Chapter Nine

The recreation building at Foreverglades had been designed with the elderly in mind, whether hale or infirm. Leading to the front entrance was a ramp as well as a short flight of stairs with a metal banister down the center. Inside, the doorways were wide enough to accommodate a wheelchair, and the walls all sported handrails for those unsteady on their feet. The main floor consisted of a wide-open space that could be used for large gatherings—a stretch class was in progress—one end of which was a community kitchen. At the other end, a sign with an arrow pointing downstairs said, THIS WAY TO FITNESS CENTER, LOCKERS, POOL.

I'd passed the busy tennis courts, fenced swimming pool, and concrete patio, where it looked like a chess tournament was in progress, when I'd walked to the rec hall, as Sam called it, from my apartment, trying and failing to find a shady route. Having left my hat on the shelf of the closet, where it did me no good, I moved as quickly as I could to get out of the burning sun, to which the other pedestrians seemed immune. To my surprise, particularly given how hot it was, the pool was nearly empty. One woman in a skirted black-and-red swimsuit and a bathing cap studded with rubber flowers stood at the shallow end, splashing water onto her arms. Other women, their skin tobacco-colored from years in the sun, sat at three tables under umbrellas, smoking and playing mah-jongg. However, from what I could see through its plate glass windows, the gym was crowded with people riding stationary bicycles and jogging on treadmills.

The cool interior of the building was a welcome relief from the blast furnace outside, and I wandered around, exploring the facility while my body temperature slowly fell back to normal. Spurning the elevator, I climbed the stairs to the second floor, poking my head into meeting rooms, a combination game room–computer center, a small library in which a lecture on ancient Egypt was taking place, and at least three studios where elderly people, their hands stained gray from modeling clay or blackened by charcoal pencils, explored their artistic sides, until I found Mark Rosner's office.

For a big man like Mark, it must have been difficult to work in such a cramped, windowless space with its battered metal filing cabinets, desk piled high with papers, and antiquated computer. A bulletin board on the wall above the desk was so full that I wondered if he ever removed anything once he'd tacked it up. Rosner was on the phone, his white shirt open at the collar, the ends of his bow tie dangling on his chest. He waved me in and pointed to a chair, which I took while waiting for him to conclude his conversation.

"The tennis pro doesn't have any more hours on Saturday, Mrs. Lazzara, but he has openings on Wednesday. Bridge day. I see. Forgot about that. Maybe you can switch with one of his Saturday students. No, I have no influence with him. You'll have to talk to him yourself." There was a long pause. "I can't help that. Ms. Kotansky pays for her lessons just like everyone else. Try the community bulletin board. That might work." Another pause. "All right. I'll talk to him, but I can't guarantee anything. You're welcome. Good-bye."

Rosner hung up the phone and grinned at me. "Everybody wants special consideration," he said, leaning back in his chair, which squeaked under the pressure. "Wish I could accommodate all the requests, but sometimes . . ." He shrugged. "Maybe I can help you. What are you looking for?"

"I'm Jessica Fletcher, Mr. Rosner."

"Ah, yes, one of our hotel guests. How do you like the accommodations? Nice, aren't they? Did you notice how the kitchen has dishes and utensils? I think there's a couple of pots, too. You don't need to bring a thing."

"The apartments are lovely," I said. "We're not cooking, so we haven't taken advantage of your kitchen."

"Lots of people like to cook, though. Saves a lot of money, especially if you're here for a long spell."

"That's what I'd like to talk to you about."

"You know the units you and your friends are in just came on the market. I have a few brochures you can take with you." He reached into the top drawer of his desk.

"Well, actually, we weren't interested—"

"Here you go. This one talks about the financing available. And this one details all the services we have here. You won't find a better buy in all of south Florida." He made a little pile of pamphlets in front of me.

"I'm sure that's true, but—"

"They won't last, these units. Inventory is tight.

Usually sell out in a couple of days when they come on the market. I sold one last week to a couple from Michigan."

"Thank you, but I'm really not interested in moving to Florida."

"It's an opportunity to get in on the ground floor. The prices will only go up, you know. Good-sized rooms, lots of services included—no extra charge— beautiful views."

"You'll probably lose those views when the proposed development goes up, won't you?" I said, thinking maybe that would halt his sales pitch long enough for me to get a few words in.

"Where did you hear that?"

"There's a sign advertising luxury towers down at the beach."

He made a face. "Shouldn't be there."

"Even if it weren't," I said, "many people have mentioned it to me since I arrived. It sounds as if your residents are very upset about the proposal."

"There are great views right now," he said. "Those buildings aren't there yet. You never know about those things. What if they never go up? You might miss out on a great buy. Foreverglades is still a bargain. You know the old saying, 'Gotta strike while the iron's hot.' Don't worry about what's not here."

I envisioned the disappointment of the couple from Michigan when they found out their view would be obliterated by three high-rise buildings. Apparently truth in salesmanship was not Mr. Rosner's strong point.

"Do you think our rental units will still be available next week?" I asked. "Dr. Hazlitt and I plan to go down to Key West tomorrow, but I'm hoping to stay

here again when we return. I'd like to make the arrangements now."

He tapped his fingers on the desk. "I don't know.
We might sell the apartments by then."

"If you think that's the case, perhaps you can recommend a hotel or motel nearby," I said, gathering
the brochures he'd piled in front of me and handing
them back to him.

"Keep those. I'm sure we can work something out.
Since it's you, I'll make the sale contingent on accom-
modating guests for a week or so. How does that
sound?"

"Oh, I wouldn't want to inconvenience your buyers."

"No problem. I'll deal with it." He studied my expression. "Sure you don't want to buy a unit?"

"I'm sure."

"Yeah, well, no hard feelings. Can't blame a guy
for trying. Gotta earn my commission somehow." He
hesitated, then said, "These are prime units, you
know. They'll go fast."

I nodded but said nothing, fearing any words would
launch him into a new sales pitch. I had a feeling there
were many more empty apartments in his inventory
than the three Seth, I, and the Metzgers had occupied,
but didn't voice that opinion. I gave him my credit
card number for the deposit and left.

As I walked back down the hall, Minnie Lewis came
around the corner.

"Hello, Jessica. You're just the person I want to
see. Are you exploring our facilities?" she asked.

I explained my reason for being there.

"I'm giving a cooking class in a half hour," she said,
"but thought I'd e-mail my grandchildren first. Have
you seen our computer room?"

"I saw it in passing," I said, "but didn't go in."

"Do you have a minute? I'll show you around."

"I do," I said.

"I've also been meaning to ask you something."

"Yes?" I said.

"Let's wait till we can close the door," she said in a low voice.

The computer center, unlike most of the other rooms, was empty. It consisted of a long lopsided counter, held up on one end by a chair that had been wedged underneath. Perched on the slanting top were two large desktop computers of the same vintage as Mark Rosner's. Attached to each was a combination printer, scanner, and fax machine. Lying next to each monitor and keyboard was a thick instruction book, set in large type, and a credit card device to pay for using the Internet. A bookshelf at the far end of the room held an assortment of board games—chess, Scrabble, checkers, Monopoly—as well as decks of playing cards, and a caddy holding poker chips. Four square tables and a stack of chairs were pushed against the wall.

Minnie closed the door behind us and pulled two chairs over to the counter.

"These are pretty old," she said, gesturing toward the computers. "Then again, so am I. I'd better not complain."

I laughed. "It's still a nice convenience for the residents."

"It is for me," she said. "A lot of people have their own computers. Portia did. That's why the management didn't bother to put too many in here, and doesn't update them. But Sam did business for fifty years with an adding machine, paper, and pen, so we didn't see the point in buying a computer at our age."

"That makes sense."

She fussed with her handbag, pulling out a handkerchief. "Speaking of technology," she said, her voice shaky, "I understand the results from the laboratory tests on Portia came back." She looked at me, waiting to see my reaction. "Do you know anything about that?"

I nodded.

She cleared her throat. "Tell me it didn't say that she died from a heart attack brought on by diet pills."

"Where did you learn that?" I asked.

"Foreverglades is very small, and there's no such thing as a secret. Helen called me. I don't know where she heard it—her beauty parlor, probably. Is it true? Do you know?" She dabbed her mouth with her handkerchief.

I wondered how Helen had come to that conclusion. I hadn't mentioned the autopsy report when I'd visited her, but she might have guessed, based on my questions. Or perhaps Clarence had confided the results to someone, and the Foreverglades grapevine had taken care of the rest.

"Yes. It's true," I said.

"They make mistakes sometimes, don't they? They could have mixed up two people, maybe."

"Everyone makes mistakes," I said, "but in this case it's highly unlikely the results are from someone else and not Portia."

"I was afraid you'd say that." She shivered. "That's not good, not good at all."

There was a knock on the door, and Minnie and I turned to see the Simmons twins march in one behind the other. They wore matching canvas carpenter's aprons around the waists of their overalls. Hammers and screwdrivers hung from loops at their hips. They pushed up the peaks of their orange baseball caps and nodded at us in unison.

"Here to fix the counter," said Earl. I'd noticed he was slightly heavier than his brother, a clue to his identity.

"Fix the counter," Burl echoed.

The pair busied themselves with their project. It was interesting to see that they needed little or no verbal communication to coordinate their efforts. Together they wrestled out the chair that had been propping up the counter, and while Burl held up the end, Earl crawled underneath and started hammering, the racket especially loud in the small room.

Minnie covered her ears with both hands and stood. "I guess I'll have to use the computer later," she shouted over the noise. She waved for me to follow her.

Out in the hall she walked quickly, pulling me along to a broom closet, where she flipped on a light and closed the door behind us. "I don't want us to be heard," she said in a low voice. "No one will interrupt us here."

"I understand," I said, thinking Sam was not the only eccentric in the family.

"Listen, Jessica, Portia was my best friend. I would have known if she was taking diet pills."

"People sometimes keep secrets, Minnie, even from their best friends."

"You'll never convince me," she said, pacing in the small space. "If Portia died from taking diet pills, then someone poisoned her."

"Do you know what you're suggesting?" I asked.

Tears filled her eyes, and she wiped them away angrily. "Yes, and I didn't sleep half the night thinking about it."

"Let's look at this logically," I said. "How could someone put a tablet in Portia's pillbox without her noticing?"

"Clarence filled her pillboxes every day," she replied. "I'd hate to think he would do that, but he certainly could have smuggled an extra pill into her regimen without her realizing. She trusted him. She would just pour out a handful of pills and swallow them down. She never even looked at them, much less counted them."

"How many pillboxes did she have?" I asked.

"One for each mealtime, I guess," she replied. "I don't know if she had more than that. I do know she carried one with her in her bag in case she wasn't home when it was time to take the next dose."

The closet door was flung open to reveal matching expressions of shock on the faces of the Simmons twins.

"Pardon us," I said, squeezing by them, Minnie close on my heels. "Where now?" I asked her.

We hurried down the staircase and Minnie guided me into the kitchen, where her class would soon be held. She closed the door and leaned against it. "They won't come in here."

"Let's say it wasn't Clarence," I said, trying to gather my thoughts. It was hard to carry on an interview on the move. "How could someone else sneak another pill into her supply?"

"Oh, it would have been so easy." Minnie said, dabbing at her eyes. "She was very careless about her handbag. She never remembered where she'd left it. When the Residents' Committee would meet, she'd just drop it on some table and go off buttonholing people, urging them to vote on whatever issue she was working on. Plus, her vision was terrible. I can't tell you how many times I had to help her hunt for her bag after a meeting. Sometimes it was just sitting on a table in the hallway, or on the floor by her seat. Once I found it here, in the kitchen. She'd brought in some snacks, stopped to put them on a plate, got distracted, and forgot all about her bag."

"And people knew this about her?" I asked, thinking that if someone had evil intent, there would have been ample opportunities to get into Portia's bag and pillbox.

"I warned her she was going to get her wallet stolen one day. I always thought someone would be taking something out, not putting something in. I should never have let her be so cavalier. Why didn't I think of it?" She was crying in earnest now, the tears falling faster than her wadded handkerchief could contain them.

"Minnie, you can't possibly think you're to blame for Portia's death." I pulled a packet of tissues from my purse and gave it to her. "No one could have prevented this except the person who gave Portia the pills."

"I'm sorry to fall apart like this," she said, taking a deep breath to calm herself. "The idea that Portia might have been killed—on purpose—is overwhelming. I just can't believe that anyone hated her so much. She was so nice." She looked at me hopefully. "Do you think it could have been an accident? Maybe someone thought they were doing her a favor, helping her to lose weight."

I shook my head sadly. "Everyone knew she had a heart condition. She made no secret of it. If someone gave Portia diet pills, that person intended to kill her. That's no accident," I said. "That's murder."

Chapter Ten

I pulled open the heavy glass door to DeWitt Wainscott Enterprises, and walked inside. In the center of the reception area was a large table on which was a model of Foreverglades, its pink buildings rendered in miniature, down to the white-painted grilles on the terraces and the concrete walkways in the courtyards. I paused, fascinated by the detail of the model, and walked around the plastic box that covered the display. Next to the blue paint that represented the bay were three tall white structures, dwarfing their pink neighbors. Due to the angle of the spotlight shining down from the ceiling, long shadows were cast over them. In addition to the three high-rises, several smaller blocks occupied space on the property, as well as a swath of beach made from what looked like real sand. On the model, the gazebo and boardwalk I'd trodden a few days ago were missing, but the dock was considerably enlarged, with tiny yachts anchored to the new pier. A ribbon draped around the top of the model buildings said WAINSCOTT TOWERS AT FOREVERGLADES.

It occurred to me that the model made an authoritative statement. It presented the proposed construction as a fait accompli, something already established, not merely the vision of the developer. It said, "This is what will be," not, "This is something to consider." I thought of Portia tilting at windmills, fighting people who had more power, influence, and money than she could ever hope to secure. But could her persistence as a gadfly, constantly circling the ears of the developer, have irritated someone enough to call for her extermination?

"Good afternoon," a voice said from behind me. "May I help you?"

I turned to see Amelia's sister-in-law, Marina. She was a broad woman in her late forties, her long red hair braided and twisted into a chignon. She was dressed in a navy pinstriped suit, white blouse with a floppy bow at the neck, and high-heeled sandals, the shoes making her pitch slightly forward as she walked, spoiling the corporate image she was trying to project.

"I saw the sign at the beach," I said, hesitating.

"And came to find out more," she finished my sentence for me. "How wonderful. Let me show you around. Where are you from?"

"Cabot Cove, Maine."

"That's pretty far north," she said, smiling at me as if I were a student who'd just given the right answer. "It must be frigid up there this time of year."

"It's pretty cold."

"Of course it is. Hard on the bones. Well, you've certainly come to the right place. Wainscott Towers is a new community, perfect for retirement, wonderful weather year-round, all the amenities, right on the water. How many places can boast that? By the way, what's your name?"

"Jessica Fletcher."

"I'm Marina Rodriguez. And you know, Jessica, even if you're not retired yet, it's a wise woman who plans for her future. However, if all you want to do is escape the cold for a few months, what better place than here?"

She sounded like she'd memorized the sales brochures. I let her usher me over to the wall, where schematic drawings of the different apartment layouts in the yet-to-be-built towers were displayed.

"We have apartments with one, two, and three bedrooms, depending on how much space you need, and whether you'll be using this lovely residence as a permanent home or simply a wintertime getaway. We have lots of people who do that. They look upon the building as an investment. What we can do for you is arrange to rent out your unit when you're not in residence. That way, with the income from rentals throughout the year, you'll be able to pay for the apartment in no time at all. And everyone can use that extra income, no matter what their financial situation, don't you think?"

"It sounds almost too good to be true," I said. "What happens if everyone wants to do that, and you can't rent them all?"

"I wouldn't worry about that. A high-rise overlooking the water is always in demand."

I wondered if the same promise had been made to the buyers of Foreverglades whose "investments," as well as their panoramic views, were imperiled by the new construction.

"Let me ease your mind with a few statistics. People love coming to Florida for the warm weather. You did, am I right? We had twelve million visitors last winter alone, almost thirty-nine million for the whole year. And every day, nine hundred people make Florida their permanent home."

"Those are impressive statistics," I said, not bothering to tell her I had come south for a funeral. "However, I understand there's a lot of opposition to this project from the people who live in Foreverglades."

"Oh, just a few malcontents, not serious opposition, I assure you. Anyway, this project is poised to go forward. We expect to break ground next month, and nothing will stop it. Mr. Wainscott will see to that."

"He has that much influence?"

"He certainly does," she said, grinning. "And I'll let you in on a secret. Mr. Wainscott confided in me that he expects this area to become the next big resort and retirement destination, kind of a Boca south. So if you buy now, chances are the value of your apartment will skyrocket in the years to come. He's the best thing to happen to this part of Florida."

His assistant was painting Wainscott as an ambitious man, but I hoped her braggadocio was merely meant to impress me. Marina rattled on, while I mused about the myriad difficulties the towers-to-be would bring into the lives of the earlier residents of the area.

". . . That's why he's putting so much into this, and those who get in on the ground floor, so to speak, will really make a killing. Are you married or single?"

"I beg your pardon?"

"I asked if you're married or single?"

"I'm a widow," I said.

"I'm a single woman myself—or soon to be, if you get my drift—and I'm planning to move into the first building as soon as it's up," she said. "Mr. Wainscott has promised I can have a penthouse on the twenty-first floor, right next to his. If you buy in, we could be neighbors. Us single girls have to stick together."

I decided not to comment on her vision of "us single

girls," and asked, "Is your employer really giving you an apartment? That's extremely generous of him."

"Not *giving* it to me, of course. I'll have to contribute something. After all, we're in business to make money. That's what he always says. He's been very good to me, but then again, I do everything I can for him."

"Why haven't you started construction yet?" I asked.

"Just some legal technicalities to work through."

Her answer was interrupted by the ringing of the telephone. She excused herself and hustled into the office, leaving the door open while she rounded the desk and picked up the receiver.

I didn't intend to eavesdrop, but the large reception space was like the wide end of a megaphone, and her conversation was easily overheard.

"Did you call your lawyer yet? I'm waiting for the papers. . . . What are you talking about? Those aren't the grounds we agreed to. . . . I don't care what Amelia said. Your sister is nothing but a common gossip. Tell her something and the whole community knows. I can't believe you listen to anything she has to say, but then you always did favor her over me. . . . Yes, you did. . . . Well, he's a gentleman and he treats me like a lady. . . . I am not his *puta*. You have some nerve. . . . I don't have to listen to this. I'm busy now. I have a client here. . . . Well, at least I have a job. That's more than we can say about you, isn't it?"

I heard her slam down the phone. It rang again.

"What do you want now? Oh, I beg your pardon. No, he's not. . . . Of course he's good for it. What do you think he is? I'm sure you'll receive the check soon. . . . I'll have him call you back on Monday."

She replaced the receiver and stood for a moment staring at the phone.

I tried to look interested in a photograph of Foreverglades that had been left on a table of pamphlets by the wall. The picture, mounted on a board, was covered by a sheet of clear acetate. An artist had painted a series of tall buildings on the top layer, showing what Foreverglades would look like with white high-rises instead of the low pink buildings currently there.

Marina returned to the reception room with a big smile affixed to her face.

"What's this?" I asked, lifting the board so I could study the design.

Marina stopped next to me. "Where did you get that?" Her tone was chilly.

"It was right here on the table."

"That's private," she said, lifting it out of my hands. "You shouldn't have touched that." She placed the board on the floor, with the picture facing the wall, and gathered up a sheaf of pamphlets from the table. "Well," she said, making an effort to be friendly again, "have you decided which size apartment is right for you?"

"I don't know," I said, affecting uncertainty. "Perhaps I could talk with Mr. Wainscott. Is he here?"

"If you have any questions, I'm sure I can answer them."

"I'd really like to meet him," I said, "before I decide if there's any possibility of buying an apartment."

"I'm sure he'd be delighted to discuss the details of your purchase with you, but he's not here right now."

"Could I come back tomorrow?"

"You could, but he won't be back for a while. He's down overseeing our Key West property."

"What a coincidence," I said. "I'm going to Key West myself, driving down tomorrow. I should be there by midafternoon."

"Are you going to look at real estate?" Her expression was concerned. She could foresee losing a sale to another building, and she wasn't happy at the prospect. Of course, she would have been less happy had she known I wasn't a real client at all.

"I won't be looking at real estate there," I said, grateful for the truth. "Just visiting a friend of a friend."

She brightened considerably. "Key West isn't half as nice as this part of Florida," she said. "Too crowded, and too many of the wrong type of people."

"What type of people would that be?" I asked, thinking she made quite a lot of assumptions about her "client." I wasn't flattered.

"You'll see what I mean when you get there. By the way, Mr. Wainscott doesn't keep office hours on the weekend. That's his golfing time. Boys must have their games. Am I right? However, I'm sure he'd be happy to talk with you during the week."

"I wouldn't dream of disturbing his weekend," I said, amused that she envisioned DeWitt Wainscott as a boy playing a game. "I'll be there for a few days. Maybe you can let him know to expect me."

"I'll be happy to tell him that you and I talked, and that you have a few more questions for him. He'll be so pleased that you're interested in Wainscott Towers." She shoved a pile of brochures at me and escorted me to the door, all the while extolling the virtues and amenities of the development.

The temperature outside was cooler than it had been earlier in the day, but the air was still sticky. Nevertheless, I was grateful for the respite from Marina's constant barrage of sales talk. That the woman considered herself a confidante of Wainscott was obvious. Whether their relationship was more than a business one was up for debate. Amelia had said her sister-in-law had a crush on her boss, and the beautician's penchant for gossip notwithstanding, I was inclined to agree.

I flipped through the leaflets Marina had thrust in my hand and saw they were almost duplicates of the ones pressed upon me by Mark Rosner, but with *Wainscott Towers* replacing *Foreverglades* in the copy. As if by thinking of him I'd made the man materialize, I looked up to see Rosner approaching the office.

"I hope you didn't fall for that broad's phony sales pitch," he said, climbing the steps till he was next to me, forcing me to tilt my head to look up at him. "Foreverglades is a much better deal."

"Frankly, I think it's a little expensive, considering the views will be obliterated by Wainscott Towers once they go up."

"If they go up, you mean."

"What makes you think the towers might not get built?" I asked, taking a step backward to ease the tension in my neck.

He moved closer and whispered, "Let's just say the odds are against it."

"You're being cryptic, Mr. Rosner," I said.

He studied his fingernails, a small smile playing over his lips. "I'm trying to convince Wainscott to drop the plan," he said, looking at me. "There are plenty of other properties in Florida ripe for development."

"I don't mean to be rude," I said, "but does your word carry weight with him? The impression I've been given is that he just rolls over anyone in his way."

He laughed. "His reputation precedes him, I see. I

think my opinion 'carries weight' with him, as you say. He owes me. I manage Foreverglades for him, and broker the sales of the units. I'm sure he doesn't want to do it himself. He's too important for that."

Before I could ask him anything more, Rosner saluted me with two fingers and went inside the headquarters of DeWitt Wainscott Enterprises. It was interesting that one of his employees opposed the developer's plans for expansion. Of course, Rosner knew that Portia was my friend. He could be telling me what he thought I wanted to hear. Then again, since he was charged with selling the apartments in Foreverglades, and not in the potentially more profitable Wainscott Towers, it could be wishful thinking on his part. Perhaps he coveted Marina's job, and wanted to see her fail so he could take her place. Even so, Wainscott was a fool if he thought he had a loyal employee in Rosner. And Wainscott was no fool; so why did Rosner think the developer "owed him"?

I walked back to Foreverglades, thinking about Wainscott's plans, and the picture I wasn't supposed to see. Were there plans to demolish Foreverglades to make way for more towers? If Wainscott's ultimate end was to replace Foreverglades with a larger, more profitable development, one catering to a wealthier clientele, then Portia had even more reason to oppose the construction of Wainscott Towers than it seemed at first. Had she—like me, just now—found out something she wasn't supposed to know? And had someone killed her to keep it secret?

I looked over my shoulder. The street was deserted, the heat of the day having chased people inside. There were no cars in sight except for a black BMW sedan, just like the one driven by Tony Colombo. It was parked on the far side of the building facing my direction. Did I detect movement behind its dark windshield? Could he be following me? A shiver passed over me. *Foolish to feel nervous*, I told myself. *Colombo's not a hit man. That was just a figment of Sam's imagination.* But all the same, I picked up my pace and walked quickly in the direction of Foreverglades.

Chapter Eleven

"Every time I go to pack my bag, its contents seem to have grown."

"Did you buy anything in town?" I asked.

"Only a package of razor blades."

"Well, that explains it then."

"Very funny, Jessica."

Seth and I were getting ready to leave for Key West. It was Saturday morning, the sun not yet over the horizon. We sipped our tea on the terrace of his apartment and munched on granola bars. We'd become tired of restaurant meals and had purchased a box of tea bags and a package of breakfast bars to tide us over till lunchtime. Seth had decided that we'd miss most of the traffic if we took off at dawn, and I, being a morning person anyway, was happy about the early start.

"What time is Truman expecting us?" I asked.

"I told him we'd make Key West by noon. He said he'd leave the door open if he had to go out, but he expected he'd be there to greet us."

"Are you sure we won't be imposing by staying with him?"

"To the contrary. He insisted we stay there, says he's swimmin' in room and will be grateful for the company. You know, Jess, I get the feelin' he's a bit lonely down there at the end of the continent, all by himself. We'll be doin' him a favor. You don't mind, do you?"

"Now, Seth, you know I don't. It's very generous of him to have us. And it will be a pleasure to put a face to the name I've been hearing about for all these years."

"You'll like him. Nice chap. Solid head on his shoulders. Good doctor, too."

"Darn," I said.

"What's the matter?"

"We were so busy yesterday, I never thought to buy him a gift. We'll have to stop along the way."

"What do we need a gift for?"

"We're guests. I don't want to arrive empty-handed."

"Plenty of miles between here and Key West. We'll find something. What'd you have in mind?"

"I thought perhaps a nice food basket, or something else we can all share," I said. "He shouldn't have to feed us as well as put us up."

"Truman said not to worry about groceries," Seth said, gathering up his mug, plate, and napkin from the metal table. "According to him, his refrigerator is so full it won't hold a scrid more, and his cupboards are overloaded. We can take him out to dinner while we're there. I'm sure he won't object to that. Can't tell if he's on a restricted income. He'd never let you know. Let's let him be a host, if that's what he wants. Give the man some dignity. And if you see a gift store on the ride down, just sing out and I'll pull over." He slid open the glass door and ambled toward the kitchen.

I followed him, placed my mug and plate on the

side of the sink, and picked up a towel to dry our dishes as he washed them.

"Tell me what Detective Shippee said to you when you called him," I said.

"How'd you know I called him?"

"He stopped by last night."

"He did?"

"Yes. He brought one of my books for me to sign for his wife."

"Well, he wasn't happy when I spoke to him, I'll tell you that. What did he say to you?"

"I asked you first."

Seth handed me a clean mug, and I wiped off the water. "I told him I'd taken Portia's pillbox from the top of her dresser," he said, "because I wanted to check out certain pills I'd seen in one of the compartments."

"And he said . . . ?"

"Well, I won't repeat his language word for word—it was pretty colorful—but the gist of it was I might've interfered with state's evidence."

"He said 'state's evidence'?"

"Ayuh. I asked him why a pillbox would be evidence. Did he suspect any criminal activity in Portia's death? He clammed up real fast."

"What you *did* do was add hand- and fingerprints to the pillbox," I said. "But, of course, we couldn't have known that would be a problem at the time." I wiped the last of the dishes, musing about the situation.

"I can always tell when you're runnin' something around in your head," Seth said, putting the mugs and plates back in the cupboard. "What is it?"

"There are two other pillboxes, according to Clarence. I wonder if the police have those, and if they were the same color as the white one you took."

"Who cares about the color? It's what's inside 'em that's important."

"That's true, but the color might be important, too."

"How so?"

"If all three of Portia's pillboxes were the same color, then she would just take one and put it in her purse. But let's say she used a white one for breakfast, a yellow one for lunch, and a pink one for dinner. In that case, she'd be more likely to take the pillbox for the next mealtime that was coming up. In other words, if she went to a meeting before lunch, she'd take the yellow one, and if she went to the Residents' Committee meetings on Thursday afternoons, she'd take the pink one because her next meal would be dinner."

"Why couldn't she just go home and take the pills?"

"She could, but that's not what she did," I replied. "Minnie said she always carried her pills with her in case she got delayed."

"So if the white box was the breakfast pillbox, then most likely it would be Clarence who put the diet pill in with her supplements and medicines."

"Exactly. That box would be filled fresh every morning—by Clarence. Nobody else would be there."

"It should be easy enough to find out. Ask your pal Detective Shippee. And you never told me what he said to *you* last night."

"He didn't say anything until I told him I'd seen the autopsy report."

"And then?"

"And then he asked what I thought of the results. I told him that, from what I'd heard from Portia's friends—and husband—it was highly unlikely that Portia would knowingly take a diet pill."

"And what did he say?"

"He agreed with me."

"He did?"

"Yes. But he wouldn't tell me if the police were doing anything about it, and I asked him several times. I also told him about Sam suspecting Portia was killed by a hit man. He said he'd heard that."

"What did he say about me?"

"About you? Nothing."

"But you said—"

"I knew you'd spoken to him because you're a responsible person. You told Clarence you'd call the police and tell them you'd taken Portia's pillbox, and I knew you'd keep your word." I walked into the living room to get my handbag.

"That was pretty tricky, Jessica," Seth sputtered.

I smiled at him. "I'm ready to leave. Are you?"

After making sure both apartments were locked up, we loaded our bags into the white sedan—which Seth had come by with the assistance of Sam Lewis, who'd provided a lift to the closest auto rental agency— dropped off the apartment keys in a box at the rec hall, and drove through the arched entrance to Foreverglades toward the main road, passing a number of joggers running to and from the development. The temperature was expected to rise to near ninety, but the early-morning air was cool. We kept the windows open, the freshness of the breeze adding to our enjoyment of the adventure ahead.

I sat in the passenger seat with a map of southern Florida on my lap. My help was needed only until we found our way to U.S. 1, after which it was a straight shot south all the way to Key West. I hadn't taken a car trip in a long time and looked forward to what is often billed as one of America's most scenic drives, the Overseas Highway—more than a hundred miles of archipelago, skipping from island to island over the forty-two bridges linking them, driving through desert landscape and thick jungle, past tangles of mangrove and smooth sandy beaches.

The roads were fairly free of traffic until we connected to Route 1; plenty of other like-minded drivers had decided to get an early start, too. We crossed the Jewfish Creek drawbridge, a span more than two hundred feet long, marking the division of Barnes Sound on our left and Blackwater Sound on our right, and entered Key Largo, the longest and perhaps best known of the Keys, thanks to the classic movie starring Humphrey Bogart and Lauren Bacall.

Even at that early hour, T-shirts waved in the breeze in front of souvenir shacks, and cars lined up alongside roadside eateries, some with long fishing poles strapped to their roof racks. Myriad signs advertised day trips aboard seagoing vessels fishing for marlin, wahoo, and sailfish. Dive shops promised face-to-face meetings on the coral reefs with sea urchins, anemones, and manta rays for snorklers and scuba divers. And glass-bottom-boat tours offered the same views for those who didn't want to get wet. The jumble of signs, billboards, and business establishments might discourage some vacationers seeking unspoiled landscapes and less commercial encounters with nature, but I took delight in the jaunty, informal seaside atmosphere, and felt a pang that Seth and I were not donning orange life vests and going off for a day of fishing.

"I've seen so many signs for conch chowder, conch fritters, and key lime pie that I'm getting hungry," Seth said.

I checked my watch. "It's still early," I said.

"It's not early for breakfast, and we barely had any."

"We should be in Key West well before lunchtime, provided the traffic doesn't get worse."

"My stomach is making noises now," he groused.

"Can you hold out till we're a little farther south?" I asked. "Maybe I'll see a store where I can get something for Truman, and you can get a snack at the same time."

Seth frowned but assented to my request. We continued south, the markers on the side of the road counting down the miles to the end of the highway. We passed through Tavernier and across our second bridge to Plantation Key. By the time we reached Islamorada, not even a quarter of the way, Seth—more accurately his stomach—had lost patience.

"This place looks good," he said, turning off the road into a space in front of an outdoor food stand with five stools pulled up to a counter, and large signs advertising the menu. While I walked around a bit to stretch my limbs, Seth ordered a cup of chowder and a slice of pie.

"I got two forks if you want to taste the pie," he called to me as he sat at a picnic bench on the side of the stand.

"No, thanks. I'm not hungry yet."

"Don't see how. You had the same nonbreakfast I did."

"I'm fine," I said, raising my arms over my head, "but maybe another cup of tea would be nice." I ordered it and waited for the lone server, a young man not more than sixteen by the looks of him, to pour hot water over a tea bag. A large sign behind him said, THE ORIGINAL AUTHENTIC KEY LIME PIE.

"What makes your key lime pie original?" I asked when he set the paper cup in front of me and I paid.

"My great-grandmother had one of the first key lime trees down here—today they really only grow 'em on the mainland—and she invented the recipe," he said, tapping the glass dome covering the pie. "Ours has a graham-cracker crust and meringue topping. Sometimes people make it with a regular crust. That ain't right. And it's supposed to be meringue, not whipped cream. That's what my mom says." He smiled at the pie, from which a large piece was missing. "Best there is. Want a slice?"

"Can you give me a sliver? I'll pay for a whole slice. I'm not really hungry, but that's very tempting."

"Tell you what. I'll just give you a taste. No charge. Then you see what you think." He cut a thin piece of pie, scooped up a spoonful of custard, crust, and meringue, handed the spoon to me, and waited, smiling all the time.

"Just delicious," I said, thanking him and savoring the mixture of crunch, sweet tartness, and creamy meringue.

"Don't let nobody sell you a green key lime pie," he said. "The juice is yellow, kind of, but it definitely ain't green."

"Someone else told me that," I said.

"And make sure you buy from a reputable place. Sometimes, if they run out of key limes, they pass off lemon meringue as the same thing."

"I'll keep that in mind."

"Want a slice now?"

"No, thanks, but do you sell the whole pie?" I asked, thinking this might be the perfect gift to bring Truman. I had no idea of his taste in home furnishings or reading matter, but a wonderful dessert is always welcome.

"How far you going?"

"Key West."

He shook his head. "Can't do it. Don't have no dry ice to give you, and judging by the traffic, you've got hours ahead. The pie wouldn't be as good as what you just had, sitting in a hot car for that time. I can't let you do it."

"Too bad," I said, impressed by his willingness to forgo a sale to maintain his product's quality. "It's wonderful."

"Best in the Keys," he said proudly. "Tell you what. I'll give you the name of a place I heard of farther down where you can get a pie. Not as good as my mom's, of course, but it's a lot closer to Key West." He wrote the name on a napkin and handed it to me. "Stop by here on your way back up and have a whole piece."

"I'll do that," I said, "and I'll tell my friends to stop by, too."

He waved as Seth—now a happier driver—and I got back in the car.

I told Seth of my plan to bring Truman an original key lime pie, and put the napkin into the glove box so we wouldn't forget to visit the place the young man had recommended outside Key West.

"How was the chowder?" I asked.

"Good! Kind of like a combination of Manhattan and New England," he said, "with tomatoes and corn."

The remainder of our trip was a combination, too, of frustrating stop-and-go traffic and uplifting stop-and-view panoramas, especially the Seven Mile Bridge linking the Middle and Lower Keys. With the Atlantic Ocean on one side and the Gulf of Mexico on the other, the concrete path snaked over aquamarine water, filling us with wonder and true appreciation for the miracles both nature and human effort can achieve.

A large amount of the Lower Keys was dedicated to wildlife refuges, but civilization—and the development it brings—was clearly in evidence well before we reached Key West. I wavered between disappointment at how much of the land was paved over, and understanding the lure such a tropical paradise held as a human refuge for those escaping a more intense lifestyle.

We stopped as instructed on Stock Island to pick up a key lime pie from the stand recommended by the young man. Another THE ORIGINAL AUTHENTIC KEY LIME PIE sign, affixed to the front of the screened porch, greeted us when we drove up. Inside, a ceiling fan circled lazily over the single counter and half a dozen tables. As the proprietress put the pie in a box, I could see that it had a pastry crust instead of a graham-cracker one.

"We've been making it that way for generations, ever since my family moved to the Keys during the great Depression," she said when I queried her about the authentic recipe. "Those graham-cracker crusts have only been around since the fifties. Must've been a Nabisco invention. True conches"—she pronounced it *conks*—"know their pie is supposed to have a pastry crust."

"What's a conk?" Seth asked, coming in to see what was keeping me.

"It's what we native Key West islanders call ourselves," she replied. "It's spelled C-O-N-C-H, but it's not said that way. Remember that and you'll endear yourselves to the residents."

She tied a bow of string in the middle of the box, pulled off a tiny blossom from a jelly jar of wildflowers perched on the counter, and twined the stem around the string. "Have a good time," she said, handing me the box. "Come back again."

With our house gift safely stored on the backseat, we crossed the final bridge into Key West, both the island and the city. Truman's instructions guided us into a neighborhood called Old Town, past Victorian mansions with white picket fences.

Downtown, the city was filled with people; they wandered in and out of the stores and myriad art galleries, holding shopping bags and soda cups, and licking ice-cream cones. They filled the tables at outdoor cafés, and tied their bicycles to every palm tree along our route. At times the sidewalks were so congested, people walked in the street to make their way around the crowds. We shared the roadway with scooters, mopeds, bicycles, tricycles, and even a unicycle. At one intersection we stopped to make way for the Conch Train, which provides tours of the city, its passengers sitting in bright yellow open cars shaded by a green striped awning. The "locomotive" pulling it was a gussied-up tractor.

Seth turned into a residential side street, strangely quiet after the hubbub of the more commercial thoroughfare. We drove slowly, looking for the number of Truman's house. Most of the homes were pastel colored or white, except for a vivid lavender one at the far corner. They were large and imposing, with columns and gables, broad verandas, and shaded galleries on the second floors, reminding me of the older homes I remembered seeing in New Orleans. The plantings on the relatively small lots were lush, in some places nearly concealing the front of the house. Despite the cracked and buckled sidewalk where the roots of banyan trees had pushed up the pavement, there was a look of prosperity to the street, of new money spent on old houses.

We drew up in front of the purple house, peering out the window, searching for the house number Truman had given Seth. A man in shorts and a pink-blue-and-yellow Hawaiian patterned shirt was sitting on the porch in an old-fashioned double rocker. When he spotted our car, he rose from his seat, shaded his eyes, and waved.

"Seth! Seth!" he called, slipping his bare feet into sandals and shuffling toward the stairs. He was tall and spare. His gray hair, what there was of it, was pulled back into a wispy ponytail that hung down his back.

"Truman?" Seth said, clearly astounded at the alterations in the companion of his youth.

"The very same," he called out.

Truman hurried down the path and pointed away from the house. "You'll have to go 'round the corner to the driveway and pull into the back. You can't park here. You'll get a ticket." He squatted down so he could see into the car. "Seth, you old coot, it's good to see you." He pounded Seth's shoulder. "Hi, there, Jessica. I was hoping I'd get to meet you." He pushed his arm past Seth and shook my hand. "Go on around. I'll meet you in the driveway. I'm glad you guys don't have an RV. I wouldn't know where to tell you to park it. It would never fit, and the town hates them. They barely tolerate cars, much less trailers. See you in a minute." He turned and trotted back up the path.

Seth sat for a moment, his mouth agape, before clearing his throat and releasing the brake.

I cocked my head. "He's changed a bit, I take it."

"More like transformed," Seth said. "Always perfectly groomed. Never without a tie. Used to make me feel like a poor relation standing next to him."

"Retirement often encourages people to explore new directions," I said. "Or maybe it simply allows a person's true nature to emerge."

"But he's a completely different man."

"You may seem different to him, too."

"I haven't gone from a normal person to a hippie."

"Seth, you've only just said hello. It's been years since you've seen each other. Give it a little time."

"Ayuh," Seth said, stopping at the corner before making the turn. "I know. I know. You can't judge a book by its cover. But, Jessica, I think the contents may have changed here as well."

"He seems genuinely happy to see you."

He didn't say anything more, but frowned as he drove beneath the low-hanging branches of a tree that arched over Truman's driveway. The gravel crunched under the tires as we pulled to a stop before what I assumed had once been a garage. It was painted the same intense hue as the house, and still had the broad, multipaneled garage door, but a smaller door, painted blue, had been cut into it. A matching sign with white letters tacked up on the right said, DISPENSARY.

Truman was halfway down the path when we climbed out of the car and took in our surroundings. The back of the house had a second-floor balcony that looked down on an overgrown but charming garden. Enough of the overhead foliage had been cleared to allow a little pool of sunlight to reach a stone patio, where a wrought-iron table and chairs—and a canvas hammock on a stand—created an inviting area to relax. A young woman in a long, gauzy dress was doing precisely that. She was stretched out on the hammock asleep, an open book on her chest, one forearm resting across her eyes, shielding them from the sun, a little black dog curled at her feet.

"Let me see what you look like, Boomer," Truman said, grabbing Seth by the shoulders and turning him around.

"Boomer?" I said, noting the blush rising into Seth's cheeks.

"Got quite a front porch there," Truman teased, poking a finger into Seth's abdomen, "but you've got more hair than I do. Good for you." He gave Seth a bear hug, and turned to me with outstretched arms. "I've heard so much about you, I feel like we're old friends."

I was the recipient of another hug, and then Truman, beaming at both of us, ushered us up the path toward his home.

"Oh, wait," I said, rushing back to the car.

"I'll get Benny to bring in your luggage later."

"It's not the luggage I want," I said, opening the back door on the passenger side. "We brought you a key lime pie. I think it may need to be refrigerated."

"How wonderful. My favorite."

"I hope it's not like bringing coals to Newcastle," I said.

"Not at all," Truman said, reaching for the pie. He lifted a flap on the box to peek inside. "Must be the original, authentic recipe."

"How did you know?" I asked.

He laughed. "There are probably a hundred places

down here that boast that their key lime pie is the original, authentic recipe."

"You mean it's not?" I was crestfallen. The young man whose pie I'd sampled had seemed so sincere, and I'd purchased this one on his recommendation.

"Don't worry," Truman said, taking my arm as we walked to the house. "I haven't tasted a bad key lime pie in thirty years. It's always good, just a little different every time. Some are chiffon; some are custard; some are frozen. Use meringue; don't use meringue. Pastry crust, graham-cracker crust, cookie crust. Every baker has another idea of what's authentic. And they'll swear their grandmother invented the recipe."

I nodded and sighed. "It's not often I'm taken in, but I was."

"Don't think twice about it. Making key lime pie is a competitive sport down here. I'll take you over to La-Te-Da on Duval. The baker makes theirs with chocolate ganache. Delicious, but definitely not authentic. At Louie's Backyard, it has a gingersnap crust and is served with a raspberry sauce."

"What *is* the authentic recipe then?" Seth asked.

Truman shrugged. "I've no idea," he said. "But I'll tell you a little secret. You have to swear not to reveal it or my reputation will be ruined in Key West." He winked.

"I think your secret will be safe with us," I said.

"My favorite key lime pie isn't made in the Keys at all. The one I love best is made in South Beach at a restaurant called Joe's Stone Crab. But as a freshwater conch, I don't dare reveal my preference."

"And a freshwater conch would be someone who *wasn't* born here?" I asked.

"Exactly. A true conch would never prefer the pie

of an off-islander. There must still be some Boston in my bones."

"Not much," I heard Seth mutter.

Truman laughed. "Gave you a start, huh, Boomer? Not exactly the Dr. Truman Buckley you knew and loved." He grinned at Seth. "We'll have to catch up later, but let's get you settled first. I'll show you to your rooms and then we can have lunch."

If Seth had thought Truman was living on a limited income, that impression was corrected as soon as we entered French doors leading into the back parlor. The house may have had Victorian origins, but someone in the past twenty-five years—and I suspected it was Truman—had put a large fortune into renovating the interior. Marble floors and whitewashed plaster cooled the air in the old house, which was filled with antiques and reproductions of antiques that any decorating magazine would have been proud to display on its pages.

Truman led us through the parlor to the front hall and up a broad staircase, which had elaborately carved newel posts and spindles.

"The house dates to the late eighteen-hundreds," he explained. "It was a mess when I got it, the plaster falling down, floors all rotted. I ripped them out and replaced them with marble. It'll never rot in this humidity, and it feels delicious underfoot in the summer on days when you can barely move because it gets so damned hot."

"Very nice," Seth said, pausing to catch his breath and look back at the stained-glass transom over the front door, and the crystal chandelier hanging from the end of a long chain.

Upstairs, Truman led us to guest rooms at opposite sides of a carpeted hallway. Seth's was at the front of the house, looking out on the street. Mine faced the rear, with French doors leading to the balcony I'd seen earlier.

"I'll give you guys a few minutes to unwind," Truman said. "Find your way to the kitchen when you're ready."

He closed the door behind me and I looked around. The room wasn't large, but it had an iron four-poster bed hung with yards of white gauze, and an Eastlake Victorian chest with a rolltop desk above the drawers, on which was a telephone, pad, and pen, just like in a hotel. At the foot of the bed was a blanket chest with an inlaid design of birds and vines. A wing-back chair and small ottoman completed the furniture. Two doors side by side took up half one wall. I opened the first to reveal an empty closet except for a folded luggage rack and an array of hangers. The other door led to a private bath. It had been restored but maintained its old-fashioned appearance, with small octagonal white tiles on the floor with a line of black tiles set as a border, pedestal sink, claw-footed tub, and a commode with a pull chain of a type I hadn't seen since my grammar school days.

The sound of a knock drew me back to the bedroom. I opened the door. A young man, attired in crimson from hair to shirt to shoes, stood in the hallway with our two bags. He had tattoos on both arms and more piercings than I could comfortably look at.

"Hi, I'm Benny. Which one is yours?"

"That one." I pointed to my bag. "I'm Jessica Fletcher. It's nice to meet you. Do you work for Dr. Buckley?"

"Work for Truman? No. I just hang out here. We do favors for each other. Today I'm his bellboy."

"Oh."

"But you don't have to tip me," he said. "This must be his, huh?" He pointed to Seth's bag and cocked his head at the door across from mine.

"Must be," I said, smiling.

He turned and knocked on Seth's door.

I pulled my bag into the room, not waiting to see Seth's reaction to the "bellboy," and unpacked the things I would need for our stay, changing into a fresh blouse and khaki skirt. I washed my hands and face using the fluffy washcloth and towels Truman had provided, went into the hall, and knocked on Seth's door. "I'm going downstairs," I called through it. "I'll see you there."

There was a muffled reply I didn't catch.

"This is like a lovely hotel," I told Truman when I found him in the kitchen. "How do you ever persuade houseguests to go home?"

"I enjoy the company," he said, clearing off the clutter on a marble-topped island to make room for a tray of crackers. He gathered newspapers and unopened mail and piled them in one corner, and pushed a portable telephone out of the way. It was one of two in the kitchen.

"Can I help with anything?" I asked.

"I'm just about done, but thanks for the offer." He unwrapped a package of Brie, placed it on the tray with the crackers, and pressed the blade of a knife into the wedge of cheese. He picked up the tray and I followed him into the back parlor through which we'd entered the house.

It was a peaceful room, the upholstered furniture all in beige silk with cushions soft enough for comfort, but not so soft as to hinder getting up. In the corner by a window, a round table, covered in a white cloth, was already set for lunch with a platter of sandwiches and a bowl of fresh fruit salad. Truman had placed three tall glasses of iced tea on coasters on top of the coffee table, and he slid the tray of cheese and crackers next to them. I sat on the sofa while he took one of the armchairs. It was interesting to see that this decidedly informal man chose to relax in such a formal setting.

"It's the Boston influence," he said, reading my thoughts. "I can't quite shed it, but I've been trying to for years."

"You've been here for thirty years, you said?"

"Just about. Not full-time, of course, at least not in the early years. You know, President Truman had his summer White House here. There's an avenue named for him, although I tease the kids and tell them it was named for me. Maybe it was fate that brought me here."

"It must have been quite a change from what you were used to."

"I liked Key West precisely for that reason. It was such a departure from my life in Boston. I'd joined my father's practice right out of medical school; never had a chance to look around and see what else was available. It was just by chance I came here. My first wife had a cousin who lived about three blocks away and we came down for a visit." He stopped, smiling at the memory.

"And you were charmed," I said.

"Charmed? I was overwhelmed. I couldn't believe the freedom of it. Key West has always been a place for free spirits. It was so accepting, so nonconformist, so totally opposite everything I knew and had been raised to value. There were artists and writers and musicians. Philosophical discussions in the cafés. Creativity virtually shimmered in the air. It was like Paris in Picasso's day—at least I thought so."

"Is it still that way?"

"Good question. I'd have to give you a provisional yes. We've come close to being ruined by our best qualities. The tourists are rampant. The chain stores and the cruise ships have moved in. There's a lot more glitz these days, a lot more money going into bourgeois construction, whether it's a resort or housing. I must sound like a terrible snob, but it saddens me to see the changes. But there's still an independent spirit. And the gay community here really supports the arts. I've been to more plays and concerts than I ever went to in Boston."

"Are you artistic yourself?" I asked.

"Not in the least," he replied. "My main talent is living well, which I have a knack for. But money has always come easily to me, with little effort on my part."

"Pretty fancy digs, Truman," Seth said from the doorway. "You've put a lot into it, I can see."

Truman looked over his shoulder at Seth. "My inheritance at work. Come sit down, buddy, and join us. We're talking about my love affair with Key West."

Seth had changed into a white golf shirt and tan slacks. He looked ready to attack the links, a goal I knew he harbored. "Nice place to retire," he said. He sank down on the sofa next to me and leaned forward to spread some cheese on a cracker.

"Retire? Who's retired?"

"But you gave up your practice in Boston."

"I did. My son took it over. His specialty is internal medicine. I told him he didn't have to. There's a wide world out there, but unlike his father, he actually wanted to stay in Boston. I moved here permanently with the intention of consulting every now and then. But little by little the practice has grown."

"Have we interrupted your office hours?" I asked.

"Not at all. The weekends are mine. I like being lazy."

"Ever get out on the golf course?" Seth asked.

"Not really my game. Do you play?"

"Oh, yes. Great sport. Good exercise," Seth said, neglecting to mention that he was relatively new to the activity.

"There aren't many courses. Land down here is at such a premium. But there's a new private club several miles up. I can probably arrange a tee time for you, if you like. I know some people."

"Oh, no, I couldn't impose," Seth said, "at least not unless you'd join me." He looked at his host hopefully.

Truman would have had a hard time missing the hint. He smiled. "If you insist."

Seth sat back, satisfied. "What's your handicap?"

"Don't know. It's been a while since anyone forced me onto a course. Are you sure you want to play with a rank novice like me? You might prefer more of a challenge. I can make some calls to see if you can make up a foursome with experienced players."

Seth rushed to head him off. "Not necessary at all. I want to spend my visit with you. We can take our time. I'll give you a few pointers if you get in trouble," he said, happy in the knowledge that Truman was likely a worse golfer than he was. "Only problem is I didn't bring my clubs."

"I'm sure you can rent them," Truman said. "I don't have any of my own, either." He turned to me. "Jessica, would you like to play?"

"No, thank you," I said. "But please go ahead without me. I'm sure I can find lots to do while you two get your exercise."

Truman stood. "It's a little late for today, but let me see what I can do for us for tomorrow. I'll give Wainscott a call and see what he can arrange."

"Wainscott?" I said.

"Yes. He's a real mover and shaker down here. I'm sure he'll know someone on the board of the new golf course. Have you heard of him?"

"I have," I said.

"He built Foreverglades, where our friend Portia lived," Seth added.

Truman snapped his fingers. "Right. That's what brought you to Florida in the first place. I'm sorry. I never gave you my condolences." He shook his head. "That's what happens when you have a poor memory. I must have forgotten to take my gingko biloba. Let me make that call before I forget again." He ambled into the kitchen, and I followed.

"Just out of curiosity," I said, "how do you know Wainscott?"

"Hmmm?" He was rummaging through the newspapers.

I plucked the phone out from under the pile and handed it to him.

"Ah, thank you. What was it you said?"

"Wainscott," I repeated. "How do you know him?"

"DeWitt? He came to my office."

"He did?"

"Yes. He's one of my new patients."

Chapter Twelve

The crowd that gathered to view the sunset at the docks behind Mallory Square was young, cheerful, and loud. There was a carnival atmosphere to the occasion, a tradition Truman insisted we had to experience at least once or we wouldn't be able to hold our heads up back home and say we'd *really* visited Key West.

"Fortunately, there are no cruise ships in port tonight," he said, "so we might actually get to see the sun go down. But even if all you can see is the sky above, it's worth the visit."

We had walked to Mallory Square from Truman's home, about ten blocks away, and had already experienced the "happy hour" atmosphere of Duval Street, with its myriad bars including Sloppy Joe's, its name illuminated in neon, and reputed to be Ernest Hemingway's favorite watering hole, and the nearby Captain Tony's Saloon, the original location of Sloppy Joe's in Hemingway's day.

In front of one bar, a rapt audience assembled to watch two long-haired men taking bodybuilding poses to show off the muscles of their chests, arms, and necks. They were shirtless, perhaps the most incongruous part of their show, given that there were more T-shirts offered for sale on Duval Street than I had ever seen in one place before.

We'd made a detour to buy stone crab claws from a fisherman friend of Truman's, whom we'd found sitting on a wooden lobster trap behind a restaurant—tubs filled with shaved ice and heavy plastic bags of fish arrayed around him—and selling his catch to the proprietor.

"How's it going, Gabby?" Truman asked after the restaurateur disappeared with his purchase. "Got anything left for me?"

"Always save something for you, Doc," Gabby replied, pulling out a plastic bag and lining it with fistfuls of shaved ice. He was a man of indeterminate age. The sun had tanned his hide to a burnished bronze and bleached his hair to a color somewhere between brown and gray. It stuck straight out from his head and jaw like that of a cartoon character who'd poked his finger into an electric socket.

Truman introduced us, then squatted down to inspect the claws and select the particular ones he wanted for our dinner.

Seth leaned over to watch the process. "What happened to the rest of the animal?" he asked.

"We throw 'em back," Gabby said. "We only take one claw. Don't want to leave the little fellers defenseless. They'll grow a new one, and we get to eat good. Works out for everyone." He grinned up at Seth, two gold front teeth gleaming.

"Don't think we ever tried that in Maine."

"Might not work with your lobsters," Gabby said. "Florida lobsters got no claws. That's why we catch these guys. I ate one o' your lobsters once. Ours are sweeter."

"Well, I don't know about that," Seth said, straightening, his home state pride ruffled.

"Didn't mean to offend. Takes all tastes, o' course.

But you try my stone crab claws tonight and come back tomorrow and tell me what you think."

"I'll do that."

Truman filled the bag with claws and dickered with Gabby on the price. "Don't go charging me what you twist out of those fancy-pants down at Wainscott's development," he said.

Gabby chuckled. "You're not so easy to hoodwink, Doc."

"Right you are," Truman said, patting the pockets on his shorts. "I don't have any cash on me. Stop by the dispensary on Monday and Sunshine will pay you."

"I'll be there. You got any of that tonic left? Did me a world of good last time."

"If I don't, I'll make some up for you."

"Gotta keep the ladies happy," he said, winking at me. To Truman: "I'll leave the claws right here by the door. You can pick 'em up after the ceremony."

The "ceremony" on the dock wasn't so much a rite as it was a party. Enterprising saloonkeepers had set up outdoor bars and sold rainbow-colored cocktails to those of drinking age. Jugglers and tumblers, good enough to be circus acts, entertained for small change and dollar bills tossed into hats that lay on the wooden planks. Parents hoisted children onto their shoulders, and people sat on the side of the dock facing west— some in folding chairs they'd brought for the occasion—as if waiting for a parade. There was an air of excitement at the "event" to come.

"Is it always like this?" I asked Truman.

"Every night. Don't know how it got started. It's been a tradition for as long as I've been here, a real tourist attraction. But I can't begrudge them what I get to see every day." He smiled at me. "Wait till the sun goes down and the last color comes up," he said. "See if it doesn't remind you of something."

"You certainly get a crowd down here," Seth said, turning in a circle to take in the whole panorama of entertainment.

"Yes, and keep track of your wallet," Truman said. "They're all friendly, but they're not all honest."

We watched a young man in a top hat twist long balloons into fanciful animals, and bought ice-cream sandwiches from a tap-dancing vendor holding her wares on a wooden tray.

"They say if you come to the sunset every day, you'll eventually meet everyone you know," Truman said, waving at a young family eating dinner from a bag of fried chicken. "I've had that experience several times." He turned to Seth. "Remember Johnson Werbel?"

"The big blond who fainted in our first autopsy lab?"

"The very same. He's a pathologist up in St. Louis. Used to be a medical examiner, but now he confines his exposure to death to what he can see under a microscope. Came here with his third wife and three towheaded kids."

"No kidding. Haven't seen him since med school."

"Yoo-hoo, Jessica."

I heard my name and turned to see Maureen and Mort Metzger squeezing through the crowd to get to us. Maureen, a big smile on face, had gotten into the spirit of Key West and was wearing a long paisley skirt, sandals, and a T-shirt tied at the hip. Her hair was tied back with a colorful bandanna. Mort was in matching shorts and shirt with a pattern of large yellow leaves on a turquoise background. He also wore a black fanny pack wrapped around his waist, and looked decidedly uncomfortable. I guessed he wasn't pleased for friends to see him in his new attire.

"That's quite the outfit," Seth said, raising his brows.

"Maureen bought this for me," Mort said, color rising to his cheeks, "but I told her she'll never catch me wearing it at home."

"Honey, you look terrific in that color," Maureen said. "Doesn't he look terrific, Jessica?"

"You look like you belong here," I said to Mort.

We introduced Mort and Maureen to Truman, who promptly extended an invitation for them to join us for dinner, and it began to feel as if we'd started a party of our own on the dock.

"We were hoping to meet you down here," Maureen said. "We've come for the ceremony every night."

The "ceremony" didn't disappoint. With the help of rolls of scudding gray clouds edged in limey yellow, the sky turned all the colors of a prism as the sun slowly melted into the horizon, the water providing a wavering reflection of its path. A drummer kept the beat while two dancers in Native American dress performed, drawing scant attention away from the real star of the moment. When only a sliver of brilliant light hovered over the water, there was a momentary hush; then, when the last beam of red slipped away, the crowd burst into applause. But the color show wasn't over. Streaks of peach and saffron painted the sky and gradually dissolved into a vibrant violet that I'd seen before.

"That's the color of your house," I said to Truman. He smiled. "I wanted to be reminded of the sunset when I don't get down here," he said. "I try not to get complacent about what inspired me to live in Key West in the first place."

"It's easy to forget to appreciate familiar blessings," I said. "It's when you lose them that you become most conscious of their value."

We left to collect our dinner and walk back to Truman's home. The party on the dock was still in full swing, with competing music, both live and recorded, rising into the air like thick smoke. During our absence, the throngs on Duval Street had increased, but there were fewer young children and more teenagers. Some of them waved to Truman, who returned their greetings.

"You're certainly a popular fellow," Seth said.

"Some of them are runaways I've treated from time to time," Truman said. "I try to move them off drugs and into a healthier lifestyle."

"Are you successful?" I asked.

"Only occasionally. But you've met one of my successes."

"Who's that?" Seth said, looking at me.

"Benny," I said. "Am I right, Truman?"

"You are, Jessica. And Sunshine, who manages my dispensary and handles my mail-order business. I don't think you've met her yet."

"Was she the young woman napping on your patio this afternoon?"

"What an observant lady you are! Yes, I believe so. I have several outbuildings on the property. If one of the youngsters needs a place to crash, they know they can come to me. My only rule is no drugs unless I prescribe something. Plus, they have to work for their keep and comport themselves in an appropriate manner. Sometimes it takes them a while to figure out what that is."

"Is Benny that fellow with all the metal sticking out of his face?" Seth asked.

Truman laughed. "Hard to look at that, isn't it? I think he considers it part of his charm. Doesn't seem to turn off the young ladies."

"Do you help them reconnect with their families?" I asked.

"If they want to. Often the relationships that pushed them out of the nest are not ones they're eager to reestablish. I encourage them, but I don't make an issue of it. I'm more interested in helping them be healthy. But the telephone is always available."

The bag of ice and crab claws was waiting for us, as promised, along with a second bag containing fish fillets.

"Gabby must've had leftovers," Truman said, picking up both bags. "We're going to have a feast tonight."

"Here, let me help you carry them," Mort said, relieving Truman of one of the bags.

"Be careful of your shirt, honey," Maureen said to Mort. "Don't hold the fish so close."

"I'm bein' careful," he said, but I noticed that as soon as Maureen turned away, he tucked the bag a little closer to his side.

"You're going to end up smelling like Mara's kitchen on a fish-fry night," I said to him as the others filed down the alley at the side of the building and back onto the main street. "Why don't you just tell Maureen the truth?"

"Gee, Mrs. F, I can't tell her I hate these clothes. She picked them out for me special."

"I think your wife will understand. Disagreeing about taste in clothing doesn't mean you don't love her."

"Yeah, but she's real sensitive."

"You'll end up with a closetful of clothes you don't wear."

"It's lucky I wear a uniform to work."

We both laughed. At the end of the alley Maureen turned around, a quizzical look on her face.

"Say, Mrs. F.," Mort said as we hastened to follow our host, "you learn anything from that autopsy report I asked Doc to drop off at your place before we left?"

"Nothing we didn't already suspect," I said. "Portia died from a heart attack, in all likelihood brought on by diet pills."

There must have been something in my tone of voice, because Mort said, "But you're not buying it, huh?"

"I don't know why someone would want to kill Portia," I said, "but the people who knew her best are convinced she would never knowingly have taken diet pills. That means she took them unknowingly."

"By accident?"

"I don't think so."

We reached the street and saw Truman, Seth, and Maureen cross at the corner a block away. I waved when Maureen looked around to see where we were.

"So you figure Sam was right?" Mort asked.

"Sam thinks Portia was killed by a mob hit man," I said. "That doesn't ring true."

"Sounds a bit far-fetched to me, too. Did you discuss it with that cop we met, Shippee?"

"I did, but he dismissed the idea. I think he suspects something's not quite right, but he's still looking for proof."

"And you are too, huh?"

"What do you mean?"

Mort cocked his head and squinted at me. "I was trying to figure out how the doc managed to lure you down to Key West. If you suspect murder, I would have thought wild horses couldn't get you away from Foreverglades and an investigation. Unless there's something to investigate here in Key West."

"I'm afraid you know me too well, Mort," I said, smiling. "There *is* someone in this city I want to talk to."

"Who's that?"

"DeWitt Wainscott."

"No kidding! I saw the man this morning."

"You did?"

"Maureen and I went to look at an apartment in his new development—Wainscott Manor, it's called. It's right on the water. We knew it was going to be too rich for our blood, but she likes to pretend we're interested."

"And Wainscott was there?"

"Well, not in the apartment, but we stopped by his office to pick up some brochures, and he was showing plans he has for another construction project to a couple of men. He was throwing around some big numbers."

"Maybe he's looking for investors," I said.

"Sounded that way to me."

"Do you think he got them?"

"I don't think so. Not yet, anyway. When the men said they had to think about it, Wainscott told them not to waste too much time. Said he has a lot of people coming in Sunday to check the place out."

"You mean like an open house?"

"I guess. Maureen and I plan to go. Why don't you

join us? They're opening up the first building to show off the model apartments."

"But I thought you already saw them."

"We did, but we don't mind seeing them again. Besides, tomorrow they're serving refreshments."

Chapter Thirteen

It was early Sunday morning. Truman and Seth were scheduled to tee off at eleven, and I planned to ask them to drop me at the Wainscott development on their way to the golf course. I would be early for the festivities, but that would give me time to look around before I tried to beard the lion developer in his den.

Over breakfast, Truman had offered to take us on a tour of his property.

"Not that there's that much to show you, but you might like to take a look at the restoration work I did on the house," he said as he sliced fruit and put it in a juicer. "The kitchen, as you can see, is completely new, all the appliances, even the cabinets, although I had the carpenter finish them to look old. Here, try this." He handed me a glass of juice and I took a sip.

"Delicious," I said. "I've never tasted such sweet orange juice."

"A tangelo isn't exactly an orange, but I guess it's close enough."

"What exactly is it?" I asked.

"It's a hybrid, a cross between a grapefruit and a tangerine."

Seth reached for his glass. "Is this something new?"

"Just the opposite," Truman said. "The first tange-los came from Asia a couple of thousand years ago.

Then, it was a cross between a Mandarin orange and a pomelo. That was the ancestor of the grapefruit. You'd be amazed at how many oranges on the market are mixes of particular varieties. These are the Honeybell tangelos. You can only get them three months out of the year, December, January, and February."

"Aren't we lucky we're here at the right time?" I said.

"You are."

"How big is the house?" I asked as he squeezed more juice.

"Six bedrooms, two sitting rooms—I guess you'd call one of them a family room these days—dining room, front hall, library, kitchen. There's maid's quarters in the attic, but I just use that for storage at the moment. I'm not sure of the square footage. I put in extra bathrooms for each bedroom when I decided to go forward with the renovation."

"It would make a great bed-and-breakfast," Seth said, buttering a piece of warm seven-grain bread Truman had baked in his bread machine. "Ever consider that?"

"Actually, I had an offer once from a group that wanted to turn it into a hotel. They promised to name it Buckley Inn, after me, if I agreed to sell. Offered me over a million to move."

"Dollars?" Seth said, almost choking on his bread.

"And that was a couple of years ago," he replied. "Probably worth even more now."

"Why didn't you take it?"

"And go where? Real estate is crazy down here. Besides, after all the work and money I'd put into this place, I didn't see any point in selling. I'd like to get a few years out of it, anyway. Enjoy all the improvements for a while before I put it on the market. But it costs a bundle to keep up. That's why I went back into medicine."

Truman walked us around the four buildings on his lot, which was larger than it had initially appeared. The garden behind the main house stretched to what once had been the house next door and was now part of Truman's property, and which he rented out. In addition, there was a two-room guest cottage— currently Benny's residence.

"And this is the dispensary. I opened it about five years ago when I became interested in the whole supplement field." Truman unlocked the blue door of what had once been a garage and pushed it open. "I'd been reading about ancient healing arts and I thought those early doctors and healers and medicine men might have been onto something. After all, medicine didn't just sprout full-grown in the twentieth and twenty-first centuries."

His dispensary was a combination doctor's office and herbal pharmacy. In addition to multiple cupboards, their glass doors revealing shelves stacked high with plastic bottles, there was a lineup of window boxes set beneath pink fluorescent bulbs and containing an array of homegrown herbs. Tubular skylights, ten inches in diameter, let in abundant natural light, and there were several long vines and trees in two corners. I wasn't sure if they were meant to be decorative, or were medicinal plants as well.

"You never learned about this in medical school," Seth said, eyeing the rows of bottles with a scowl.

"Yes, and it's a shame that conventional medical education in this country is so ignorant about complementary medicine."

"Seems to me that a conventional medical education stood you in good stead for a lot of years," Seth said.

"But there was so much more to learn that we never touched upon, Seth. In Europe, doctors routinely prescribe herbs and minerals in place of artificially manufactured pharmaceuticals."

"Might be. But you can't tell me their patients get better treatment than they do here."

"Well, I tend to disagree with that—"

"Uh, Truman," I interrupted, trying to head off an argument. "Yesterday you said DeWitt Wainscott was one of your patients."

"What? Oh, yes, Jessica. He is."

"I'm going to see him today. Shall I send him your regards?"

"By all means."

"If you don't mind my asking, what did you treat him for?" I heard Seth harrumph behind me.

"I don't mind," Truman said. "He came to me complaining of fatigue. He said he knew he was overweight, said he thought if he took off a few pounds, the fatigue might abate. I complimented him on his insight—it's not everyone who realizes the link between weight and fatigue."

There was more coughing and throat clearing from Seth. I knew he was likely to be horrified at the breach of patient confidentiality I so blatantly requested and Truman so blithely provided. I would have been understanding had Truman declined to answer my question. But since he hadn't, I persevered.

"And were you able to help him?" I asked.

"Of course. I suggested a strict fat-free diet, and gave him some E-z-waytoff tablets to help him get started."

"Never heard of that drug," Seth said, his curiosity as well as his temper piqued. "What is it?"

"A popular brand of diet pill."

"What's the active ingredient? Don't tell me. I already know. Ephedra, right?" Seth was working himself up.

Truman nodded.

"Don't you know people have died from that?" Seth said.

"You're thinking of those athletes a while back. You can't control people who abuse dosage or take medications without consulting a physician. But for someone under medical care, ephedra can be safe and effective. I took a very detailed history of Wainscott, stressed that if he had ever had a stroke or a heart condition, this was not the drug for him. He assured me he was in perfect health except for the paunch. I gave him a limited supply and was very specific about when to take them and for how long, told him all the potential side effects. He seems to be doing well. When I called him to see if he could help arrange our tee time, he told me he's taken off several pounds following my recommendations." Truman tucked his hands in his shorts pockets and rocked back on the heels of his sandals, certain he'd satisfied Seth's objections.

"Do you have any of them here?" I asked. "The pills you gave Mr. Wainscott."

"Jessica! After Portia—"

I put my hand on Seth's arm and squeezed.

"I might have an extra bottle," Truman said. "But you don't need to lose weight."

"Thank you. I'd just like to read what it says on the label."

He surveyed his cabinets and opened one, using a

key he wore on a chain around his neck. He pulled bottles off the shelf and pushed others aside. "I don't see them where they usually are. Sunshine probably has them on the inventory. I can check if you want. Just have to boot up the computer."

"Don't bother," I said. "It's not that important. Do you happen to remember what the pills look like?"

"They're just little blue pills," he replied. "I don't know if they have any other marking. I haven't looked at them in a while."

Seth, who'd been perusing the bottles in another cabinet, couldn't resist commenting. "Blister beetle. Chinese thorowax root. Smoked plum. Surprised you don't have a bottle of snake oil here," he said.

"You're old-school, Boomer," Truman said. "There's a whole world of medicine we were never taught, ancient Chinese practices, African medical arts, Native American rituals. That's only three cultures. There are so many, and we only learned about biology, chemistry, and technology. You should open your mind; you might learn something."

I could see Seth struggling to hold on to his temper. A challenge to his medical knowledge was the last thing he expected from his friend of long standing. "I may be old school," he said, "but I take good care of my patients. I don't experiment with their health."

"Seth, Seth, Seth," Truman said, shaking his head. "I've discovered so much since I started exploring the natural world. Wait, let me show you this." He unlocked a cabinet and took a brown bottle off the shelf.

Seth raised his chin and peered through the bottom of his glasses to read the label. "Tincture of feverfew. What's that?"

"Last month I read an article about it. It's an effective treatment for migraine headaches. But here's the rub. This is why it's so important that you do your homework, because if you took the dried herb, it would do you no good. Might even make you worse. It's got to be the tincture. Or, if you can get it, you can use the freeze-dried herb in capsules."

Seth looked at him skeptically.

"I'm telling you, there have even been *studies* that show it stops the pain and nausea," Truman said, carefully replacing the bottle on the shelf, "and even reduces the frequency of migraine attacks."

"Don't remember reading about a clinical trial on—what is it?—feverfew in any of my medical journals. What kind of study was it? Did it follow established guidelines? Did it get a peer review?"

"Of course not. Conventional medicine is not ready to hear about natural drugs," Truman said, locking up his cabinet. "The drug companies will see to that. Why use something we can grow ourselves when they can charge millions of dollars for their products?"

"So you're going to take it on faith that this feverfew works?"

"Not faith, experience. I gave it to one of my patients and she told me it was a miracle drug. That's better than established guidelines or peer review."

"You know that anecdotal evidence is not applicable to a wide population. You might have had the same reaction giving her sugar water."

"Gentlemen, gentlemen," I said, feeling it was time to intervene before an old friendship went up in flames over a disagreement on medical practices. I looked at my watch. "You don't want to be late for your tee time, and if I remember correctly you still need to arrange to rent golf clubs. Are we taking the car, Truman, or can we walk there?"

"Too far to walk, Jessica. Usually I'd take the bus

to that area, but since you have a car, let's take advantage of that."

We followed him out the door.

"Are you sure you want to play with an old man who hasn't held a putter in twenty years?" he asked Seth.

"Whatever you forgot, I'll teach you," Seth replied. "I'll probably be a little rusty myself. Haven't really put in time on the golf course since last summer. We'll be duffers together."

"Sounds good. I'll let Benny know we're leaving, and I'll join you in the driveway." He locked the dispensary and trotted toward the guest cottage.

"Can you believe it?" Seth exploded as soon as Truman was out of sight. "The man has become a witch doctor."

"Seth, we're staying in his home, benefiting from his hospitality. You don't want to quarrel with him."

"I knew something was wrong the second I saw him. What man our age wears his hair like that?"

"He does," I said, smiling.

"Can you imagine him treating patients in Boston, looking like that? Shorts. Sandals. No socks."

"I doubt he dressed that way in Boston. But even if he did, he doesn't live there anymore. And in Key West, neither his attire nor his hairstyle is the least bit unusual."

Seth shook his head slowly. "I don't know, Jess. It's not what I thought it would be. I just don't know the man anymore."

"You haven't seen him in a long time, Seth. People change. But he's being a wonderful host. He's taking you golfing because that's what *you* like. Let's be good guests."

"I know you're right." He sighed heavily. "But all the same, when you want to leave, I'll be ready."

"Why don't you find other topics to talk about while you're playing? Ask him if he's read any good books lately."

"Probably reading about casting spells and making potions," he muttered.

"Are we ready, Truman?" I said brightly when he appeared from around the corner.

"All set," he said, holding up a pair of rolled socks. "I figure they'd like me to put these on when I rent golf shoes."

"Good thinking," Seth said.

Chapter Fourteen

"You're going to be awfully early, Jessica, if the opening is at noon," Truman said from the backseat. "You've got time to sightsee if you want. It's not even ten yet."

"How do you know the time?" I asked. "You don't wear a watch."

"I cheated," Truman said. "I looked at yours."

"You don't wear a watch?" Seth said, carefully backing the car down the driveway.

"Threw it away years ago."

"How do you manage if you don't know what time it is? What about your patients?"

"It's not really hard. I just tell my patients to come in after breakfast, before lunch, or after work. No point in giving them a specific time. They don't wear watches either. On occasion they may have to wait, but no one's in a hurry, so it works out fine."

"Well, I'm not in a hurry either," I said, "so where would you suggest I go?"

"There's a lot of history down here. I think I mentioned that President Truman had his summer White House here. There's that, and Mel Fisher's museum. It's got some of the treasure he salvaged from a sunken Spanish galleon. Great stuff—doubloons, pieces of eight, gold bars. Kids love it there. The Audubon House is nice, too. But I imagine as a writer, you'd like to see the museum they made of Ernest Hemingway's place."

We agreed on Hemingway's house, which Truman assured me was within walking distance of Wainscott Manor, although he cautioned me against long walks in the sun.

"It's not too hot today, so it's easy to forget the sun can still damage your skin. Do you have sunscreen?"

"I do. And I also have a hat," I said, holding up my handbag to which I'd fastened a canvas cap. "Foreverglades had a heat wave when we left, so I came prepared."

"Do you have an umbrella?"

"No, but it doesn't look like rain." I looked out the window up at the sky. It was clear except for some scattered puffy clouds.

"You can't go by that. It rains a lot down here. If you get caught in a shower, you can duck for cover and wait it out. It won't last long."

Truman gave Seth directions and we drove across town, slowly navigating the narrow streets we shared with people on bikes and mopeds.

"It's just over there," Truman said when he and Seth dropped me at the corner of Whitehead Street. "Have a good time, Jessica. The back door is open if you get home before us."

"And don't do anything foolish at Wainscott's," Seth added.

"Why would you tell her a thing like that?" Truman said, extricating himself from the back of the car and climbing into the passenger seat I'd vacated.

"I'm just concerned for her safety."

"I'll be fine," I said.

"She's only going to visit model apartments," Truman said, pulling on his seat belt. "What kind of trouble can she get in?"

"You have no idea."

I waved as they drove off, happy to be freed from referee duty and hoping they could get through nine holes without constant bickering. They'd stayed in touch for so many years, it would be a shame to let these new disagreements jeopardize their friendship. Good friends, even ones we see only once in a long while, are precious. I hoped they'd find a way to tear down the walls they'd been building between them and, if nothing else, tolerate the differences that each had accumulated over the years. If they did, it would be rewarding for both of them, and pleasurable for me, although I really hadn't suffered from their conduct.

Since I hadn't expected to visit many tourist attractions in Key West—I had an ulterior motive for being here, after all—I was pleased that the opportunity arose to see one of the city's most popular sites, a place where a great writer had lived.

Surrounding the Hemingway property was a redbrick wall, which blocked the view of its neighbors, reinforcing the impression that this was a private retreat. The grounds were lovely, with tall trees shading the Spanish colonial home with its mansard roof, iron balcony, arched windows, and long green shutters. In the garden I was delighted to find purple-leafed caladium, areca palms, and tall Schefflera umbrella trees, grown-up versions of much smaller houseplants we had at home. Two long-haired calico cats accompanied me as I explored, admiring the luxuriant foliage and colorful beds that Hemingway was said to have put in himself. In addition to my companions, I caught glimpses of other feline residents—some sixty of them,

I later learned—descendants of the author's beloved pets.

I toured the elegantly furnished house filled with fascinating antiques Hemingway and his wife, Pauline, had collected on their travels, and many photographs and a large painting of Papa, as he was first dubbed by his Key West friends. The crystal chandeliers and formal furniture were at odds with my image of the brawny outdoorsman who wrote such sensitive yet muscular prose. But in the hushed, book-lined study, with its mounted trophies and other mementos of an adventurer's life, the man emerged. It was set away from the rest of the house to ensure the writer's concentration would not be disturbed. There, seated on a cigar maker's chair at a dark, round drop-leaf table, far from the bullrings of Spain and the soaring peaks of eastern Africa, Hemingway wrote some of his most famous works, like *Death in the Afternoon* and "The Snows of Kilimanjaro," laboring over the pages that would later thrill his readers.

By the time I left the house, the sky had clouded over. I consulted a map Truman had given me, and walked down Whitehead toward the water, musing on the life of a writer. As I crossed Truman Avenue, a dilapidated pickup truck that might once have been red rattled to a stop on the corner. Given the piquant fumes wafting from the bed of the truck, it was apparent that the vehicle was used to transport fish.

"Off on your own today, missy?" said the driver.

It was Gabby, the fisherman from whom Truman had bought our dinner the night before.

"Good morning," I said. "Did you go out fishing today?"

"Nah. But I've got a buddy's scraps, and I know just where to unload 'em. Where are your boyfriends?"

"Playing golf."

"Truman?" he said, cackling. "That old bird never played golf."

"There's a first time for everything."

He hooted. "I'd give a day's catch to see that."

"Not I," I said. "I just hope their friendship can survive it."

"Doc Buckley's an easygoing feller. He's no fighter. Must be the other guy."

I wasn't sure how well Gabby knew Truman, and decided discretion would be served by staying away from this topic. "No comment," I said.

"So where are you off to? Doing the sights?"

"I'm on my way to Wainscott Manor," I said.

"Well, this is your lucky day. I'm on my way there m'self. Got some regular customers in the neighborhood. I'll give you a lift."

I looked down at my slacks and wondered if Gabby's truck was as dirty inside as it was on the outside.

He saw my hesitation, leaned over, and opened the door. "You won't muss yourself. It's only the bed that has the fish in it. Hop in. You could walk to Wainscott's, but no sense getting tuckered out in this heat."

I put my foot on the running board, my hand on the door, and pulled myself up into the truck. Aside from fishing charts beside me on the bench seat, and an empty paper coffee cup rolling on the floor, the cab of the truck was presentable. I had second thoughts, however, when I looked around for a seat belt. There wasn't one.

"We had a feast last night, thanks to you," I said. "My friend Seth was delighted with the crab claws. I probably shouldn't give away his secret."

"It's no secret. No one can resist 'em," he said, pulling away from the curb. He glanced over at me.

"What's your name again? Memory's not what it was."

I told him, and he said, "Mine's Gabby. Least that's what they call me."

"It's not your real name?"

"Nah. Some tourist once said I looked like Gabby Hayes, and the name stuck."

"Gabby Hayes?"

"Remember him?"

"I do," I said, recalling the character actor with wiry gray hair and whiskers, who played a cantankerous cowboy. "He was on *The Roy Rogers Show,* if I remember correctly."

"Righto! He was Roy's sidekick. Handsome devil, didn't you think?" He winked at me.

I laughed. "You're taking me back to my youth."

"Yeah, well, it was an old-timer who named me. Between the hair and the beard, he said, I was a dead ringer. I told him I'd rather be a live ringer." He laughed at his own joke.

"Young people won't remember the reference," I said, "unless cable television airs reruns of the show."

"Well, I don't watch much TV, so it don't matter. How come you're going over to the Manor? Got friends there?"

"No. I don't know anyone there."

"You're not thinking of buying, are you?"

"No," I said, surprised at his sharp tone. "I'm hoping to talk to DeWitt Wainscott."

Gabby screwed up his face and spat out the window. "Can't imagine what you'd want with that ugly, bottom-feeding miserable shark, who never gave a decent person the time of day. You can't trust him worth a damn. He'll steal you blind and take away your cane."

Although I was no fan of DeWitt Wainscott, Gabby's tirade took me aback. "You certainly have strong feelings about the man."

"He's a thief and a murderer," he said, clamping his jaw till the muscle in his cheek quivered.

"That's quite an accusation," I said.

"It's the truth."

"Who did he steal from, and who did he kill?"

"He steals from everybody."

"Well . . ."

"I knew a guy worked for him for years for pennies—that's all he ever paid—and no health insurance, of course. He can't afford it, the big man says. Course, *he's* living high," Gabby said in a snide voice, "but his men got to scramble to pay the bills. Rudy got sick, no money for the doctor, much less the hospital. Wainscott wouldn't even lend him the dough, just fired his ass—'scuse my language—for 'malingering on the job,' he says. And the guy was dead in six months. You can't tell me that man ain't responsible for Rudy's death."

"That's a terrible thing to have happened," I said. "It's cruel and immoral, but it's not the same as murder."

"Yeah, well, what about Denny Carimbolo?"

"What about Denny Carimbolo?"

"When they built the first building at Wainscott Manor, the boss was ordering this cheap-grade lumber, nowhere near code. Denny was superintendent on the job, threatened to report it if Wainscott didn't change the order. And didn't he end up dead a few days later?"

"What happened?"

"Got hit in the head with an I beam."

"How awful."

"The guy operating the crane was some thug Wainscott had brought down from up north. A 'terrible accident,' the paper said." Gabby sneered. "That weren't no accident."

"You think the man on the crane hit Denny intentionally?"

"My mother didn't raise no idiot. The guy disappears right away, too. Wainscott sent him off to another site to get him out of Key West."

"But what about the police? Did you tell them your suspicions?"

"No way, missy. I ain't about to put my head in the way of a steel bar."

"Did you work for Wainscott, too?"

"I did, but not anymore. Went back to fishing. No money, but at least you don't have to watch your back, like in construction."

"I'm from Maine," I said, "and I happen to know fishing isn't exactly a safe occupation, either. We've lost too many men to the sea."

"True. But if you know the signs, you can anticipate Mother Nature. You got no idea what Wainscott is gonna do."

Chapter Fifteen

Wainscott Manor was on the Atlantic Ocean side of the island, between the airport and the Fort Zachary Taylor State Historic Site. There were supposed to be two buildings on the site, but only one was completed. The other, surrounded by a chain-link fence, was no more than a structural skeleton of steel beams and concrete platforms. Stairways were visible through the plastic tarpaulins that had been hung to shield the open floors from the elements, and to protect the nearby swimming pool from the dust and other debris kicked up by construction. Forklifts and cranes stood abandoned. Piles of lumber, reels of wire, and other materials littered the ground within the fenced-off site. It looked as if there were many months to go before this building would match its neighbor.

Gabby pulled his truck into the broad circular driveway and jammed on the brakes, the crates in the back slamming into the cab, then sliding back against the tailgate. I braced myself against the dashboard, grateful to have arrived in one piece.

He looked at the abandoned site and shook his head. "He ain't never gonna get that sucker built."

"Why do you say that?"

"Just a hunch."

"I can see they haven't worked on it for a while,"

I said. "That wire is beginning to rust. But that doesn't mean they won't start again."

"The wire is the least of it. Between the rain and the sun, the wood will warp, and if the tarps leak, his cement bags'll be stone." He cackled, exposing his gold front teeth. "I hope he runs out of money and goes bankrupt," he said. "That'd serve him."

I climbed down from the truck, thanked Gabby for the ride, and walked to the entrance. Red, white, and blue pennants, fluttering in the breeze, had been strung across an arched porte cochere. Flanking heavy glass double doors were lush tropical plantings, each with an artificial waterfall, the pleasant sounds accompanied by cool mist. I pulled on each door but they were locked. A sign advising residents to use the back entrance surprised me. I'd thought the open house was to attract buyers, but apparently there were already some people living here.

I cupped my hands over my eyes and leaned close to the glass door to peer inside—a crew was setting up tables in the lobby. I knocked on the glass. Eventually a woman wearing a long apron over black slacks and a white shirt came to the door and gestured with her finger, pointing at her watch. "Come back in an hour. We're not open yet," she called out, her voice faint on my side of the glass.

I followed a stone pathway around to the side, down a series of long steps toward a swimming pool nestled between the two buildings. A trail to the left led to the chain-link fence and a padlocked gate. Several people were stretched out on chaises, but it didn't look as if many residents took advantage of the pool, and I wondered if its proximity to the construction site was a deterrent. From the pool, another patio led to stairs that gave access to the beach. It was tempting to shuck my shoes and walk on the sand. But I was here for a purpose, and looked instead for a rear entrance to the building. As I approached the back door, a woman in overalls and a Florida Marlins baseball cap came out of the building carrying an insulated cooler. She stuck her foot out to hold the door for me.

"Thanks," I said, grabbing the knob and leaning against the door to keep it open for her.

"No problem," she said. "Did you see where Gabby went?"

"Gabby?"

"Yeah, you know, the old guy who sells the fish."

"He just left."

She set down the cooler and slapped her hands on her hips. "Can you believe it? My neighbor said she just saw him pull into the driveway."

"Were you expecting him?"

"Well, sure. He's here every Wednesday and Sunday. I buy all my fish from him. He's a little pricey, but you know you're getting the freshest fish, right off the boat."

I didn't tell her Gabby was selling leftovers from yesterday's catch. "Perhaps he's planning to come back," I said. "Where does he usually sell his fish when he's here?"

"Oh, he moves around. The management has chased him off a few times."

"Really? Why?"

"Someone complained that his tubs left a slimy puddle on the property. What do you want? It's fish. Fish don't smell so nice." She lifted the cap, ran a hand from her forehead across her bright red hair, and snugged the cap down again. "They think they're so elegant in this place. But they're going to have to learn to lighten up. This is Key West, not Palm Beach.

Us conches are freethinkers. Anyway, when the big boss isn't around, they don't usually bother Gabby, but they're having some sort of do downstairs today."

"That's why I'm here," I said, glancing at my watch. "It doesn't start until noon."

"They won't let you in early, that I know, not if they've closed off the lobby. I'm Reena, by the way." She stuck out her hand. "Thinking of moving in here? We could use some more neighbors."

"I'm Jessica," I said. "I thought I'd just see what's being offered."

"Well, I hope you like it. I'm afraid the builder's never going to finish the other one till this one is sold out. Doesn't make for a pretty view, a half-finished building."

"I don't imagine it does. Who's the builder?" I asked, knowing the answer, but curious as to what she might say about him.

"His name's DeWitt Wainscott. He's pretty much a newbie in Key West, but I heard he built stuff up north. He fought tooth and nail with the city over this development, but finally got his way. It'll be nice if he ever finishes it."

"What do you think is holding him up?"

"Ran out of money is my guess, although if he doesn't get moving on the second building, his permit might expire. Then who knows when it'll get built? The city doesn't want any more luxury buildings— what we really need is middle-income housing—so it gives these developers a hard time."

"So you think he doesn't have the funds to complete the project?"

"Who knows? These guys always find banks to give them more money. It's just us little people they cold-shoulder. I'll tell you this: If he's broke, you'd never know it by the looks of his office. It's just off the lobby." She looked around and covered her mouth with one hand, as if to keep from being overheard. "See if you can get a peek in there. A million dollars' worth of furniture and paintings. My neighbor says he has gold fixtures in the bathroom."

"My goodness. But you say he fought with the city; it seems he won."

"Sure, he got the go-ahead, but the city commission made him jump through a lot of hoops. Must've cost him a lotta dough to keep fighting."

"Putting up a building like this is expensive, too," I said.

"You're not kidding, but he'll get it back. The carrying charges are no small change, and these apartments aren't cheap to begin with. Sorry, I don't mean to discourage you."

"You aren't."

"I'd better see if I can find Gabby. It was nice to meet you. Look me up if you decide to move in. I'm on the third floor, west corner."

"I'll do that."

The lobby was abuzz with workers from a catering company getting ready for the reception. I leaned against the wall, next to a closed door, and watched as three men unfolded long wooden tables, pushed them against the wall, draped white linens across the tops, and clipped on spring-green skirts that fell to the floor. Two young women in black shorts, white short-sleeved shirts, and bow ties squatted in front of one table, lifted the cloth, and shoved boxes and crates out of sight. Styrofoam coolers were stacked along one wall, waiting to be unloaded onto silver trays standing on their sides in a crate. Insulated bags of chipped ice sat dripping on a rubber mat.

The woman who'd given me instructions to return in an hour hefted a platter covered in pink cellophane onto a table and loosened the ties at the top. She glanced in my direction. I could tell when she recognized me because she put on an annoyed expression, wiped her hands on a towel flung over her shoulder, and steamed in my direction.

"I'm sorry, madam," she said, scowling and blocking my view of the room. "As you can see, we're not set up yet, and we only have a short time to finish. I can't tolerate any distractions. I already told you, you'll have to come back later."

"I'm here to see Mr. Wainscott," I said. "I believe he's expecting me."

He would be, that is, if Marina Rodriguez had informed him of my impending visit. Of course, that didn't mean that he wanted to see me, or even that he would consent to see me. But I was hopeful I could capture his attention, at least for a few moments.

"I beg your pardon," the caterer said, backing away, her expression now conciliatory. "I didn't realize. Can I get you anything? Would you like a glass of water?"

"No, thank you," I said. "But you can tell me where Mr. Wainscott's office is located?"

"It's that one, over there."

She indicated the door I'd been standing near. There was no sign, only the round peephole, doorbell button, and fluted brass knocker I'd seen on the other doors I'd passed as I walked down the hall. A small square below the doorbell read ONE A, spelled out instead of the usual numeral.

I looked at my watch. "I'm a few minutes early," I said. "I'll wait here, if you don't mind." I didn't want her to witness my rejection if he declined to talk to me.

"Shall I get you a chair?"

"Oh, that's not necessary. I'm perfectly happy standing and watching your preparations. I'll try to keep out of the way."

"You're not in the way at all. I hope you'll stay for the reception after your appointment with Mr. Wainscott. He says we're his favorite caterer. We're setting up a wonderful buffet."

She went back to her tasks, and I waited, giving myself a moment to compose what it was I wanted to ask the builder. Suddenly the door was flung open and an enraged DeWitt Wainscott in shirtsleeves, his tie askew, came storming past me, a cell phone pressed to his ear.

"Don't tell me what I can and cannot do," he yelled at the person on the other end of the line. "Tell them I'll close the whole damn beach if they continue protesting. I don't care what the law says. They'll never set another foot on it again. Go fill the place with alligators. If you can't do it, I know someone else who can." He listened for a second to the reply. "The hell with the village. Those weak-kneed hicks cost me money every time they sit down. They always have their hands out. Tell them to take care of those old biddies, or I'll do it myself." He snapped the phone closed and descended on the caterer, bellowing, "Marian, why isn't the food out yet?"

"We're working as fast as we can, Mr. Wainscott. One of the trucks broke down and—"

"Don't give me your excuses. I want the food out and I want it out now."

"Of course, Mr. Wainscott. Here, I've just unwrapped the tray of steak sandwiches. Would you like to try one?" She pushed a stack of china plates next to the platter, flattened the pink cellophane on the table, and stepped back.

"The cookies. Where are the cookies?"

"Right here, sir," said one of the men, holding out a plate of artfully arranged dark- and white-chocolate lace cookies.

Wainscott took a fistful, toppling the design, then dropped the cookies on a dish the caterer thoughtfully handed to him. She took the plate back from him and said, "Let me put together lunch for you," she said. "I know what you like."

"Make it snappy," he growled, and, wheeling around, he stomped back to his office. He banged open the door, and I followed him in, grabbing it and closing it softly behind me.

He whirled to see what had prevented the satisfying crash of the slammed door. "What the . . . ? Who the hell are you?" he said.

"How do you do, Mr. Wainscott?" I said. "I'm Jessica Fletcher. I believe your associate informed you I was coming. I missed seeing you in Foreverglades, and she said you'd be delighted to talk to me down here, since I was coming to visit a friend in the city." Without being asked, I sat down in the chair across from his desk.

He reached for his suit jacket, which hung from a leather chair, thought better of it, and sat down, buttoning his collar and tightening his tie.

"Well, isn't this lovely," I said, looking around.

The office was actually an apartment—or would be, whenever the developer decided to vacate the premises. It was furnished with a startling mixture of elaborately carved French antiques and upholstered modern pieces in dark green leather with hand-painted details.

Wainscott had commandeered a gleaming mahogany dining room table to serve as a desk, and added, incongruously, a lateral file cabinet on the wall behind it. Hanging along with oil paintings—fair copies of Impressionist masters—was a row of framed color photographs and newspaper clippings showing Wainscott grinning at the camera with various celebrities.

"You know the governor?" I said, popping up from my seat and examining the pictures on the wall. "Oh, my."

"What?"

"Nothing," I said, taking my seat again.

There was a knock on the door and the caterer came in, placed a plate on his desk, and left. I noticed that she'd given him a much more balanced meal than he'd planned for himself, complete with sandwiches, green vegetables, fruit, and a few cookies. He didn't bother to thank her.

His cell phone, which he'd placed on the desk, vibrated and danced around the polished surface as if it were a windup toy. He snatched up the phone and walked into the next room. I popped up from my chair to look again at one of the photos on the wall, groping in my bag for my magnifying glass. I thought I recognized a man standing in the crowd behind Wainscott and the governor. The face was familiar. Who was it? I held up the magnifier. It was Tony Colombo. I was sure of it.

In the room next door, Wainscott was talking loudly. "Was anything missing? Dammit, Marina, didn't you lock up? Call the security people. I want an alarm on that door right away. I don't care if it's Sunday. Do it!"

There was a pause, and I scooted back to my seat.

"Do you have the letters ready?" I heard him ask. "Good. Deliver them. . . . Put them off. I'm working on the deal now. Johnson is bringing the big-money guys with him today. Oh, yeah? Why didn't you tell me before? Once I get this out of the way, we can line up the ducks in Foreverglades. I don't care. Do whatever you have to do."

I returned the magnifying glass to its pocket in the side of my bag and felt Wainscott looming behind me before he rounded the desk and sat again.

"Mrs. Fletcher, how can I help you?" he said.

"I came to ask you about Wainscott Towers in Foreverglades."

"Beautiful project," he said, smiling. "Going to be the start of great things. The area will be the next Boca Raton, if I have anything to do with it. If you buy now, you can get in on the ground floor. Would you like a cookie?" He pushed the plate in my direction, but not before taking one.

I doubted cookies were part of the diet Truman had prescribed for Wainscott.

"Mrs. Fletcher?"

"I beg your pardon?"

"You didn't answer. I said we have detailed brochures on the project. Didn't my girl give them to you?"

My girl? Marina wasn't held in as high regard as she supposed.

"Do you mean Mrs. Rodriguez? Yes, she gave me brochures."

"They should tell you all you want to know. The towers are going to offer everything. Health club. Shopping mall. Restaurant—we have a chef coming over from Tuscany. Full luxury units. You can choose the flooring, paint colors, optional appliances—only the best quality. It'll even have a spa for facials, massages, that kind of thing."

"It sounds very extravagant."

"Not extravagant, Mrs. Fletcher. Reasonable." He was well into his sales pitch. "After all, don't you deserve to live in luxurious surroundings at this time of your life? You've worked hard. This is your reward."

"I see. Well, when do you anticipate the towers will be built?"

"We should be breaking ground next month. Once we start, they go up pretty fast. There's quite a bit of prep work that has to take place, of course, but occupancy could take place within the year."

"That soon?"

"It could be. You can't *guarantee* a date. Things come up and cause delays."

"Is that what happened with the building next door? I noticed it's only half-finished."

He leaned back in his chair and chuckled. "Don't let appearances deceive you, Mrs. Fletcher. That's coming along right on schedule. We're just taking a break while we give this building a chance to reach a higher level of occupancy. That's what today's reception is all about—attracting buyers. Then we'll zoom along on the other."

"You don't say? I thought it was customary to complete construction from start to finish so you don't lose your crew to another project, or have your permit lapse."

"Not always," he said, running a finger under his collar. "We work in stages. Our crews are very loyal. They'll be back as soon as I snap my fingers." He hooked his thumbs under his suspenders.

"How interesting."

"I wouldn't expect a little lady like you to know how development works."

"No, of course not."

"If you're interested in seeing what the units will look like, stick around. The model apartments we're showing here are similar in layout to the plans for Wainscott Towers, and you can see all the amenities we offer for retirement living." He stood up and came around the desk, obviously ready to escort me out. "Plus, you can have lunch on me." His eyes twinkled.

"One more thing, Mr. Wainscott," I said, standing to face him. "I understand there's some objection to the towers being built on that particular piece of land in Foreverglades."

"Not a problem. My lawyers are taking care of that."

"The residents of the development next door say you promised them never to build on that land. Does that mean you're not a man of your word?"

He continued smiling, but the light went out of his eyes. "Mrs. Fletcher, you wouldn't understand. I'm a businessman, a builder. A builder of beautiful projects, I might add. My buildings are designed to add architectural presence to an area and stature to the community."

"Whether the community wants them or not?"

The smile faded. "I don't know what you've heard, but just because a few old ladies want to keep a beach to themselves is not a reason to stop progress. Florida is one of the fastest-growing states in the nation, and nothing can stop it. Nor can they stop me."

"Even if someone dies trying?"

"What are you talking about?"

"Portia Shelby."

His eyebrows shot up. "Mrs. Shelby had a heart attack," he said, his voice hard. "You can hardly hold me responsible for that."

"Denny Carimbolo?"

"Our visit is over. You're obviously not interested in buying an apartment. If you're here to make trouble, I'll have you thrown out."

"Mr. Wainscott, does someone who opposes you die on every project of yours?"

"Out!" he roared. He grabbed my elbow, dragged me to the door, and flung it open, ready to hurl me outside.

A young man holding a pad and pen was poised to knock. "Hi, Mr. Wainscott. I'm Jared Levin from the Key West *Citizen*. My editor called about an interview."

Wainscott stopped, nonplussed. He released my elbow, put a hand on my back, and shoved me out. "Come in," he said to the reporter. "Mrs. Fletcher was just leaving."

"Thank you, Mr. Wainscott," I heard the reporter say as the door was shut firmly behind me.

I paused to collect my wits. I'd wanted to raise the topic of the diet pills, to accuse the builder of supplying, if not administering, the ephedra that caused Portia's death. But without sufficient evidence to prove my suspicions, not to mention treading on Truman's trust by revealing his indiscreet comments about a patient, I'd remained mum. Wainscott was a ruthless man, but was he ruthless enough to have ordered a murder—or two? I'd taken a chance referring to Denny Carimbolo. I hadn't had an opportunity to verify Gabby's accusation. But it was too late now.

I straightened my shirt, patted down the back of my hair, hooked my bag over my shoulder, and looked around. In the time I'd spent with Wainscott, the caterers had finished setting up the buffet in the lobby. They had thrown open the double doors, and a good-size crowd was spilling in, some already lining up for the food. I scanned the faces in the throng, wondering which ones were the "big-money guys." One face was familiar.

"Jessica, we've been looking all over for you." Maureen came to my side and waved to where Mort was standing in the buffet line. "Honey, I found her."

"I'm sorry," I said. "I've been here awhile, but I was in the office talking to the builder."

"That's nice," Maureen said, absently tugging on my arm. "Come on. Mort's holding a place for us. Wait till you see what they're serving: stone crab claws, shrimp, sushi, and—"

"Steak sandwiches," I finished her sentence.

"Yes. How did you know?"

Mort had reached the buffet and had already taken three plates, handing one to Maureen and one to me. From the amount and variety of the food, not to mention the ice sculptures and the floral arrangements, I gathered that Wainscott had some very important people coming to the reception, and hadn't spared any expense. I ate lightly, not entirely certain I wanted to take advantage of the largesse of a man who might have been responsible for Portia's death.

"After lunch, we'll take you around to see the model apartments," Maureen said to me.

"Won't you be bored? You've already seen them," I said.

"But *you* haven't, Jessica. Besides, I brought my camera today. I could never describe what they look like to the ladies back home."

Mort was on his second piece of key lime pie when

I thought I saw someone I knew among the attendees. "Isn't that Mark Rosner?" I said, pointing out a man standing in Wainscott's doorway.

"Who's Mark Rosner?" Mort asked.

"He's the manager of Foreverglades," I said. "I arranged our apartments at Foreverglades with him. That's funny."

"What's funny, Mrs. F?"

"He never mentioned that he was coming down here when I told him we were driving to Key West."

"Maybe he decided to come at the last minute. Kind of like us driving down to Boston for the weekend."

Rosner surveyed the room, looking for someone. When his eyes met mine, he turned back to the door, said something to someone inside, and moved across the room in our direction. At the last moment he swerved away from us and went out the front door. I had the feeling he had something to say to me, but changed his mind when he saw Maureen and Mort.

"Excuse me," I said. "I want to check on something. I'll be right back."

"Do you feel okay, Jessica?" Maureen asked. "Want me to come with you?"

"No, thanks, Maureen. I'm fine. I just need to talk with someone."

I walked out the double doors into the broad driveway and looked for Rosner. He was starting down the stairs for the pool. "Mr. Rosner," I called, waving, hoping to flag him down. But he didn't hear me. I followed him to the stairs, only to see his back as he disappeared to the left, in the direction of the construction site.

There was a low rumble from above. I looked up. Dark clouds had moved in and were rolling across the sky. I reached the bottom of the stairs, took the path to the construction site, and was surprised to see the gate standing ajar. Up ahead, Rosner lifted a corner of the plastic sheeting and slipped under it, into the ground floor of the half-built structure.

What's he up to? I wondered. I picked my way across the construction site, skirting a rusting reel of electrical wire, and careful not to trip on the many bolts, nails, and screws that littered the ground. A large drop of water hit me in the head; another splashed on my shoulder. Then it began to rain in earnest. I sprinted the last few yards to the tarp, pulled it aside, and ducked into the building.

It was the smell that first assaulted me, a combination of damp cement, raw wood, lubricating oil, and the indefinable tang of steel. I stood for a moment in the dim interior and listened, to make out whether I could hear where Mark Rosner might be. On clear days the sun would illuminate the building—at least when the angle of its rays allowed light to pour in. But the dark skies overhead let little light penetrate the gloom. And the pounding of the rain on the equipment outside and the slap of water when the wind blew the drops against the long tarpaulins made hearing difficult.

"Mr. Rosner," I yelled. "It's Jessica Fletcher, Mr. Rosner. Are you there? I'd like to talk to you, Mr. Rosner."

There was no answer, but I thought I detected a muffled sound from somewhere inside.

I fumbled in my bag for the flashlight I always carry and flicked it on. The floors were dusty but clear of debris, other than a scattering of crushed cigarette butts in the corner. The light bounced off the massive steel beams that connected the floors. The workmen had begun framing out the spaces to be enclosed—

wooden studs stood every sixteen inches, limiting visibility—but the electrical and plumbing connections had yet to be installed. A box of nails and tendrils of wires had been left lying along a stack of two-by-fours. I moved toward the concrete stairs, swinging the light, hoping to capture some movement in its ray. As I put my foot onto the first step, I heard a scraping sound overhead.

I shone my light up to the second floor, but the beam disappeared into the gray ceiling. There was no railing to steady myself as I climbed slowly, keeping my eyes and the flashlight on the next step to avoid stumbling on some unseen obstacle. Behind me, the wind whipped the edges of the tarps, making them flap against each other and setting up a deafening clamor. A gust blew up the stairs and raised the hair on the back of my head. I whirled to see whether someone or something was there. No one. I was alone.

On the landing I turned, training the light down what would eventually be a hallway, and crept forward. The thicket of studs standing upright on either side cut off what little light filtered in from the outside and shielded the rest of the space from view, except those areas directly to my right and left. I aimed the flashlight at a piece of equipment far down the hall sitting atop a wooden ramp. It was a large rolling trash receptacle—the kind with a hinged front panel that tilts down to make it easier to empty. I walked up the ramp to take a look at it. The cart was too tall for me to peer inside, but two split beams and a crumpled canvas dropcloth were visible poking out the top. It was also too wide to squeeze past, and too heavy to move. I tried pushing against it. It wouldn't budge.

I retraced my steps, intending to search for Rosner on the other side of the stairwell, when I heard the scraping sound again. It was behind me this time. I turned to see the dump cart rolling slowly in my direction. The weight inside must have shifted when I'd pushed on it. Suddenly the hinged front panel dropped down with a terrible thud, exposing the contents of broken beams, shredded cloth, and shards of metal. As the cart bore down on me, its wheels made an earsplitting squeal.

I heard a faint voice calling my name. "Mrs. F?"

"Mort? I'm up here." There wasn't time to say more. I had to get out of the way. The dump cart picked up speed, thundering down the ramp, spears of splintered wood aimed at my head. I turned to run and the strap of my bag snagged on an exposed nail, jerking me backward. The flashlight flew from my hand and crashed to the floor. I stumbled, losing my balance, falling, falling. Then everything went black.

Chapter Sixteen

"Dang it, Truman, I've got her."

"Hell, it's my hospital, Seth, let me do it."

"This thing's like a shopping cart with a bad wheel."

"You just don't know how to steer it."

I sat in a wheelchair in the hall of the Lower Keys Medical Center on Stock Island, where I had spent the night under observation. I knew I was fine, but the doctors had been adamant. They'd wanted to be certain I hadn't sustained a concussion. I had a bump on the head and some bruises, but overall I'd escaped serious injury. I could have insisted upon being discharged, but didn't. When I saw how pale Seth and Truman were when they tumbled through the door of the emergency room and rushed to my side, I decided I would probably get more rest—and so would they— if I stayed in the hospital rather than returning to Truman's home, where the two of them would have fussed over me like a pair of hens fighting over one egg.

The wheelchair lurched forward, and I gripped the arms as I was propelled down the corridor.

"Got it now, Jess," Seth said.

"I can walk, you know."

"Sorry, Jessica," Truman said from behind me. "Hospital rules. You have to be wheeled to the door."

I sat back and sighed.

Mort had brought me to the hospital, but I didn't remember getting there, and I was eager to ask him the details of my accident. I only knew—or thought I did—that I'd been hit by the trash container. It wasn't a head-on collision. If it had been, like a cowcatcher on a train, the heavy metal cart would have scooped me into its maw, and I'd have been skewered by the sharp debris. That hadn't happened. While I was bruised, I wasn't cut.

"Did you sleep all right, Jessica?"

"I did, Seth, considering how many times the nurses woke me to see if I was sleeping."

"And you got to sample our delicious hospital food," Truman said, a smile in his voice.

"It was fine," I said. "I wasn't terribly hungry, but I wouldn't mind a cup of tea when we get back to your house."

"We'll give you a lot more than that," Truman said. "We left the lunch preparations up to Maureen and Benny. They promised a feast by the time we get back."

"Truman, don't you have office hours today?" I asked.

"Don't even think twice about it. Sunshine canceled my appointments, but she'll be there in case someone shows up unannounced. You had a message, by the way."

"I did?"

"Yes. Someone called last night. Sorry, I can't remember the name, but I wrote it down."

"I wonder who it could be," I said. "So few people know where we are."

Truman took a clipboard from a nurse at the door to the hospital, signed a form, and I was officially free.

Seth had parked nearby, and I declined to have him pull the car up to the door, preferring to walk. I wanted both men to see that I was well. Which I was. Physically, anyway. Mentally, I was a little shaky. I'd spent a good portion of the night in my hospital bed going over in my mind the circumstances leading up to my injury. It *was* Mark Rosner at the reception. I was sure of that. He had spoken to someone in Wainscott's office, presumably the builder himself. I'd followed him, convinced he intended to deliver a message. Perhaps he had. Had he lured me into the construction site for the purpose of scaring me—or worse? Was my accident not an accident at all? Was this a warning? Or an attempt on my life? *Now, don't get paranoid, Jessica. You observed him enter the empty building, but you didn't see him inside.* I turned the incident over in my mind, examining it from every angle. I could be certain of only one thing: Rosner had been in that building. Why couldn't I find him? I would ask him that question when we returned to Foreverglades.

Mort was waiting in Truman's driveway when Seth pulled in. From the sheen of perspiration on his forehead, I suspected he'd been pacing up and down the gravel for some time. "How're you doing this morning, Mrs. F?" he asked, opening the passenger door.

"Just fine, Mort," I said, taking the hand he extended to help me out of the car. "And I have you to thank for it."

"No trouble, Mrs. F. I was just on the scene at the right time."

"Thank goodness for that, or who knows where I'd be right now."

"You were lucky. It could have been worse. You weren't wearing a hard hat. Everyone knows you're supposed to wear a hard hat on a construction site. Why did you go into that building anyway?"

"Mort, give the woman a chance to get inside before you give her the third degree," Seth said.

"Oh. Sorry, Mrs. F."

"No need to be," I said. "I'll tell you all about it after I've had a cup of tea. There are some questions you can answer for me, too."

"Like what?"

"Like, would you happen to have seen my handbag? It wasn't with me at the hospital. I'm hoping you took it with you."

"Maureen did. She brought it back to the hotel for safekeeping."

"Thank heavens. I have an extra pair of glasses in there, and I didn't relish having to cancel my credit cards if my wallet had gone missing."

Maureen, with Benny's able assistance, had put together an elaborate luncheon for us—two different seafood salads, a spinach quiche, fresh-baked bread, orange and grapefruit juices, string beans vinaigrette, a platter of tomatoes, cucumbers and radishes with a creamy avocado dip. I had the feeling she'd been influenced by the spread DeWitt Wainscott's caterer had supplied, and I was grateful. Contrary to what I'd told Truman, the hospital cuisine left something to be desired.

We gathered around the oval table in Truman's dining room, under the crystal chandelier, and above a hand-hooked rug with all the colors of the sea, and celebrated my return. Maureen and Benny had set the table with flowers, and used Truman's silver and fine china. Benny had removed the studs from his chin, nose, and eyebrows for the occasion and, except for the row of rings up the side of each ear, looked almost wholesome, his scarlet hair washed, his face scrubbed, a smile on his lips.

Sunshine joined us from the dispensary, along with her affenpinscher, Harriet. She was a quiet and serious girl, but her pet expressed all the joie de vivre the owner lacked. The little black dog scampered from guest to guest, showing off how well she could sit, shake, and roll over, in hopes of being rewarded with a morsel or two from the table. She ate very well.

No one wanted to disturb the festive atmosphere with talk of what might have happened if Mort hadn't found me, and I was happy for the diversion.

"How come I haven't gotten any questions about my very first golf game yesterday?" Truman said. "It's not every day I pick up a six-iron. Is that right, Seth?"

"You went golfing?" Benny was flabbergasted.

I heard Sunshine giggle.

"Okay," I said. "I'll bite. How did you fare on the golf course?"

"I was terrible!" Truman said, laughing. "If anyone I know saw me, I'll never live it down."

"You weren't that bad," Seth said. "You were starting to get the hang of it at the end."

"I could live to be a hundred and ten and never get the hang of it."

"The course only had nine holes. If we'd gone another round, you would have seen improvement."

"You're far too generous, my old friend. I think I'll stick to tiddlywinks, and save my ego from a beating."

Happy to see that Seth and Truman had set aside their differences, I got up to help Sunshine clear the table while Truman regaled the others with stories of his ineptitude at golf.

"You don't have to do that, Jessica," Maureen said, rising from her seat.

"Please sit down, Maureen. You took care of all the preparations," I said. "Now it's my turn. I'm perfectly fine, and I want to help."

"I'll give you a hand, Mrs. F.," Mort said, picking up his plate, and winking at Maureen. "We need to talk anyway."

I carried two dishes into the kitchen and set them on the counter next to the sink, while Mort collected more in the dining room. Sunshine rinsed the plates before she put them in the dishwasher.

"You have a charming little dog," I said.

Sunshine smiled. "She was a present from Truman."

"She was? How lovely. Was it for your birthday?"

"No," she said, blushing. She mumbled something, her chin on her chest.

"I'm sorry, dear. I didn't hear what you said."

"I said he gave her to me on my first anniversary of being off drugs." She busied herself with the dishes in the sink, obviously worried about my reaction.

Mort had come into the kitchen and left a stack of plates on the island. I picked them up and brought them to the sink. "That was quite an accomplishment," I said, "and worthy of such a precious gift."

She smiled, relieved. "She was really mine anyway. I rescued her from the pound. But Truman wouldn't let me keep her."

"No?"

"He took her away and said he'd give her back when I was clean. Harriet will go with anyone. She's very friendly."

As if she knew she was the topic of conversation, Harriet pranced into the kitchen, her claws tapping the floor. Tail wagging, she gave a sharp bark.

"You ate enough, you little devil," Sunshine said fondly. She filled a plastic cup with water and put it on the floor near the door. "Truman told me I had to take care of myself before I could take care of another living thing."

"That was good advice, don't you think?"

She nodded. "Having a dog is a little like having a baby. You know, you have to feed them and clean up after them. That was part of our agreement. Harriet's not allowed to mess the yard."

"Owning an animal is a great responsibility. They rely on you for everything, but it's worth it, don't you think? They also give you a lot of love."

"Do you have a dog?"

"No," I said. "I travel a lot. It wouldn't be fair to have an animal if I couldn't be home to care for it. But I do love dogs—and cats."

"You can borrow Harriet, if you like. She loves everybody."

"Yes, I can see that." I bent to scratch Harriet's neck and pet her head.

Mort brought in the serving dishes, and with Sunshine's direction we packed up the leftovers and put them in Truman's refrigerator.

I retrieved a handful of silverware from the island and handed it to her. "I think we might want to do these by hand," I said.

"No," she said. "Truman throws everything in the dishwasher. He says if he has to take special care of it, he won't use it."

A phone rang, and Sunshine picked up the one on the wall. "Healthy Stuff," she said. "May I help you?" She clapped her free hand over her ear to hear better as Seth and Truman came into the kitchen, followed by Maureen and Benny with the last of the dishes.

"Anyone for coffee?" Seth asked.

"I'll put up a pot," Truman said, pulling the coffeemaker forward on the counter. "You guys did enough." He looked from Sunshine to Mort to me. "I'll take over from here."

"Do you have any decent decaf?" Seth asked.

"Are you going to criticize my coffee, too, Boomer?"

"Benny, get the pie out of the fridge, please," Maureen said. "I'll put out the plates."

The party had moved to the kitchen, as it always seems to manage to do in my home.

I cocked my head at Mort and we slipped out the back door into the garden. I didn't want to talk about yesterday in front of Sunshine, although I suspected Truman might have told her what happened, at least what he thought might have happened.

It was hot, but the trees shielded the yard from the intensity of the rays. I walked to the little patio where I'd first seen Sunshine napping in the hammock and took one of the wrought-iron chairs. Mort sat in another.

"It's so pleasant here," I said, tilting my head back to look up into the canopy of leaves.

"Yeah, but I miss being home. I think we're going to start back up in a day or two."

"Why don't you turn in your car and drive back up with us? We're leaving tomorrow."

"Yeah? I'll check with Maureen. I like that idea." He looked at me closely. "How are you really feeling? Are you up to a long car ride?"

"I'm a little sore," I said, "but I don't feel nearly as bad as I would have expected after being hit by that cart."

"You weren't hit by the cart. Or if you were, it just

knocked you to the side. When I found you on the floor, it looked like you'd fallen between the studs and tumbled over a pile of two-by-fours."

"You mean I tripped?"

"I couldn't say for sure, but you weren't in the hallway; you were one room over."

"And the cart?"

"I had to duck out of the way when it rolled past the stairwell. Those things are so wobbly, they're always dangerous, especially if the weight of the load is uneven. It hit some bump and spilled its trash all over the floor. Made a heck of a racket."

"How did you know where to find me in the first place?"

"You left me a clue."

"I did?"

"I saw your hat lying on the ground inside the fence, and figured you must've gone into the building."

"And I had. Why don't I remember what happened?" I said, shaking my head.

"You got knocked on your noggin, that's why. You gave me quite a scare."

"Did you see anyone else in the building?"

"No. Was someone else there?"

"I thought so."

"I didn't see or hear anyone until I yelled for assistance. Then some guy shouted up to me from the first floor and I told him to call for help."

"And you didn't see who it was?"

"Nope. He was just a voice. I wasn't surprised. I figured the loud crash made when the cart tipped over might bring someone in to investigate. What's going on, Mrs. F?"

"I had a long talk with Gabby yesterday morning."

"The guy Truman buys his fish from?"

"Yes. He used to work for Wainscott, but left when another man was killed on the job."

"Construction can be very dangerous."

"Yes, it can. But in this case Gabby thought the man's death was no accident. He had been complaining about shoddy materials being used in Wainscott's building. I just find it interesting that two people who objected to what Wainscott was doing both end up dead."

"But what's this guy you were chasing yesterday got to do with it?"

"Mark Rosner? I can't figure out his part in this. Back in Foreverglades, he gave me the impression that he was opposed to Wainscott Towers. That would put him on Portia's side."

"If someone did kill Mrs. Shelby, it might have nothing to do with the development, Mrs. F. After all, whoever did it would have to be pretty close to her to put something in her pillbox without her knowing."

"I know. I may be following the wrong scent."

"What about her husband? He could've done it."

"I haven't forgotten about Clarence."

"And that chatterbox who joined us for breakfast the other day said a lot of women in Foreverglades had their eyes on him. Maybe one of them wanted Mrs. Shelby out of the way."

"You see the problem? I'm no closer to finding the murderer than I was in Foreverglades. And there's another strange thing."

"What's that?"

"When I was in Wainscott's office, I saw a framed photograph of Wainscott and the governor, and in the crowd in the background was a man I could swear was Tony Colombo."

"The guy Sam has been following?"

"Yes." I looked at Mort. "What do you make of that?"

Mort stood and stretched. "No idea. We can ask when we get back, but there's nothing you can do about it here," he said. "Let's go in. They must have dessert and coffee on the table by now."

"What are we having?" I asked.

"It's going to be great. Maureen and I found this neat little place in town. They make the only original, authentic key lime pie in all the Keys."

I'd started to stand, but fell back in chair.

"What are you laughing at?" he said.

Later that day, after Mort and Maureen had left, Sunshine and Truman had reopened the dispensary, and Seth and Benny had gone off to see the Spanish doubloons at Mel Fisher's Treasure Exhibit, I climbed the steps to my bedroom intending to rest. The events of the day before had taken more out of me than I'd first thought. Maureen had left my shoulder bag on the bed along with a plastic sack containing my canvas cap, a bit ragged for having spent some time in the mud at the Wainscott construction site. The bag, too, had a long scrape on one side and a small tear on the strap where it had been hooked by the nail. Since it was the only pocketbook I'd brought, it would have to do till I got home to Cabot Cove, unless Truman had shoe polish I could use to cover the scratch in the leather—an unlikely expectation.

I put the bag and hat aside, and pulled down the coverlet on the bed. A piece of paper I hadn't seen earlier fluttered to the floor. I picked it up and tried to decipher Truman's handwriting, feeling sorry for the pharmacists who must have struggled to read his prescriptions for so many years. I finally discerned that

Sam Lewis had called, but the message was illegible. At least the numbers were fairly clear. I sat at the desk and dialed the Lewises' apartment in Foreverglades. How had Sam known where to find me?

There was no one home to answer, and after four rings a machine picked up. I left a message that we'd be returning to Foreverglades tomorrow and I would call again when we got back. Then, achy and weary, I slid under the covers and was immediately asleep.

Chapter Seventeen

We pulled into Foreverglades the following afternoon. The midweek traffic flowing north from Key West had been blessedly light along the way. Oddly, although we were still in Florida, in the tropics and close to the water, there was a difference in the air when we crossed the Jewfish Creek drawbridge from Key Largo. The island ambiance, with its water borders, was gone, the fresh marine breeze missing. We were back on the mainland. The air was heavier, hotter, and more humid.

Seth pulled in front of the Foreverglades rec hall and sat in the idling car with Mort, while Maureen and I went upstairs to get the keys for our apartments. I'd called ahead and left a message on Mark Rosner's answering machine that we'd need a place for the Metzgers, who planned to stay a few extra days before continuing north to Miami, and from there home. I had no illusions that I'd find him at his desk. But if I had, there wouldn't have been time for that earnest chat that I was determined to have with him.

The rooms on the second floor, so busy at my last visit, were quiet, the library empty, the art studios dark.

"I wonder where everyone is," Maureen said.

"Perhaps there's some event we don't know about," I said.

"It's a little eerie with no one around."

"I was surprised when I saw the tennis courts empty," I said. "I'd gotten the impression the residents battle for court time."

"I hope everything's all right."

"I'm sure it is," I said, not sure at all.

Rosner's office door was locked, but a manila envelope taped to it said, *Mrs. Fletcher*. Inside were keys to the three units, their numbers printed on tags dangling from the key rings.

We rejoined Seth and drove to the building we'd occupied the previous week, across the courtyard from Clarence's unit, and dragged our luggage upstairs. Once in my room, I unpacked swiftly and placed a call to the Lewises. If something was going on, Sam and Minnie would certainly know about it. They weren't home. I left a message that we had returned, hung up, and tried Helen's beauty parlor. The number was busy. After several fruitless attempts to get through—if Amelia was on the phone, it might be a long time until the line was free—I gave up and called Seth.

"I'm going to take a walk into town," I said. "Would you like to join me?"

"Can you wait fifteen minutes? I was just about to call Truman to let him know we arrived, and to thank him for his hospitality."

Seth and Truman had made peace with each other on the golf course, and had agreed to steer away from discussions about medicine, despite the fact that both were doctors. Fortunately they'd found an abundance of topics on which they were not in conflict, and their friendship seemed to have been not only sustained, but also deepened. I'd even seen Seth leafing through one of Truman's complementary medicine journals.

While waiting for Seth to meet me, I used the time to check with my agent in New York, Matt Miller, about an upcoming publicity tour. My latest novel had made the Barnes & Noble top-fifty list, and Matt thought a round of radio and TV interviews would help boost it into the top ten. I promised to call again when I was back in Cabot Cove.

Restless and impatient to walk into town to find out what was going on, I went downstairs to the courtyard, sat on a bench, and rummaged through my shoulder bag, taking inventory. I needed to buy a new flashlight since leaving mine behind in Wainscott's unfinished building, and a new sun hat would come in handy, now that my canvas cap would have to be relegated to the pile of fishing hats I kept in a bin in my kitchen back home. I'd tried to wash it, but the water had left an ugly stain on the peak.

I pulled my new sunglasses from their case and put them on as Seth finally came through the door, and we started down the hill.

"What do you think is going on?" he asked.

"I don't know," I said, "but I have a feeling it has something to do with Wainscott."

"What makes you say that?"

"When we were in Key West, I heard him on the telephone threatening to close the beach and fill it with alligators to get rid of the demonstrators."

"Nice fellow."

"Not even close."

As we approached the intersection, we saw groups of three, four, and five people walking toward the beach. Many of them carried signs, although I couldn't read them from my vantage point. Cars lined both sides of the road coming into the village from Forev-erglades, and all the way up the hill as far as the chapel and Weinstein's Pharmacy. It reminded me of the Fourth of July at home when everyone in town congregates at the beach for the annual fireworks dis-play. There was an atmosphere of excitement.

"Do I hear singing?" Seth asked.

"It sounds like the civil rights anthem, 'We Shall Overcome.'"

"What do you think they mean?"

"We'll soon find out."

Seth and I walked faster, following the crowd walk-ing down the unpaved road leading to the shore.

"This looks like a senior citizen convention," he said.

It was true. Every person we saw was over sixty-five. There were a few people in wheelchairs, some others with walkers or canes, but the majority were able-bodied, in robust health, tanned from the Florida sun. But all showed the years in their features if not their gaits.

As we got closer to the beach, we heard loud voices, including one blaring through what sounded like a bullhorn. We passed police cars, four of them, pulled over on an angle, as if the drivers didn't have time to park properly before leaping from their vehicles.

We trooped down the sidewalk and rounded a curve that led down into the gravel parking lot to the right of the beach and in front of the small dock. From our perspective, which was slightly higher than the parking lot, we could see that the beach had been blocked off with a hastily constructed fence about ten feet high, on which a huge sign had been posted, reading, PRIVATE PROPERTY, KEEP OUT. It was now evident why hundreds of people had assembled. They were protesting the closure of the beach.

Wainscott had posted three security guards in front of the fence. They were big men with sullen faces. Their presence, I was sure, discouraged anyone who might have had the urge to rush the fence and topple it. The wooden stockade didn't look particularly sturdy, anchored as it was in the sand.

Standing to the side of the guards and looking distinctly uncomfortable were the Simmons twins in their orange caps and matching suspenders, their arms around each other's shoulders, looking like Tweedledum and Tweedledee. As employees of Foreverglades, I imagine they'd been expected to side with Wainscott or lose their jobs. But the brothers were not happy facing off against the residents they usually served, and who were much more a part of their lives than the callous developer.

Uniformed policemen stood off to the side, monitoring the situation but not interfering.

In the thick of the crowd in the parking lot was Sam's pink Cadillac with the top down. Sam stood on the backseat, a bullhorn in his hands.

"Where'd he get hold of one of those?" Seth muttered.

"Leave it to Sam," I said. "I wouldn't be surprised if it belongs to the Dade County Police Department."

We headed for Sam's car. He spotted us, waved, brought the bullhorn to his mouth again, and shouted into it: "Two, four, six, eight, who don't we appreciate? Wainscott! Wainscott!"

A group of seniors gathered near his car and, carrying crudely made signs, picked up his chant. "Two, four, six, eight . . ."

I suppressed a smile. It was like a high school pep

rally, except that the "cheerleaders" were in their seventies and eighties, the men's bald heads glistening in the sun, the women's carefully coiffed gray and blue hair waving in the stiff breeze off the water.

"What brought this on?" Seth shouted up at Sam.

"What?" he yelled.

"This rally," I said in as loud a voice as I could muster. "What triggered it?"

"Oh." Sam leaned over, picked up a sheet of paper from the seat, climbed out of the car, and handed it to me. "What do you think of this?"

It was a letter from a law firm, addressed to *Residents of Foreverglades*.

> This is to advise you that effective this date, your access to the beach heretofore open and available to residents of Foreverglades through the generosity of the owner of said beach, Mr. DeWitt Wainscott and Wainscott Associates, Inc., will no longer be accessible to you, pursuant to applicable laws of the State of Florida and Dade County. Trespassing on private property is a criminal offense, and anyone failing to heed this warning shall be prosecuted to the fullest extent of the law.

It was signed by one of five names on the letterhead, whose title was general counsel to Wainscott Associates, Inc.

I handed the letter to Seth, who frowned as he read it. "Looks like Mr. Wainscott is playing hardball," he said, passing the letter back to Sam.

"This beach was supposed to be part of Foreverglades," Sam said. "It was in all the brochures. Wainscott's reneged, but we're not going to let him get away with it. He thinks he can push us around 'cause we're old. We may be old, but we're not dumb.''

"Do you think making a lot of noise will make him change his mind?" Seth asked.

"No," Sam replied. "He'll never listen to us. He figures he's already got our money."

"Then what good will the demonstration do?" Seth said.

"The power of the press," Sam said. "I called all the papers and television stations. We're a great pop photo.''

"I think you mean photo op, Sam," I said.

"That's it. If we can get the press to cover us, it'll push the authorities to pressure Wainscott to reopen the beach." Sam looked at me. "I called you to let you know what was going on," he said. "Didn't want you to miss an opportunity for publicity. Stick with us and you could sell some more books.''

"That's very thoughtful," I said. "How did you even know where to find us?"

Sam grinned. "Good police work," he said. "Helen told me where you lived. I figured out the doc's office would probably know where you went. Told the lady who answered that it was a police matter, and we needed to locate your whereabouts. She gave me the telephone number.''

"Good grief," Seth said. "They must think I've been arrested.''

"You'd better call them today," I said. "You know how rumors spread.''

Sam climbed back into the Cadillac and returned to shouting words of encouragement into his bullhorn. Seth and I gravitated to a large knot of seniors, many of whom we recognized from our stay at Foreverglades. Monica Kotansky, in hot-pink Capri pants and a tight white T-shirt, Snowy nestled in her arms, saw us coming. She broke away from the others and came directly to Seth.

"Oh, Seth," she said, batting her long, false eyelashes. "I'm so relieved you're here. I was worried about you."

"Worried about me? That's very flattering, but why?" he asked, straightening up and drawing in his stomach.

"I was looking all over for you, but you seemed to have disappeared. I was hoping I'd see you at the gym, but—"

"Just away for the weekend," Seth said, smiling.

I touched Seth's arm, hoping to signal him to move on, but he seemed content to remain talking with Monica.

"I'll be with the others," I said, walking away. I glanced back to see my dear friend from Cabot Cove still transfixed by the alluring Monica.

"Hello, Jessica," Minnie Lewis said. "How was your trip to the Keys?"

"Just fine, but I see we almost missed the action here."

"Isn't this something?" she asked.

"I saw the letter," I said.

"Sam was so incensed, he hasn't stopped organizing since we received it. I'm so proud of him. Once Sam gets going, Wainscott won't know what hit him."

"The nerve of that man," Helen Davison said, "trying to bully us with his highfalutin law firm and all that legal mumbo-jumbo. I closed up my shop today, told all my customers to come down here and demonstrate. If we don't stand up for ourselves, no one else will do it for us."

"Did he give a reason for closing the beach?" I asked.

"Oh, sure, he gave a reason," she replied, indignant, her voice getting louder. "His ugly face shows up on TV last night and he says there are too many alligators in the area, and it's dangerous for the old folks. Can you imagine? He actually called us 'old folks.' Said he was concerned we'd get hurt and that he was only doing this to protect us from attack. Baloney! He's doing this to get even with the protesters who oppose his construction. We'll show him 'old folks.' Won't we?"

A cheer went up at the conclusion of Helen's tirade.

A young man with camera equipment strung around his neck approached, focused on individual faces, and took a quick succession of shots, going from one face to the other.

Clarence put his hand up in front of his face. "What newspaper are you from, young man?" he snapped.

The photographer said nothing as he took a few more pictures and moved on to another group.

"*Caramba!* I'll bet he's from Wainscott's office," Amelia said. "Spying on us, taking our picture. My sister-in-law probably sent him. Then she'll turn our pictures over to those goons, and we'll be in trouble." She pointed to where Wainscott's security men stood with their arms crossed defiantly on their chests, their grim expressions saying loud and clear they weren't enjoying this impromptu beach party.

"Hush, Amelia," Helen said. "You're only going to scare people away, and we need everybody here."

"Too many of us to arrest," Minnie said with a satisfied nod. "They tried to get us to leave, but we stood our ground. Strength in numbers, that's what I always say."

Miles Davison, who had been leaning on his two canes, raised one and shook it at the police and security men. "I dare 'em to arrest me," he said, stepping away from us and hobbling in their direction.

"I don't think you should confront them," I called after him.

But he wasn't to be deterred.

"Oh, my," Helen said. "Miles, don't egg them on. You'll get hurt."

"Hope they don't shoot the damn fool," Clarence said.

All eyes were on Miles as he walked unsteadily but with purpose, in order to lay down a face-to-face challenge. The policemen, too, seemed to brace for what would come next. When Miles was within fifteen feet of them, the security guards dropped their arms and took a few steps toward him. Earl and Burl gasped and hurried over to stand on either side of the old man, protecting him from the brawny guards. A cheer went up from the crowd.

Detective Zach Shippee appeared from behind the officers and confronted the guards, who stepped back into place.

"Who's that?" someone in our group asked.

"He's from the police," I said, relieved that he'd shown up when he did. The detective stopped close to Miles and the Simmons twins and said something to them. The trio simply nodded and turned back in our direction, Earl and Burl assisting Miles till Helen ran to help him.

I looked to where Seth had been talking with Monica. They were gone from view. Coming from that direction was a two-person crew from a local TV station. One carried a video camera, the other a microphone tethered to the camera, and a clipboard. They approached us, and the young woman carrying the microphone, who I assumed was the reporter, took us in, fixed on me, and said, "You're Jessica Fletcher." She said it as though delivering a revelation.

"I'm afraid I am," I said.

"And you're part of this demonstration."

"Well, no. Actually, I'm not. We were in Key West and—"

"And returned for the demonstration," she said, again a statement of supposed fact.

"No," I said. "We didn't know that—"

She turned to her cameraman and said, "Get a two-shot of Mrs. Fletcher here."

"Now wait a minute," I said, raising a hand. "I'm just a visitor. It's Sam you should interview." I pointed to Sam standing in the pink Cadillac.

Her microphone suddenly appeared in front of my mouth. "Why have you lent your considerable celebrity, Mrs. Fletcher, to this demonstration? Are you now living in Foreverglades?"

I stepped back and to the side, out of camera range.

"Hello, Mrs. Fletcher," a male voice said. I turned to see that Detective Shippee had come to my side. "Grabbing fifteen minutes of fame?" he asked, not unpleasantly.

"The last thing I want," I said. I looked to Miles, who'd now rejoined us, and the Simmons twins, who were surrounded by well-wishers, and said to Shippee, "Thanks for intervening with them."

"We're supposed to be keepers of the peace," he said. "Got a moment?"

The TV reporter had repositioned herself and her cameraman to take another stab at interviewing me.

"Please," I said. "This is inappropriate."

"Later," Shippee told the reporter, taking my arm

and leading me to an unoccupied area of the parking lot.

"Thanks," I said.

"Won't make any difference," he said. "You're a celebrity. That's what the media thrives on. Your face will be all over TV tonight."

"I suppose it will."

"Mrs. Fletcher," he said, "did you know this demonstration was going to take place?"

"Goodness, no. My friend Dr. Seth Hazlitt and I were totally surprised. We just came back from a trip to the Keys and noticed no one was at Foreverglades. Now we know why."

"It's a touchy situation, as I'm sure you can understand. Wainscott has a legal right to close the beach. He owns it."

"And that's a shame," I said.

"Yeah, sure, I agree with you. But the law's the law."

"And I respect that, although there are many times when the law should be changed. These are good, decent people who moved here to live out their retirement years with the expectation that the beach was among the good things in life they would enjoy. Wainscott is guilty of false advertising at a minimum, perhaps even fraud. Frankly, Detective Shippee, I find him to be an arrogant bully, without any sensitivity to the needs of others."

"I warned you about him, didn't I?" Shippee smiled and looked out over the water, his eyes squeezed almost shut against the glare. He drew a deep breath and again faced me. "This sort of situation happens in Florida every day. Land is precious. Men like Wainscott grab it up and build what they hope will make them millions of dollars. Citizens like your friends from Foreverglades get hurt in the process. I understand why they're angry. They have a right to demonstrate, and I respect that. They buy a place with beautiful water views, and along comes a developer like Wainscott who takes it away from them."

"But . . ." I said, reading that in his voice.

He grinned. "Yeah, that's right, Mrs. Fletcher. There's always a 'but' involved."

"The law."

"The law. That's right, although I don't think Wainscott has ever come up against a gang like this."

"Gang?"

"All these golden-agers. They're old enough to not care what people think about them anymore. They're not concerned with image. They're concerned with what they think is right, and they fight for it. Tip over one of their wheelchairs and they'll find a way to get up and keep fighting. They don't let their walkers or Coke-bottle glasses stop them when they think they have a just cause. They may have become weaker physically, but they haven't lost a thing when it comes to commitment."

"I'm sure they'd be pleased to know you feel that way," I said.

"I've got a mother and father getting on in years," he said.

I nodded.

"Even so, Mrs. Fletcher, I'm sure you realize that in the end, Wainscott will win. The moneymen always do."

"Perhaps," I said.

"In the meantime," he said, "there's Mrs. Shelby's death to solve."

"Solve?" I said. "You don't think it was from natural causes either?"

"You and I were on the same page all along, but I couldn't go public without proof."

"And now you have it?"

He nodded. "And now I'm going to do something about it." He looked around at the demonstrators, and started walking toward Sam standing in the Cadillac.

"Not Sam," I whispered. "Never Sam."

The detective called up to Sam, who put down his bullhorn and leaned down to hear what Shippee had to say. He straightened up again and looked out over the crowd, pointing to the group I'd recently been standing with.

Shippee turned toward them and I followed quickly, in time to hear him say, "You're under arrest for the murder of Portia Carpenter Shelby. You have the right to remain silent. Anything you say can and will be used against you in a court of law."

The people around us were stunned.

"Portia was murdered."

"Can you believe it?"

I heard the murmurs as the realization spread through the crowd.

Then Detective Shippee pulled out his handcuffs and Clarence Shelby held out his hands.

Chapter Eighteen

"Where are you going?"

"What makes you think I'm going anywhere in particular?"

"You don't wear shorts very often, Seth."

"Don't know why a man can't put on a pair of shorts without raising suspicion."

It was the morning after the demonstration and the shocking arrest of Clarence Shelby. Although according to Amelia, who told everyone who would listen, she had suspected him all along. Minnie had cried, and Helen and Miles had helped Sam take her home.

Seth and I walked down the stairs from our respective apartments. He opened the building door for me.

"Are you going to play tennis with Mort?" I asked, stepping outside.

"No, I'm not going to play tennis with Mort."

"Good, because I asked him to meet me at the police station."

"The police station, huh? Going to see Detective Shippee?"

"Yes. I want to talk to him about Clarence. I thought he might be more amenable to answering questions if another police officer was present."

"What are you questioning him about? You suspected Portia was murdered. I didn't think so, but you were right. The police have arrested her murderer. I should think you'd be satisfied."

"I was. I am. I just want to assure myself they have the right person."

We crossed the courtyard and paused on the sidewalk. "So where are you going?" I asked.

"Just out for a little walk."

I raised my eyebrows at him. He was obviously concealing something.

"Well, if you must know, I'm going over to the gym."

"That's wonderful, Seth. Why didn't you say so? You've been talking about starting an exercise program. The trainers are supposed to be very knowledgeable, although I'd heard it was difficult to get an appointment."

"Yes. Well, we'll see."

"You did make an appointment, didn't you?"

"Why are you so danged nosy about what I'm going to do at the gym?"

I laughed. "Because you're usually not so secretive about your activities."

A car horn sounded, and I turned to see Monica Kotansky driving a red convertible. Snowy was sitting in the passenger seat. She pulled over to the curb. "Seth? Oh, Seth," she called out.

Seth raised one hand in a sheepish wave.

"I'm sorry I'm late," she said. "I just got back from the store, and I still have to change and walk Snowy. Why don't you go on over? I'll be there in two minutes. Hi, Jessica. Nice to see you again." She drove off without waiting for my reply.

Seth's face was the color of Monica's car. "She's going to show me how to use the equipment."

"It's not my business who you meet at the gym," I said.

"Yes. Well. She offered, and I thought it would be a good opportunity."

"Just be careful," I said. "Take it easy the first time. You haven't used the machines before. You don't want to pull a muscle."

"I know that. You don't have to tell me to take it easy. I've been telling my patients the same thing for years."

I glanced at my watch. "I've got to go," I said. "Have a good time. I'll see you later."

As Seth started walking toward the rec hall, I couldn't resist teasing him. "I'll phone you this afternoon," I called after him. "We can go back to Portofino for dinner. Unless you have other plans."

He batted a hand at me behind his back, and I laughed.

The station house in Foreverglades was on a side street, away from the busy shopping area, in a low brick building with a white façade. Mort was already there when I arrived.

"He said he can see us in about ten minutes. That okay, Mrs. F?"

"Sure, Mort. I'm glad he'll see us at all."

We took seats on a wooden bench in the narrow lobby. The desk sergeant in uniform was at a desk behind a glass partition. Working with him was an elderly gentleman who answered telephones. Behind them was a wall-size corkboard covered with papers, clipboards, visitors' badges, and pictures of the FBI's Ten Most Wanted fugitives. A glass door off to the side allowed a view of a corridor leading to other offices.

"What do you want to talk about with him, Mrs. F?"

"I want to let him know what Gabby said about the Key West project, in case it has any bearing on the evidence. Detective Shippee mentioned an accident once, and I think that's what he may have been referring to."

"You mean about the crane operator and the guy who was killed?"

"Yes."

"Could just be a coincidence."

"It could. I'd also like to find out how they came to suspect Clarence."

The elderly man at the desk tapped on the glass partition, and we looked up. "Detective Shippee can see you." He waved us over to a door and buzzed us in. "Write your name on those and put them on, please," he said, handing us orange visitors' badges and a marker.

We did as we were asked, and he led us through the glass door to the corridor, escorting us to small room furnished only with a table and four chairs. Detective Shippee met us at the door.

"Mrs. Fletcher, how are you?" he said. "Metzger." He nodded at Mort.

We sat at the table, and there was an awkward moment of silence.

"Didn't see you on the news last night," Shippee said to me.

"Just as well," I said. "Your arrest made the demonstration even bigger news."

"That wasn't my intent." He smiled. "Now, to what do I owe the honor of this visit?"

"Detective Shippee," I said, "I was hoping I could talk to Clarence Shelby."

"If he's agreeable. You could've asked the desk sergeant."

"I wanted to talk to you first."

"Here I am."

I told Shippee about our trip to Key West, including my conversations with Gabby and Wainscott, and what I considered the uncomfortable coincidence that someone opposing the developer had died both in Key West and in Foreverglades.

"If you'll remember our conversation down at the beach, Mrs. Fletcher, I told you he was a ruthless man. The Key West cops were never able to pin anything on the crane operator, much less Wainscott, and the guy disappeared shortly after that anyway. Maybe Wainscott took care of him in his own way."

"Wainscott might've been after Mrs. Fletcher, too," Mort put in.

"How so?"

"Tell him about your accident, Mrs. F."

"What accident?" Shippee said.

"Mort, I don't have any proof that it was anything other than an accident."

"Tell me about it anyway," Shippee said.

I gave him a quick summary of my encounter with the dump cart but didn't mention Mark Rosner by name. It wouldn't have been fair to accuse someone without proof, and I'd never seen him once he'd disappeared into the building.

Shippee studied me for a moment before saying, "You'd better be careful who you irritate, Mrs. Fletcher. I don't want to find *your* body down at the beach."

Mort cleared his throat and jumped into the conversation. "How'd you come to suspect Clarence?" he asked.

Shippee shifted his gaze to Mort. "We found out he'd lied to us."

"Yeah? About what?"

Shippee looked from Mort to me and smiled. "Okay," he said. "It'll come out in court anyway. Mr. Shelby said he'd been at home the whole evening his wife went down to the beach, and that he'd gone to bed early, expecting she'd be home shortly. He said he didn't know she was missing till the morning."

"And that wasn't true?" I said.

"No. The maintenance men at Foreverglades, the twins, saw him sneak out of his apartment around nine o'clock that night. He was carrying a square box. They said he came back about an hour later without it."

"Did you find the box?"

"We did. One of our investigators found it in the water. It had gotten caught in the tall grass under the gazebo down at the beach. Someone had tried to get rid of it by tossing it in the water, but it didn't sink or float away."

I leaned forward. "Was there something in the box?"

"No. It was empty, but it still had a packing slip under the clear tape, showing it had contained two bottles of diet pills, E-Z Weight Off, something like that, and it had been shipped to Clarence Shelby."

I sat back in the seat. "Were they the same pills that killed Portia?"

"We're getting a sample from the supplier to send to the toxicology lab, but we expect we'll get as much of a match as we can under the circumstances."

"Portia's three pillboxes," I said. "Did you take them as evidence?"

"We did, including the one your friend pocketed and returned," he said, a note of disgust unmistakable in his voice.

"Do you mind if I ask what color they were?"

"They're all white. Is there a significance to that?"

"No," I said. "There isn't."

"We know that Shelby's wife had poor vision and that he filled the pillboxes for her every day," Shippee said.

"Did he confess?" Mort asked, echoing my thoughts.

"No. But we're following up on another lead. Recently we found out his first wife died in a boating accident, and we're looking into those records, too."

"Did you ask him about that?" I asked.

"He says he won't say anything more till he talks to a lawyer."

"And when will that be?" I asked.

"There's a Legal Aid attorney coming down from Miami this afternoon. Couldn't make it yesterday."

"He hasn't hired a private attorney?"

"No. He said he couldn't afford one."

"Do you think money was his motive?" I asked.

"It's a domestic case, Mrs. Fletcher. These things happen all the time. He was having an affair, and he wanted to get rid of his wife. He was a little more clever than most, but he got tripped up in the end anyway. Liars always do."

"Who told you he was having an affair?" I asked.

"We heard it from several friends of the victim, and we have a witness who overheard an argument in which Mrs. Shelby confronted her husband, and Mr. Shelby threatened to kill her."

"Who was he having an affair with?" I asked.

Shippee smiled. "I'm surprised Foreverglades gossip hasn't given you her name yet."

"Monica Kotansky?"

"The grapevine is still in working order, I see."

"But the witness. We don't know who that is."

"Let me keep a few secrets, Mrs. Fletcher. Don't want to give away my whole case."

"Do you mind if we speak to Mr. Shelby?"

"Me? I don't mind. But I don't know if he'll talk to you. He's not talking to us."

"Would you ask him?"

"Sure. Wait here, and I'll see if he'll see you."

Shippee opened the door and called to another officer. "I gotta go fill out a form," he said to us. "I'll be right back."

Mort and I looked at each other.

"Be prepared, Mrs. F. Clarence probably won't want to talk to us."

"I know, but I really need to speak with him. Do you think the detective would let me send him a note?"

"Sure. Maybe. I don't know. Depends on the jail policy. But you could send in a note with the lawyer if he was willing."

I pulled a pad from my shoulder bag and scribbled a message to Clarence. But it wasn't necessary. Surprising all three of us, Clarence agreed to talk, but only to me. While Mort waited for me in reception, Detective Shippee brought in the prisoner.

Clarence, dressed in striped pajamas, his hands and feet manacled, shuffled to the chair Shippee held out for him, and sank down. He had aged a decade since the demonstration the day before. His skin had a gray cast to it, with dark crescents under his eyes. His face and shoulders sagged as if his body felt the tug of gravity for the first time. Being jailed is never a pleasant experience, but some people weather adversity better than others. I wavered between feeling sorry for Clarence and wanting to shake him out of it. If he was guilty, he deserved to be here. But if he was not, succumbing to depression wasn't going to aid his cause.

"An officer will be right outside, Mrs. Fletcher," Shippee said.

"Thank you, Detective."

I waited quietly. Shippee closed the door, and Clarence raised his eyes to mine.

His first words were: "I didn't do it."

"What didn't you do?" I asked.

"I didn't do any of it. I didn't give her diet pills. I didn't threaten her life. I didn't have an affair. I didn't kill her." His eyes blazed momentarily, then subsided into the dull expression he'd entered with.

"Let's say I believe you," I said. "I have to be honest: I'm not entirely convinced I do. But for argument's sake, let's say I don't think you killed Portia. There are some things you need to explain."

"Like what?"

"Let's go one by one, Clarence. The police have a box that was shipped to you. They have proof it contained two bottles of diet pills."

"It wasn't for me. I ordered it for someone else."

"Who did you order it for?"

"I'd rather not say."

"I can't help you if you won't cooperate."

"This is a private matter."

"Not anymore. You've been arrested. All the details of your life are open to inspection. And if the press comes down and starts its own investigation, your version of events is not likely to be put forward. Your lawyer will tell you the same thing."

He pressed his lips together, and I feared our conversation might break down on the initial point. I tried to come at him from another direction.

"Then answer me this," I said. "Why would someone ask you to order diet pills for her?"

"Weinstein's stopped selling them a while back."

I noticed he didn't correct me when I'd said "for her," and I continued to assume this person who wanted the diet pills was a woman. "Why couldn't she order them herself? Why did she ask you to do it?"

"Because I have my own computer. And I was doing all the research on Portia's medications. It was easy just to type in the name of another drug."

"Did she give you her credit card number to place the order?"

"No."

"So you used your own card?"

"Yes." He hung his head and shook it slowly side to side. "Looks bad, doesn't it?"

"It does," I said. "And if you refuse to say who you ordered the pills for, how can you convince a jury you didn't kill Portia? Keep in mind, even if you do identify her, she may deny that she asked you to buy the pills. Did you ever think of that?"

"What do you mean?"

"The person who wanted the pills might be Portia's killer."

"No. No," he said, standing and rattling the chains that bound him.

The officer outside swung open the door and glared at Clarence, who sat quickly, hunching his shoulders and tucking his chin on his chest.

I nodded at the policeman, and he closed the door again.

"She'd never do that," Clarence whispered. "Why would she want Portia dead?"

"You tell me."

"I can't."

I decided this cat-and-mouse game was getting us nowhere, and a more direct approach was needed. "Why are you protecting Monica Kotansky?" I said.

Clarence looked up sharply.

"Is it because you were having an affair with her? She wanted you for herself and Portia was in the way. Is that it?"

"No. No."

"No, what, Clarence? No, you weren't having an affair? No, she didn't want you for herself?"

He sighed heavily. "She may have wanted me at one time. God only knows why. I'm no bargain. Not rich. Not young. Nothing to offer. But when I married Portia, I made it clear that she was my wife and my loyalties lay there."

"But Monica had been your lover before."

"When I first moved down here she latched onto me, and I didn't know how to turn her down."

"You didn't know how to say no to her then, but you do now?"

"I know you won't believe me, but I loved Portia. She was everything I'm not, strong, passionate, principled. She stood up, not only for herself, but for everyone else who didn't have the gumption to defend themselves or what was right. She was a tiger when she got hold of a cause."

"And were you one of her causes?"

A small smile crossed his lips. "I never really thought of it that way, but I guess I was."

"Did Portia know you were ordering diet pills for Monica?"

"God, no! I couldn't tell her. She would have been terribly hurt. There wasn't anything going on between Monica and me. I swear it. But Portia knew our history, and Monica is so, so . . ." He cast around for a word and couldn't find one.

"Sexy," I supplied.

"I guess. I really preferred Portia's looks, but I doubt she would have believed me if I'd told her that. Anyway, I didn't want Portia to know and worry that I was having an affair."

"Then why did you order the pills for Monica? She's hardly a helpless female."

"She asked me several times, and I turned her down, but she's very persistent. When she wants something, she keeps running after you until you give in. She's always over the limit on her credit cards. She said she'd pay me back. I thought I'd get her the pills and that would be the end of it. She'd have the telephone number and address of the company and could order them herself the next time. Then maybe she'd leave me alone."

"And did she?"

"No. I ordered them for her again."

"What happened the night Portia died?"

"Portia and I had a late dinner, and—"

I interrupted him. "Did she take her pills that night?"

"Of course. She took her pills every night before dinner."

"And you didn't notice there was an extra pill."

"No. I never examined her pills. I just brought her a glass of water and went to get another for myself."

"And then what?"

"After dinner she left to take her walk on the beach." A tear slid down Clarence's cheek. "I should have offered to go with her. She might be alive now." He dropped his head, lifted his manacled hands, and pressed them against his eyes.

I gave him a minute to compose himself, and said, "Clarence, I need you to talk to me or I can't help you."

He raised his head, his expression bleak. "I'll never forgive myself."

"You didn't kill her," I said. "Someone else did. Help me find out who it was."

"What do you need to know?"

"You were seen leaving the apartment that night. Where did you go?"

"I brought Monica her pills. She was at the rec hall for a yoga class or something, and said she'd stick around. I could give them to her afterward. But I had to wait, because Wainscott's people were there for a meeting, and I wanted to keep out of sight."

"Did you go right home after you gave Monica the pills?"

"Yes. And I was so pathetically grateful Portia hadn't come back yet, that she didn't know I'd left the house in her absence, I just climbed into bed and fell asleep. It never occurred to me that something might have happened to her, that it was getting late, that she should have been home by then. All I could think of was myself." He lifted his eyes to mine. "How stupid I was. Stupid and selfish."

"Why would Monica throw the box in the water?"

"Is that where the police found it? I don't know. It doesn't make any sense. But so much of this doesn't make sense."

"How did Monica get along with Portia?"

"There was no love lost there, but I don't think she killed Portia, if that's where you're going."

"Why not?"

"She's irritating, but she's not vicious. She's a flirt but she's really very insecure inside. She's getting older. She's worried that youth has passed her by and she won't be attractive anymore. It's sad, really, but I don't think it's in her to kill."

"Is that why you're protecting her?"

"I hate this, Jessica. Don't think I don't. Jail is every ugly thing anyone ever said it is, even here where the crime rate is relatively low. I can bear it, but I don't think Monica could. I know she didn't kill Portia, but just as the evidence looks bad for me, it'll look worse for her. And she'd never survive this."

"Are you willing to bet your life on that?"

"They can't convict me. I didn't kill Portia."

"People have been convicted on a lot less evidence than what Detective Shippee is holding against you."

"He's got a box, that's all."

"He's got a witness who says you fought with Portia and threatened her life."

"Never. It never happened. We may have disagreed on occasion, but we never fought."

"Nevertheless, that's what the witness will say in court."

"Who? Who would say that?"

"I don't know. But I'd like to find out."

Chapter Nineteen

"I heard the rumor, but I don't know who it refers to," Minnie said to me when I knocked on her door and queried her. "Let's ask Sam."

Sam was lying on the couch in the living room watching a tape of a Miami Heat game, a bowl of popcorn balanced on his chest.

"Sam," his wife said, picking up the remote and muting the sound of the game. "Jessica has to ask you a question."

"Aw, Minnie, you're interrupting the best part," Sam said, sitting up and putting the bowl on the floor.

"You can rewind it when we're through."

"How do, Mrs. Fletcher," Sam said, struggling to his feet.

"You don't have to stand, Sam."

"Yes, he does," Minnie said. "The doctor said he needs more exercise. But you're welcome to sit, Jessica." She took a seat on the couch, I took one in a ladder-back chair, and Sam sank back on the couch.

"I'm trying to trace a rumor," I said.

"What rumor?" asked Sam.

"Someone said he or she overheard an argument in which Clarence threatened to kill Portia."

"Heard that one yesterday," Sam said, "at the demonstration. Don't know who it is, though."

"Who did you hear it from?" I asked.

"Minnie, you told me."

"I heard it from Helen," she said, "but I don't know where she got it."

I made a note on my pad. "What about the rumor that linked Clarence and Monica?"

"Oh, that's been going on a long time," Minnie said.

"What has?" I asked.

"Well, the affair, I guess. I heard about it a long time ago."

"Before or after Portia married Clarence?"

"Well, now, that's a good question. I guess I first heard about him having an affair with Monica about five years ago. That would've been before Portia, for sure."

"Didn't the rumor stop when he married Portia?" I asked.

"Now that you say that, I'd have to say yes," Minnie said. "Don't you agree, Sam?"

"Huh?" Sam said. He'd been watching the silent game on the screen.

"Sam, listen for a minute," his wife said. "Basketball can wait."

Sam heaved a dramatic sigh, picked up the remote, and clicked off the TV.

"I'm all ears," he said.

I had to suppress a smile, because he was—all ears, that is. They jutted out from the side of his head, making him look something like Yoda from the *Star Wars* film.

"Sam, the police suspect Clarence of having an affair with Monica, and that's why they're alleging he killed Portia. I'm trying to find out who gave them that information, and whether it's true."

"I told you this was a gossipy place, Jessica. That's why I like volunteering down at the station house."

"He goes again tomorrow," Minnie added helpfully.

"Do either of you know if the rumor is true?"

"I don't know," Minnie said. "Helen and I aren't very fond of Clarence. Frankly, we didn't see what Portia saw in him. But perhaps we were influenced by all the talk."

"Where did you hear it first?"

"From Helen, no doubt," Sam put in. "Her shop is a fountain of news."

"I think you mean fount, Sam," I said.

"Whatever. That's where you go if you want the latest gossip."

"Then I guess that's where I'll go. Thanks so much. You've both been very helpful."

"Do you think they arrested the wrong man?" Minnie asked as she escorted me to the door.

"Possibly," I said. "That's why I'm trying to separate the truth from the rumors."

"Will we see you tomorrow at the Residents' Committee meeting? Portia's memorial is on the agenda."

"I thought it was on the agenda of the last meeting."

"It got tabled. No one could agree on a proper commemoration."

"I'll try to make it," I said.

Helen's shop was abuzz with activity and talk until, that is, I walked through the door. Then it was as if someone put a muzzle on all the ladies. They stopped talking and stared at me, watching my every move as if I were about to deliver the Sermon on the Mount.

Helen was standing at her reception desk with a phone to one ear while she mixed a goopy gray concoction in a plastic bowl. "No, dear, I don't know any more than that. Listen, I've got two roots to do and a half head of highlights. I'll talk to you later."

"Helen, do you think I could talk to you a moment—in private?" I asked when she'd hung up.

"Amelia!" she shouted. "Where is that woman? She's always disappearing on me."

A young woman who'd been sweeping hair on the floor into a neat pile came over to Helen and whispered over her shoulder, "Amelia went to the drugstore."

Helen shrugged, handed the young woman her bowl, and said, "You keep stirring this till I come back. Do not let it separate, hear?"

"Yes, ma'am."

"C'mon, Jessica. We can step into my office for a moment. That's all I can spare."

"Thank you, Helen. I promise not to keep you long."

"Don't worry. You won't."

Her office was really a storage room with a table piled high with boxes of hair products, an electric sterilizer, and an old washtub sink covered in spots and drips of permanent hair color.

I asked her the same questions I had of the Lewises.

"Told you I was never fond of Clarence. There's just something so cold and calculating about him," she said. "Now someone heard him threaten Portia. I'm not surprised."

"Who overheard that argument, Helen? It wasn't you."

"No. I never saw them argue. If anything, he was too passive, I thought. You can't trust a man who never talks."

"Isn't that a bit of a generalization?" I said.

"I guess. I just never got comfortable with the man. Couldn't see with all Portia had to offer why she settled on such a milquetoast."

"But she was happy with her choice, wasn't she?"

"Yes. I have to admit she was."

"Did she ever confide in you that she thought Clarence was unfaithful?"

"No, she never did."

"Then it's possible the rumors aren't true at all."

"Anything's possible, I suppose."

"So who told you Clarence was having an affair? And who overheard him threaten Portia?"

"Well, I never got any names, but I must've heard it in the shop. This place runs on gas." She laughed at her own joke. "Ask Amelia. She's the queen of scandal. Knows them all and tells them all."

"Thanks, Helen. I'll go find her."

"You don't think Clarence did it, do you?" she asked, sobering.

"No," I said. "I think he may be the innocent victim of a smear campaign."

"If that's true, I'm very sorry," said Helen. "I know my shop is the center of gossip in this town. If you find out the truth, let me know and I'll set everyone straight."

"I'll do that. In the meantime, if you find out who started the rumor, I'd appreciate knowing who that person is."

*   *   *

Weinstein's Pharmacy had received an order of decorative items for Easter and Passover—even though those holidays were almost two months away—and the aisles were clogged with boxes of silk flowers, chocolate matzoh, marshmallow bunnies, spring-themed cocktail napkins, hand-painted glassware, flower-scented talcum, and china hens and chicks.

I found Amelia and her soon-to-be ex-sister-in-law, Marina, talking with Weinstein's saleswomen, Donna and Sandy, as they unpacked a new shipment of honeycomb candles.

"And she died from taking diet pills," Amelia was saying as I approached.

"Isn't it amazing what a little blue pill can do?" Marina said.

"Thank God we don't carry ephedra anymore," Sandy said. "Harry was smart to get rid of it."

"I've been on the Atkins diet," Donna added. "It works better than pills, anyway."

"They've got her husband in jail now," Amelia said.

"They say he might have murdered his first wife, too," Marina said.

"*No sabía.* You didn't tell me that," Amelia said. "You've been holding out on me."

"Well, I'm telling you now."

"*Hola,* Jessica," Amelia said when she spotted me.

"Hello," I replied. "I'm sorry to interrupt the conversation."

"No problem," said Sandy, stacking the boxed candles on a shelf.

"I was hoping you to talk to you, Amelia," I said. "Can you spare me a minute?"

"*Sí. Qué desea?* What do you want?"

"I have a question about my hair."

"Of course. *Hasta luego,* ladies. This is business."

Amelia left the others and followed me to a bench outside the front door, where we both sat.

"Just a little lightening up here will do it," Amelia said to me, running her fingers over the top of my head. "And maybe a touch here, too."

"You really think so?"

"You could go a bit darker on the sides. It's the contrast of dark and light that makes it attractive."

"Thank you," I said. "By the way, I couldn't help hearing you talk. It was Portia and Clarence you were discussing, wasn't it?"

"Jessica, you were there when he was arrested. Helen never cared for him. I always thought he was the strong, silent type. Unfortunately, he wasn't the faithful type, and now look at what he is. *Un asesino.*" She shook her head.

"Amelia, did you ever see Clarence with anyone other than Portia?"

"Me? *Nunca!* He was always very attentive in public."

"Then how do you know he was having an affair?"

"Well, everyone said . . ."

"Yes, but who told you the first time?"

"*No estoy seguro.* I'm not sure. Let me think."

Marina Rodriguez pushed through Weinstein's door.

"Marina!" Amelia said.

"What?" Marina said, getting angry. "Are you gossiping about me?"

"*Sentarse.* Sit down. Jessica was asking me where I heard about Clarence and Monica. I can't remember. Can you?" Amelia moved over to make room for Marina.

I leaned forward to talk to Marina. "Do you know who saw Clarence threaten Portia?"

"You told me about that," Amelia said to Marina.

"It's true," Marina said. "I saw it with my own eyes, and I told the police, too."

"The Shelbys came to Marina's office to look at the apartments," Amelia said.

"She was so high and mighty about opposing our development," Marina said, "but her husband liked the idea. That's when it happened."

"What happened?" I asked.

"He threatened to kill her."

"Ooh, Marina, are you going to take the witness stand?" Amelia asked.

"Of course I am."

"When did this take place?" I asked.

"About three days before he killed her."

"How can you be sure?"

"I marked it on my calendar. I even showed it to the police. I told them he sounded so threatening, I thought I should write it down in case anything happened to her. And you see? Wasn't I smart?"

"Poor Portia," Amelia said. "And he was so handsome, too."

"You can't trust men," Marina said.

"You're talking about my brother again, aren't you?" Amelia said. "I don't want to hear anything bad about him."

"You only want to hear bad things about everyone else."

"That's not true. *Eso no es verdad.*"

"Well, thanks for your help," I said, standing. "I'll see you tomorrow."

Seth had begged off dinner that evening, saying he was too tired, and I called him the next morning to see how he was feeling. He groaned when he answered the phone.

"Seth, are you all right?" I asked.

"No. I am not all right."

"What's the matter?"

"I am starving to death. That's what's the matter."

"I'm not surprised. You skipped dinner last night. Why don't you go to the café in the village and get some breakfast?"

"I would, if I could get out of bed. I wrenched my back on those darned machines yesterday."

"How awful. I'm so sorry."

"Don't you dare laugh, Jessica."

"I'm not laughing," I said. "Is there anything I can do?"

"Yes! You can bring me something to eat."

"Tell me what you want and I'll be over as soon as I can."

Seth's door was unlocked. I knocked, called out, and walked in carrying a brown paper bag, which held an egg-and-cheese sandwich and a cup of coffee. I'd elected not to bring him the jelly doughnut he'd also requested, and had substituted a container of fruit, knowing I was risking a tongue-lashing.

Seth was sitting up in bed, the covers neatly arranged, watching television when I entered.

"You picked a good day to stay in bed," I said. "It's raining out. I'm just going to put this on a plate and I'll be right back."

"Mort stopped by after you phoned," he called out as I walked into the kitchen.

"I see that," I said, noting the crumpled paper bag in the garbage pail and empty dish with powdered sugar on it in the sink. I put the sandwich on a plate, the fruit in a bowl, and the coffee in a mug. I even found a tray to carry them in to the patient.

Seth consumed his second breakfast, and I politely refrained from asking which machine it was he'd injured himself with, or where his athletic instructor was in his time of need.

"Feeling better?" I asked.

"Much. Just a bit sore, that's all. I'll be up and around in a trice."

"A back injury is nothing to take lightly," I said. "You should rest today."

"Thank you, Dr. Fletcher. I guess I know what's wrong with me, thank you very much."

I held up both hands and feigned innocence. "Far be it from me to tell the great Dr. Hazlitt what to do," I said.

"Dang it, Jessica. I'm uncomfortable enough as it is. Don't rub it in."

"I never said 'I told you so,' now, did I? I'm just concerned about you, Seth. I know back pain is no picnic. I don't want you to injure yourself further, that's all. You tell me how I can help, and that's what I'll do. And I won't say another word about it."

"I'm not sure it's the back at all," he said, mollified. "I hurt all over."

"Would you like me to run you a hot bath? That might relax your muscles and make you feel better. I can also stop in Weinstein's and pick up some liniment, if you tell me what you want."

After grumbling some more, Seth agreed that a bath would be therapeutic. I ran the water, testing it with my wrist so it wouldn't burn him. I offered to help him to the bathroom, but he stoutly refused and sent me off instead to Weinstein's with a shopping list. I was certainly getting my exercise this morning, walking to and from the village.

When I returned from the drugstore with various

bottles of painkillers, plus a tube of capsaicin cream—
something Harry had recommended—Seth was
dressed and had propped himself on the couch with
pillows on either side. The color was back in his
cheeks and he looked far more relaxed than when I
had left. But he was upset about something. I brought
him a glass of water. He took two pills and sighed.

"I'm sorry, Jessica."

"What are you sorry about?" I said, taking the armchair next to the couch.

"I yelled at you and made you go out in the rain."

"I don't melt. And you were in pain when you
cranked at me. I didn't pay it any mind."

"No, I was embarrassed."

"There's no need for that."

"Yes, there is. I feel like an old fool trying to act
like a young buck, running around a gym showing off.
And this is what it got me."

"A very wise friend once told me that people do
foolish things at times, even people who are conscientious and intelligent."

"Yeah, well, I'm paying the consequences today."

"But you're feeling better now?" I said.

"I am. The bath was just the thing. By the way, I
forgot to tell you I called the office. Assured Dr. Jenny
and everyone else that the police were not looking for
me in Key West."

"Good old Sam and his police work."

"Remember I'd asked her to look up Portia's
chart?"

"Yes. And what did you find out?"

"Portia was practically the same weight for thirty-
five years. I never prescribed a diet. She never asked
about losing weight."

"It's good to hear, even though we no longer need

to convince the police a murder has taken place. Although if you ask me, the evidence against Clarence is skimpy. Still, your records seem to confirm what we thought all along, that Portia didn't take those diet pills on purpose."

"Or even know she was taking them."

"True."

"Must be someone with a mighty strong reason for wanting to see her dead to go to all this trouble to kill her."

"I agree," I said.

"Do you know who did it?"

"Maybe. I'll know better at the Residents' Committee meeting this afternoon. Think you'll be up to coming?"

"Wouldn't miss it for the world."

Chapter Twenty

"Where is everyone?" Seth asked as we took seats next to Mort and Maureen. "I thought the residents' meeting was a popular event."

The chairs in the meeting room were arranged in two banks, with an aisle up the center. Less than half the seats were full, most occupied by people who'd become familiar faces by now: Monica Kotansky and her sister Carrie; their friend Olga Piper; Helen and Miles Davison; Minnie and Sam Lewis; Earl and Burl Simmons, and Amelia Rodriguez. Marina, who was there as Wainscott's designated representative, sat in the back row, a steno pad and pen on her lap. I looked for Mark Rosner, but didn't see him.

"The tennis tournament had to be postponed this morning because of the rain," I heard Minnie say. "By the time the sun came out and dried up the courts, the tournament and this meeting overlapped."

"They'll be here," Sam said loudly, referring to the tennis players. "We've got food. If you want to fill a meeting, that's what you've got to do. They always come for the food."

Tony Colombo came through the back door, wearing a white apron and carrying a large cooler, followed by a younger man, also in white, wheeling an aluminum cart on which were two foil-covered chafing dishes. I'd seen the younger fellow making pizzas at Colombo's restaurant when Seth and I had dinner there. I presumed he was Colombo's cousin and partner.

At the sight of the food being set up, the Simmons twins started getting out of their seats.

"No refreshments till the end of the meeting," Sam called out.

"Well, then, let's get started. It's already past the hour," someone said.

Sam looked at his watch. "Give 'em another five minutes, Minnie; then start."

"Hi, Seth," Monica called from across the aisle, waving to him, her bracelets jingling. Snowy, perched on her lap, bared his teeth.

Seth gave her a wan smile.

"Does she know how sore you are from yesterday's workout?" I whispered.

"No. And don't you tell her."

"Your secret's safe with me," I said. "But I do need to ask her a question. Excuse me." I moved across the aisle to the seat next to Monica.

A few minutes later, after more people had drifted in and the room began to fill up, I rejoined Seth. Minnie closed the front door, went to the officers' table, and pounded a gavel on a little block of wood.

"The meeting of the Residents' Committee of Foreverglades will come to order," she announced. "May we dispense with the reading of the previous minutes?"

"So moved."

"All in favor?" Hands went up. "Opposed? Good. I hate it when people oppose things. Now, we have two items on our agenda today—a suitable memorial for Portia Shelby—that subject was tabled at the last meeting—and the closing of the beach."

Sam jumped up. "I want to say something about that. If DeWitt Wainscott—"

Minnie interrupted. "I didn't call on you, Sam."

"So call on me then."

"Sam Lewis has the floor."

Sam tugged on the belt of his shorts and took a deep breath. "If Mr. DeWitt Wainscott thinks he can intimidate us from demonstrating by closing the beach and siccing his lawyers on us, he's got another think coming. I know my rights as a citizen. This is a freedom-of-speech issue. I say we file a class-action suit."

"We're on the first item, Sam," Minnie said, "the memorial for Portia."

"This is more important, Minnie. We can do something for Portia another time. This is affecting not only the quality of our lives, but the value of our properties, too. There are too many empty units as it is."

There was a rumble of agreement, punctuated by a sharp bark from Snowy.

"Sam's right," said a voice from the rear doorway. It was Clarence. "The best memorial for Portia would be to reopen the beach."

The rumble turned into a full-fledged roar as everyone craned to see Clarence. "He must have made bail," Mort said to me.

"Good for him," I replied, thinking it was very courageous of Clarence to brave the meeting and the scrutiny of those who believed him guilty.

Minnie pounded her gavel until order was restored.

Clarence came halfway up an aisle and stopped. "For the sake of what few friends I may have here," he said, "I loved my wife and I did not kill her, either accidentally or on purpose. Portia died in the place that she loved the best—on the beach. It was an important part of her life and she wanted desperately to preserve it for you and everyone else in Foreverglades. If you want a memorial to Portia, get Wainscott to reopen the beach."

Sam started applauding, and the Simmons twins joined him. But the rest refrained, perhaps uncomfortable with the idea of supporting anything said by a man accused of murder.

I reached out and touched his arm. "Come sit down and let the meeting continue, Clarence," I said.

"I've said my piece," he said, turning to leave.

"No, please stay," I said. "You may want to see this to its conclusion."

He thought for a moment, then reluctantly sat down beside me.

Sam Lewis, who'd remained standing, took a few steps in Marina Rodriguez's direction. He moved up and down on his toes as he asked her, "So, Mrs. Rodriguez, what does your boss have to say for himself?"

Marina jumped to her feet and dropped the pad and pen on her seat. "Mr. Wainscott does not have to make any excuses to anyone," she said. "We've been over all this before. Your contracts say access to the beach is at the discretion of the owner. The beach is his private property. The fact that he has generously allowed the residents here to use it for all these years doesn't entitle you to beach rights forever. Not only that, he's protecting you. There have been several alligator sightings—"

"He probably put them there himself," Miles Davison called out.

"Mr. Wainscott cares about all of you," Marina concluded. "He doesn't want anyone here to get hurt."

"How come he never cared about us before?" Sam shouted. "Alligators, my foot!"

Olga Piper stood. "What about the brochures? When I bought my unit here, the brochures showed people walking on the beach." There was a chorus of agreement, and Olga continued. "We were promised a beach. You can't take it away now."

"What do you expect me to do, draw in the towers on the brochures?" Marina responded angrily. "Of course the pictures show the beach, because that's the way it is now. Besides, how do you know your view will be blocked? It's possible you'll be able to see the water from some of the buildings."

"It's not the same thing," Olga said.

"No. No," a chorus erupted. "It's not the same thing." Snowy started barking again until Monica wrapped her hand around his snout and whispered in his ear.

"We won't see the water unless Wainscott's sky-scrapers are transported," Sam said.

"You mean 'transparent,' Sam," Minnie said.

"That, too."

Marina crossed her arms. "The beach belongs to Mr. Wainscott. He can do whatever he wants with it."

"That's right!" boomed a voice from the back of the room.

DeWitt Wainscott filled the doorway, his face angry and red. "It's my property," he bellowed. "If you step on the beach, I'll have you arrested. And I'd like to remind you I still own the majority of the units in Foreverglades. If you don't like it, you can sell. Or you can take it up with my lawyers. I'll sue anyone who tries to stand in the way of Wainscott Towers." He stalked into the room, followed by Mark Rosner, who was no longer dressed like the manager of the complex—no button-down shirt, no bow tie. He wore faded black jeans, a T-shirt, and heavy work boots, looking more like a bodyguard or a construction worker.

"You can't stop us from protesting," Sam shouted.

"You'll shut up if you know what's good for you," Wainscott growled.

"Are you threatening me?"

"I don't need to threaten you. I have other ways I slap down fleas who pester me."

The room fell silent, as though everyone was fearful of drawing Wainscott's wrath. Snowy growled softly from the safety of Monica's lap. Earl and Burl grabbed for each other's hands.

I stood. "Like murder, Mr. Wainscott?" I said. "Is that the way you slap down people who get in your way?"

"You again? You don't even live here. You have nothing to say that interests me." He turned to Marina. "Get out of here," he told her. "You have more important things to do than waste time with these people."

"I'd like to hear what Mrs. Fletcher has to say." All eyes turned to Tony Colombo. "I recommend you listen to her, too, Mr. Wainscott."

"I don't give a damn what she or anybody else has to say," Wainscott said, grabbing Marina by the wrist and pulling her toward the front door.

"Sit down, Mr. Wainscott," Colombo said, authority in his voice. "This meeting isn't over yet."

Wainscott, his fingers gripping Marina's wrist, glared at Colombo. "Who the hell do you think you are?" he shouted. "Stick to making pizzas and keep your nose out of things that don't concern you."

"I think you might be surprised who I am, sir," Colombo said, reaching into his back pocket.

Amelia gasped. "Ah, *Dios mío*. He's got a gun."

"I knew it. I knew it," Sam shouted, fairly jumping up and down. "I knew there was something fishy about this guy."

Colombo smiled. "It's not what you think, Sam," he said. He pulled out his wallet and held up a badge for everyone to see. "Anthony Colombo, FBI."

A ripple of murmurs moved across the audience. *That explains it,* I thought. I'd known Colombo had another purpose for being in Foreverglades. Now it was becoming clearer.

I watched Wainscott as he dropped Marina's hand; she backed away from him. He stiffened his spine and scowled at Colombo, fists clenched, the picture of fury aroused. But a tiny muscle spasm on the side of his cheek betrayed his nervousness.

"You're not going anywhere, Mr. Wainscott," Colombo said. "This concerns you."

I wondered if Wainscott would try to bolt, and what I should do if he did. But Mort came to my rescue. He stood and held up his badge, too, turning in a slow circle. "Mort Metzger, sheriff, Cabot Cove, Maine," he said, going to the door nearest Wainscott and positioning himself in front of it. "I'll see that no one leaves."

"I knew it," Sam said. "Sure, he's FBI. I knew it all along."

"You said he was with the Mafia, Sam," Miles Davison reminded him.

Colombo ignored the debate and pocketed his badge. "Now, Mrs. Fletcher, you were saying?"

Marina, who'd been inching her way toward the guarded door, finally reached it. "Sorry," Mort told her, "but nobody leaves until we say so." He looked at Colombo: "Right?"

"Right, Sheriff," Colombo said.

"I don't blame you for wanting to leave, Marina," I said. "I'd be uncomfortable, too, if I'd poisoned a beloved member of this group."

Everyone started talking at once. Colombo raised a hand in the air. "Please, let's have some order so that we can hear what Mrs. Fletcher has to say."

"How dare you accuse me of such a thing," Marina shouted at me. The color had drained from her cheeks.

"I'm certainly not happy making such an accusation," I said, "but I think it's true. You arranged it very neatly, in fact. I almost believed you. But you went one step too far when you tried to frame Clarence."

The front door of the room opened softly, and Detective Zach Shippee slipped in. His entrance went unnoticed by most of the people, who were twisted in their seats, burning to see the next scene in the drama unfolding at the back of the room.

"He did it!" Marina said in a shaky voice, pointing at Clarence. "It wasn't me. He's the guilty one. He killed his wife so he could be with her." This time her finger was aimed at Monica Kotansky.

"That's not true." Monica shrieked. "We're friends, that's all." She started to sob. Snowy whined. He stood on his hind paws, frantically licking her chin. Carrie put her arm around her sister.

"He told the police he was home all night, but he was lying," Marina said, looking around the room for confirmation.

Earl and Burl nodded in unison. "We saw him," Earl said.

"That night," added Burl. They looked at Clarence, their expressions regretful.

"We're sorry, Mr. Shelby. We had to tell the police," Earl said to Clarence.

"They asked us," added Burl.

"That's okay, boys," Clarence said.

"I saw them together the night Portia Shelby died," Marina said, encouraged now that she'd gotten some support. "He was giving her the pills to kill his wife."

"How do you know what Clarence gave Monica?" I asked.

"She threw away the box the pills came in. I found it in the garbage in the rec hall," Marina said. "The box had contained diet pills. I saw it on the slip myself."

"And what time was this, Marina?" I asked.

"It was ten-thirty, right after our meeting."

I remembered that the coroner's report had estimated Portia's time of death at ten P.M. "Portia was already dead on the beach when you say you saw Clarence give Monica the pills," I said. "They couldn't have been used to kill Portia that night."

Marina fumbled before coming up with an explanation. "Monica must have had them before," she said, "and put them in Portia's pillbox."

"But you were taking diet pills, too, weren't you?" I said.

"Never!" she shouted back, a triumphant look in her eye.

"You never took the diet drug ephedra?"

"I've never been anywhere near it."

"You knew that Portia Shelby's heart attack was brought on by diet pills, didn't you?"

"Everyone knows it. It's common knowledge here." Her confidence was growing.

"But you had nothing to do with that?"

She shook her head.

"Not even when Mr. Wainscott gave the pills to you?"

"He . . . he never gave me any drugs."

"You're saying you've never even seen these pills. Am I right?"

She nodded, a smug expression on her face.

Relief washed over me. She had fallen into my trap. "Then why, Marina, did I hear you say yesterday that it was amazing what a little *blue* pill can do?"

Amelia squeaked, "*La madre de Dios!* She did say that."

"Everyone knew they were blue," Marina said, her voice displaying less assuredness now. "Ask them down at the beauty parlor. They probably all know the pills were blue."

"This is the first I'm hearing that," Helen said. Other women in the room echoed what she'd said.

"I didn't know the pills were blue, Marina," said Amelia. "And I forgot you even said it, so I sure couldn't have told anyone."

"So what?" Marina snapped. "It doesn't mean anything." She looked to Wainscott for support, but his back was to her, a disgusted expression on his face.

"Yes, it does," Minnie shouted. "You were the one who found Portia's handbag when it went missing. Is that when you put the pills in her pillbox?"

Marina ignored Minnie's question and pointed at Clarence. "I . . . I . . . I heard him," she said. "I heard him threaten her. I told it to the police. I even put it on the calendar."

"That's right, Marina, you did," I said, careful not to show my growing excitement. "And what date was it you gave the police? I believe you said it was three days before Portia died. Am I correct?"

"That's right, and the police know it. I . . . I heard him threaten to kill her."

"You must have very good ears," I said, "because

Clarence was up north visiting relatives that week. He only returned on the day Portia died."

The room exploded with voices.

"I told you that, Jessica," Helen called out. "I'd forgotten all about it."

"You poisoned Portia," I said to Marina, "and then you tried to put the blame on Clarence. You must have been delighted to find the box that had contained the diet pills he'd ordered for Monica. So delighted, in fact, you planted it as evidence down at the beach."

Marina's bravado deserted her. Tears began streaming down her face as she confronted Wainscott. "I did it for you," she said.

"For me?" he said. "What the hell do you mean by that?"

"I thought . . ." She fought to control her voice through her sobs. "I thought that if I took care of your problem here at Foreverglades, you would take care of me the way you did Mark."

"Hey, wait a minute," Rosner said, jumping up from where he'd been sitting in a nearby chair. He looked at the crowd that now stared at him. "She's nuts," he said. "Don't listen to her."

Marina was not to be deterred. She said to Wainscott, "When that construction worker in Key West threatened to expose you, Mark arranged the accident with the crane. I knew he'd done it for you. You promoted him, made him manager here, took care of him, treated him with respect. That's all I ever wanted from you—respect."

"I'm outta here," Rosner said, heading for the door.

But Zach Shippee blocked his way. "Calm down, Mr. Rosner," the detective said. "You're going nowhere at the moment."

Wainscott, a satisfied smile on his face, announced,

"There's no reason to detain me any longer. As you've heard, this demented woman acted on her own." To her: "I'll get you a good lawyer, Marina. That's the best I can do." He looked at Mark Rosner and said, "If you killed that guy in Key West, you did it for your own reasons. I never asked you to do it. Good luck."

"You son of a—" Rosner lunged at Wainscott, but Shippee wrestled him into a chair.

Wainscott made moves to leave, but I signaled Mort to block him. "You can't get off the hook that easily, Mr. Wainscott," I said. "You gave Marina the pills, which makes you an accessory to murder."

"I don't know anything about any pills," he said.

"Oh, but I think you do."

"So do I," Seth Hazlitt said, standing. "My friend down in the Keys, Dr. Truman Buckley, prescribed the tablets for you, Mr. Wainscott, because you told him you wanted to lose weight."

"But you never intended to take the drug," I said. "You have diabetes, don't you? You knew that Dr. Buckley would never have given you the pills if you admitted that. So you lied to him and claimed you were in perfect health, except for the excess pounds."

"Your blood tests would show up as being perfectly normal as long as you were taking your insulin regularly," Seth added.

"Mrs. Fletcher?" Detective Zach Shippee asked from where he stood at the door, "How do you know that Mr. Wainscott here has diabetes?"

"I know because he sent Marina to pick up his insulin from Weinstein's Pharmacy, and we happened to be there when she did. The prescription was filed under W, which I wondered about, but didn't give any more thought to until other things became evident."

"What does it matter?" Wainscott said, his irritation rising again. "So what if I gave her the pills? I didn't tell her to kill anybody with them."

"Perhaps," I said, "but I'm sure the police will want to dig a little further into it with you."

"My lawyers will handle that. Are you finished now?" He looked around as if concluding the end of a particularly tiresome meeting.

"I'm not finished with you, Mr. Wainscott," Colombo said.

Wainscott turned and faced the FBI special agent.

"There's a little matter of investors who've been scammed by you," Colombo said. "DeWitt Wainscott, I'm placing you under arrest. You are charged with interstate felony fraud, conspiracy to commit fraud, and violations of the federal statutes on wire and mail fraud in the Securities Exchange Act of 1934." He pulled a set of handcuffs from under his apron, snapped them on Wainscott's wrists behind his back, and read him his rights.

Zach Shippee motioned to unseen people in the hallway, and three uniformed officers joined him in the room. "Take these two people into custody on suspicion of murder," he instructed them, pointing to Marina Rodriguez and Mark Rosner.

"You're never getting away with this," Wainscott shouted. "You'll have to deal with my lawyers."

"Is that why you're here?" I asked Colombo, once he'd secured his prisoner.

"Yes, ma'am. My cousin here owns the restaurant all by himself. I've been using it as a front while I built a federal case against Mr. Wainscott. He's bilked investors in several states. I came here this morning with a warrant for his arrest on those charges, but I sure didn't count on a couple of murders being solved, too."

We all watched as the various law enforcement officers led their charges from the room. Everyone seemed too stunned to speak; the only sound came from the chair next to mine, where Clarence Shelby wept softly.

Chapter Twenty-one

"If it weren't for Seth finding those blue tablets in Portia's pillbox," I said, "we'd never have known she was murdered."

"And Wainscott would have gotten away with two murders then," Mort said. "Rosner confessed to killing a construction worker in Key West. Plus he made an attempt on Mrs. F's life, too. Says it was under Wainscott's orders. Of course, Wainscott claims Rosner and Marina acted on their own, that he never told them to kill anyone. Might be tough to build a case against him."

"Even so," I said, "he's likely to be put away for a long time on the federal charges."

We were in Sam's pink Cadillac on our way to Miami International Airport and a flight to Boston, the first leg of our trip back home to Cabot Cove. I wasn't looking forward to the snowstorm that was forecast for the day after our arrival, but I *was* eager to spend some time at home before heading out on the promotion trip my agent, Matt Miller, was putting together for me.

"What exactly did Wainscott do?" Sam asked.

"Did you ever hear of a Ponzi scheme?" Mort replied. "He borrowed money from investors for construction, and when they demanded payments, he paid them off with funds he borrowed from other investors."

"He may have started out legitimately building developments like Foreverglades," I said, "but when he ran out of money, he kept lining up investors for projects that never got built, like Wainscott Towers."

"Or projects that only got half built," Mort added, "like Wainscott Manor in Key West."

"Every time an investor gave him money," I said, "he kept a portion for himself, and used the rest to pay off other investors who were putting pressure on him."

"When it got too hot for him in one state," Mort added, "he just went to another."

"Rosner must have known what Wainscott was doing," I said. "He told me he didn't think the towers would get built, and it looks like he was right. Anyway, Wainscott's days of cheating investors, and quashing protests against his properties, are far behind him."

"Jessica, how did you know that Marina found the box and threw it in the water?" Maureen asked.

I explained. "When I visited Clarence in jail, he said he brought the pills to Monica at the rec hall, but that he'd tried to stay out of sight because Wainscott's people were having a meeting. Before the Residents' Committee meeting started, I asked Monica what she had done with the box. She said it had been too bulky to fit in her bag, so she'd opened it right away and took the bottles home, leaving the box at the rec hall."

"And when Marina admitted she'd found the box in the garbage," Mort added, "she pointed a finger at herself as the one who threw it in the water down at the beach."

"I thought it was a bit too convenient that the police

found a box that had held diet pills near the beach where Portia died," I said. "It struck me as an effort to plant evidence."

"Which it was," Maureen said.

"Actually, Marina tried to plant a lot of evidence," I said. "She used Amelia to spread rumors that Clarence was having an affair with Monica, and that Clarence had threatened Portia's life. She knew that anything she said to Amelia in confidence would soon be all over town."

"It saddens me that my old friend Truman provided the pills that killed Portia," Seth said.

"I know," I said. "That would have been true no matter who used the pills to kill Portia, including Clarence. He'd found Healthy Stuff on the Internet, and had ordered many of Portia's supplements from Truman."

Sam bounced up and down in his seat. "Tell me about Colombo. How did you know he was from the FBI?"

"I didn't," I said, "but I suspected he wasn't really a restaurateur, either."

"Why?"

"When we went to the produce market, he wasn't sure what to buy and kept consulting a shopping list."

"I use a shopping list whenever I go to the market," Maureen said.

"I do, too," I said. "But Colombo's list had 'tomatoes for sauce' on it, and he bought a bushel of beefsteak tomatoes. Any cook knows beefsteak tomatoes aren't your usual cooking tomatoes. They're too watery. Tomato sauce, especially Italian tomato sauce, is traditionally made with plum tomatoes."

"So he was here all along, working for the FBI?" Sam said.

"Right you are, Sam," Mort replied. "According to

Detective Shippee, Agent Colombo has been in Florida for a long time, using his cousin's restaurant as a front, just waiting until a solid enough case was built to arrest Wainscott before he decided to skip town again."

"He's not going anywhere this time," Sam said.

"Except to jail," I added.

A few months later, signs of spring brightened the chilly Maine air. My lilacs were in bloom, and the azalea bush I'd planted the summer before was covered with fat peach-colored buds. I'd already traveled across the country and back to promote my last book, and Matt Miller had been right. The public relations push had been just enough to lift my book onto the *New York Times* best-seller list, still the gold standard for authors.

Seth and I were sitting in my kitchen, sharing a pot of green tea, an occasional break from our usual English Breakfast variety, when a FedEx deliveryman knocked on the door.

"What can it be?" I said, taking the box and signing for it.

"Open it and find out," Seth said, leaning forward to examine the label when I put the box on the table. "The return address is Foreverglades, Florida."

I pulled on the cardboard tab that opened the box, removed frozen gel packs used to keep the contents cold, and lifted out a frozen key lime pie. "Look," I said, laughing at the card taped to the box and reading it aloud: "'Only Original, Authentic Key Lime Pie. Made by Minnie Lewis.'" I turned the card over. It read:

Thought you'd like to know the news. With the help of an anonymous donor from Key

West, the Residents' Committee of Forev-
erglades raised enough money to purchase
the land along the water. We fixed up the dock,
expanded the beach, and we had a terrific
celebration when we named the whole area
Portia Shelby Park.

Monica is still chasing Clarence, who has de-
clared he wants to be a perennial bachelor.
Amelia says he just wants more attention.
Helen and Miles send you their best.

Love, Minnie and Sam

P.S. Detective Shippee gave Sam a plaque
for his dedication to law enforcement and
public safety. We have it proudly hanging in
our living room.

P.P.S. The animal control people finally
trapped that big gator they've been after for
years. Moved him to a remote swamp in the
Everglades. Come back and visit real soon.

Read on for a preview of

A Vote for Murder

The next *Murder, She Wrote*
hardcover coming in October 2004
from New American Library

"The White House?"

"Yes. A reception there."

I was enjoying breakfast at Mara's waterfront luncheonette with my friends Dr. Seth Hazlitt, and Cabot Cove's sheriff, Mort Metzger. It was a gloomy early August day, thick gray clouds hovering low over the dock, the humidity having risen overnight to an uncomfortable level.

"When are you leaving?" Seth asked after taking the last bite of his blueberry pancakes, Mara's signature breakfast dish at her popular eatery.

"Day after tomorrow," I said.

"I don't envy you, Mrs. F," said Mort.

"Why?"

"August in Washington, D.C.? Maureen and I were there about this time last year. Never been so hot in my life."

I laughed and sipped my tea. "I'm sure the airconditioning will be working just fine," I said.

"*Ayuh,*" Seth said. "I don't expect they let the president sweat a whole lot. Or U.S. senators for that matter."

Warren Nebel, Maine's junior senator, had arranged for my trip to Washington. He'd invited me to join three other writers in our nation's capital to help celebrate a national literacy program at the Library of Congress. I'd eagerly accepted, of course. And when Senator Nebel included a reception at the White House on our first evening there, my heart raced a little with anticipation.

I don't believe that anyone, no matter how sophisticated, worldly, well connected or wealthy, doesn't feel at least a twinge of excitement when invited to the White House to meet the president of the United States. I am certainly no exception. It wouldn't be my first time at the People's House, although it had been a few years since my last visit. Adding to the excitement were the writers with whom I'd be spending the week, distinguished authors all, some of whom I'd been reading and enjoying for years, and I looked forward to actually shaking hands and chatting with them. Writers, with some notable exceptions, tend to be solitary creatures, not especially comfortable in social situations. I suppose it has a lot to do with the private nature of how we work, sitting alone for months sometimes years at a time, working on a book, with only spasmodic human interaction. Those who break out and become public personalities often end up so enamored of the experience that writing goes by the boards. I've always tried to balance my life between the necessary hibernation to get a book done and joining the rest of the world when between writing projects. That was my situation when I received the invitation from Senator Nebel—a book recently completed and off to the publisher, and free time on my hands. Perfect timing.

Our little breakfast confab ended suddenly when both Seth and Mort received calls on their cell phones, prompting them to leave in a hurry, Seth to the hospital for an emergency admission, Mort to the scene of an auto accident on the highway outside of town. Seth tried to grab the bill from the table but I was quicker. "Please," I said. "It's my treat. Go on now. Emergencies can't wait."

I wasn't alone at the table very long because Mara, the luncheonette's gregarious proprietor, joined me.

"Hear you're going to Washington to give the president some good advice," she said, blowing away a wisp of hair from her forehead. She'd come from the kitchen; a sheen of perspiration covered her face.

"I'm sure he doesn't need any advice from me," I said.

"Not so sure about that," she said. "Going alone?"

"To Washington? Yes."

"Thought you might be taking Doc Hazlitt with you."

"I'd love to have him accompany me but—."

"Shame you won't have a companion to share it with you, Jess."

"Oh, I really won't be alone. I—."

Mara's cocked head and her narrowed eyes said she expected more from me. Besides being a wonderful cook and hostess at her establishment, she's Cabot Cove's primary conduit of gossipy information. She not only knows everyone in town, she seems to be privy to their most private thoughts and activities.

"I'll be meeting George," I said casually, making a point of picking up the bill and scrutinizing it.

"George?"

"Yes," I said, pulling cash from my purse. "George Sutherland."

"That Scotland Yard fella you met in London years ago?"

"That's right," I replied, standing and brushing crumbs from my skirt. "He'll be there attending an international conference on terrorism. Just a coincidence. Breakfast was great, Mara. Bye-bye."

The last words I heard from Mara as I pushed open the door—and she headed back to the kitchen—were, "You are a sly one, Jessica Fletcher."

I chided myself on my walk home for having mentioned George Sutherland. Knowing Mara, half the town would have heard about it by noon, the other half by dinnertime. Mara didn't mean any harm with her penchant for gossip, nor was she the only one. Charlene Sassi's bakery is another source of juicy scuttlebutt (what is it about places with food that seem to spawn hearsay?). Small towns like my beloved Cabot Cove thrive on rumors, and in almost every case they're utterly harmless. As far as George Sutherland was concerned, there had been plenty of speculation that he and I had become romantically involved since meeting during a murder investigation in England. There was no basis to those rumors, although he'd expressed interest in advancing our relationship to another level, and I'd not found the contemplation unpleasant. But after some serious talks during those times when we managed to be together, we decided that neither this handsome Scottish widower, nor this Cabot Cove widow were ready for a more intimate involvement, and contented ourselves with frequent letters, occasional long-distance phone calls, and chance meetings when our schedules brought us together.

The rain started just as I reached my house. I picked up the local newspaper that had been delivered while I was gone, ducked inside, closed some windows, made myself a cup of tea and reviewed the package of information Senator Nebel's office had sent, accompanied by a letter from the senator.

It promised to be a whirlwind week in Washington,

and I added to my packing list an extra pair of comfortable walking shoes. The reception at the White House was scheduled for five o'clock the day I arrived. Following it, Senator Nebel would host a dinner at his home. The ensuing days were chockablock with meetings and seminars at the Library of Congress, luncheons and dinners with notables from government and the publishing industry, and other assorted official and social affairs. Why event planners think they must fill every waking moment has always escaped me; everyone appreciates a little downtime in the midst of a hectic week. My concern, however, was that I wouldn't find time to enjoy again being in George Sutherland's company. It had been a long while since we'd last seen each other, our schedules making it difficult for him to come to the States from London where he was a senior Scotland Yard inspector, or for me to cross the Atlantic in the opposite direction. It had been *too* long, and I didn't want to squander the opportunity of being in the same city at the same time.

When I picked up the newspaper, a headline on the front page caught my eye: NEBEL'S VOTE ON POWER PLANT STILL UNCERTAIN.

The battle within the Senate over the establishment of a new, massive nuclear power plant in Maine, only twenty miles outside Cabot Cove, had been in the news for weeks. From what I'd read, the Senate was almost equally split between those in favor of the plant, and those opposed. Its proponents claimed it was vitally necessary to avoid the sort of widespread blackouts the East Coast had experienced since the late 50s, five of them since 1959 including the biggest of them all in 2003. Senator Nebel, who'd pledged to fight the plant during his most recent campaign, had pointed to the enormous cost, not to mention the eco-

logical threat the plant posed to our scenic state, and
further condemned the lobbyists behind the project
and their clients, large multi-state electric power companies that would benefit handsomely from the plant's
construction. Some members of President David Di-
mond's cabinet had enjoyed strong ties to those companies that would benefit handsomely from the
plant's construction.

But the article claimed that Nebel's opposition to
the plant could no longer be taken for granted, according to unnamed Washington insiders. The piece
ended with: *"Reports that Senator Nebel has recently
received death threats are unconfirmed, although unnamed sources close to the senator say that security has
been beefed up for him, both on Capitol Hill and at
his home."*

Death threats! Usually, they came from demented
people who have no intention of carrying through on
them. But you can never take that for granted, and
every such threat must be taken seriously. I knew one
thing; our junior senator had chosen a contentious
time to be hosting a literacy program at the Library
of Congress. Was there ever a time when something
important, something potentially earth shattering,
wasn't going on somewhere in the world, and by ex-
tension in Washington, D.C.? I doubted it.

I replaced that weighty thought with a more pleasant one, visiting the White House and meeting the
president, spending time with some of my fellow writers, and, of course, touching base in person with
George Sutherland.